KARMA'S A BITCH

A Novel

by

J. GAIL

Brought to you by Truth Hurts Publications

TH PUB Truth Hurts Publications
c/o Jazoli Publishing
P.O. Box 1316
Brookhaven PA 19015

Karma's a Bitch
Second edition (new cover) 2007
Truth Hurts Publications
an imprint of Jazoli Publishing

Manufactured in the United States of America

ISBN10 (paperback): 0-9726978-3-7
ISBN13 (paperback): 978-0-9726978-3-5
LCCN: 2006901573

Treat others the same exact way you
would want to be treated.
It's as simple as that.

TRUTH HURTS
PUBLICATIONS

an imprint of

This is real life.
It ain't no fairytale.

The beginning
of the end...

chapter 1

"Get up off my good pillow nigga!"

Tony turned slightly from the Jerry Springer Show to look at Quanisha, then turned back to the TV just in time to see Jenna, the transvestite whore, take a wild swing at her lover's girlfriend. He was laying on the bed clutching the silvery gray tassled pillow tightly.

"Did you just hear me? Give me that!" Quanisha yelled at him as she snatched her favorite decorative bed pillow from his clenched grip. When she snatched it she hit Tony's chin causing him to bite his tongue.

"Ow! Bitch! What the fuck is wrong with you?" he looked up at her incredulously as he winced, fighting back tears from the pain.

"What the fuck is wrong with *you*? Don't be acting like you don't hear me when I'm talking. This is my GOOD pillow. Your lazy ass is up in here chilling and I'm trying to get ready for work. Why don't you clean up that bed instead of laying your ass in it all the time? I swear I don't know why I even *bother* with your dumb ass. Always sitting up here doin' nothin'...." Quanisha went on with her rant as she moved about the room, grabbing her gold earrings in the shape of a "Q" and spritzing on some designer imposter perfume she had picked up from G&G.

Tony turned over on his back and put his hands behind his head with his eyes glued to the TV screen. He had stopped listening after she said the words 'good pillow' again. It was 12:40 in the afternoon and Quanisha was getting ready for her job at the supermarket. Tony, as usual, was laying in the bed with his boxers on and no shirt, watching his favorite program on TV. He loved Jerry Springer to death for the girls who didn't even flinch when asked to pull up their shirts. He had ordered the entire last season's uncut episodes, courtesy his grandmother's credit card of course, and never missed an episode. His entire day would be thrown off if he missed an episode of Jerry Springer.

"….I'm through with you. Yo' ass is more worthless than this cheap ass perfume!" Quanisha yelled as she threw the bottle of perfume down on the carpet. She went out into the living room to look for her purse. The living room was so small and bare that it could have doubled as a large closet.

"Yea you wasn't saying that shit last night when I was breaking your back out," Tony spat after her with a smirk. He spat a little too much because a line of saliva came dripping down the side of his face. He reached in a quick motion to clean it off. Quanisha already thought he was lazy and trifling, no need to have her see him drooling all over himself.

"Maybe I could get some good perfume, some Armani, some Christian Dior, some Gucci if you'd pull your weight around here. What the hell are you doing today? I know it's looking for a job!" Quanisha ranted, ignoring his little comment.

"Man quiet with all that shit. I got a few job leads, don't you worry about me." Tony's 'job leads' consisted of the UPS commercial he had just seen on TV the day before saying they were looking for part-time handlers, and a heads up from his Mom about a job at the local Pizza shop, both of which he had yet to call or inquire about.

"What you mean 'don't worry about me?'" Quanisha came back to the bedroom door and asked as she looked at Tony, still laid up in her pink cotton sheets. "I'm the one in here paying all the bills, cooking and carrying yo ass when you're not at ya mama's so you better believe Imma be worryin' bout what yo ass is doin'. Nigga."

"Yea whatever," Tony dismissed her without ever looking in her direction.

"What?" Quanisha squinted up her face and looked at Tony in disbelief. He continued staring at his beloved screen. She finally just shook her head and walked over to the closet to seek out her imitation Louis Vuitton bag.

"You know what, fuck you Tony. Man, I don't know why I even bother with this nigga…" she began talking to herself as she finally grabbed her bag and walked out of the bedroom, and then straight out the front door.

"Damn! I thought her ass would never leave. Shit!" Tony said rubbing his forehead and watching the end of the Jerry Springer show.

Time rolled by and Tony was suddenly awakened from his light nap by the sound of Quanisha's phone ringing. He looked over at her oval faced alarm clock which read 3:14pm. He picked up the phone from behind the clock and spoke.

"Yea."

"Tone, man I knew I would catch your ass over there. I been calling your cell," Tony's best boy Scoop yelled unnecessarily into the phone.

"For real? I didn't hear it. But I damn sure can hear your ass, could you take it down a notch? I just woke up nigga," Tony complained and then reached over the bed and fished through his black pants for his cell phone. When he found it, it didn't say that there were any calls missing. "This burnout been tripping on me, sometimes it rings, sometimes it don't."

"Well anyway, what you doing? I'm off today. They having a

special at Modell's on those Luggz I been trying to get man. $59.99, how bout that?" Scoop had a union job with the street workers who were supposed to go around and fill up potholes throughout the city. But don't ask your average Philadelphian why there were still hundreds of huge potholes throughout the city. Unlike his good friend Tony, Scoop worked a regular, legit job. But Scoop's main flaw was that he was a ho. A big one.

"Man I don't know why the hell you sweatin them corny ass boots. Ain't nobody in the hood rockin' them jawns like that no more man."

"Man I don't give a fuck what the hood's doin'. I tried them jawns on in the store and they fit like a glove. I need some comfortable boots for my job. They smooth as shit, and I'm going down to get 'em before they sell out my size. You comin'?"

"Do you want me to hold your purse for you too? This nigga want me to come shopping with 'im. Like we some bitches," Tony laughed.

"Fool, like you got something better to do. Git yo ass up and meet me up 69th Street in an hour." Scoop hung up the phone before Tony could say anything else.

"Dammit." Tony hung up the phone and then rolled on his side. He thought about just closing his eyes and going back to sleep but knew that if he did he probably wouldn't wake again until late that night. Plus his boy, who had 4 inches and 30 pounds on him, would probably come to Quanisha's and snatch his ass up.

His stomach was grumbling so he groaned loudly and then finally rolled out of bed. Tony was a brown skinned brother, standing at about 5'9 and weighing in at 175 pounds. He was a plain looking guy, but his quick wit and smooth "I don't care" demeanor made him a favorite with the ladies. He stretched and shuffled over to the bedroom door, stopping at the mirror to take a look. The free 'bring a friend' visits he had made to the gym with his cousin the week before had really paid off. His arms were nicely cut and he could almost make out the beginnings of a six-pack. *Well, maybe a four pack*, he thought and slapped his stomach. He usually liked to keep his hair shaped in a light 'hustler cut,' with the sideburns running a little low down the sides of his face, but right now he was woofing. He needed a hair cut badly. He continued to inspect his hair in the mirror, and after stroking his sideburns a few times he finally made his way to the kitchen.

He opened Quanisha's fridge and searched for something to eat. He saw a whole pre-cooked chicken from the Acme supermarket where Quanisha worked, and instantly grabbed it. He threw it in the mic and opened the fridge back up to grab a container of orange juice. He opened it up and drank it straight from the carton. He carried his food into the small living room and plopped himself on Quanisha's brown second hand couch. The left seat cushion had a large dark stain on it. *That shit needs to be flipped over or something*, Tony said to himself and then reached over the coffee table to flip on the TV.

* * *

Tony arrived at 69th Street sooner than the hour that he and Scoop had agreed on so that he could stand in front of the movie theater and see what fine honeys would pass his way. He was still wearing the same clothes from the night before, and hadn't even bothered to take a shower. He leaned himself against the wall and jammed his hands into the pockets of his favorite black cargo pants. A few young chicken heads passed his way, not up to his high standards, but he still took the opportunity to stare at their shapely behinds. He saw his boy Black, who was an up and coming dealer in Southwest Philly, and gave him a pound. Black gave him the low down on what was going on in his part of the hood, and he and Tony busted up in front of the theater for a good 10 minutes. Not even three seconds after Black left and headed back down the hill towards City Blue, a pretty light skinned girl wearing a green top and skin tight dark jeans walked by.

"Ay yo. Slim!" Tony called after her after getting a good look at her body. He jogged a little behind her before catching up and standing directly in her path. "What's up wit you?"

The light skinned girl smiled and shyly tried to walk past him, but he met her every step.

"Where you trynna go? What's your name girl?" Tony said with the most gangsta look on his face that he could muster.

"It's Tonya," the girl finally said, putting one of her hands on her hip.

"Okay Tonya. I'm Tony. We got a connection already; we damn near got the same name. Where your man at?"

Tonya smiled and looked off towards the street. "I don't got no man."

"Well now you do." Just as he was saying those words Scoop came up from behind Tonya and reached over the girl's shoulder to grasp Tony's hand.

"What's up my man," Tony said, smirking and giving Scoop a look. He and Scoop were always competing over women. "Yo hold up for a moment doggie."

Scoop returned the look and nodded his head. He walked up the stairs to the movie theater and greeted some people he knew standing around.

"So listen, Tonya, let me get your number and we'll go catch a flick or something," Tony said pulling out his cell phone, not waiting for an answer of 'yes' or 'no.' When he was ready he looked up and nodded to Tonya to indicate that he was ready for the number.

"747.......2382." Tonya ran off and then leaned over to make sure he got it right. Tony finished up the entry and then reached over to give her a hug.

"I'll holla at you later tonight, aiight?" he said with a smile and then walked up the steps to where Scoop had gone.

"You got that man?" Scoop asked. Scoop was a good looking chocolate brother with a goatee. He had just the right amount of weight, the right amount of height and just a little too much game. The women, especially the young girls, were damn near throwing their panties at him as if he were a Platinum selling rapper. To him there wasn't enough time in the day to deal with all the women on his roster.

"Yea, you know. That shit wasn't nuffin'. These bitches is too easy," Tony answered with a cocky smile, satisfied that Scoop had been there to witness him pulling in a number. He wasn't as good looking as Scoop, but he had a way with the ladies that more than compensated for his average looks.

They headed across the street to Modells laughing and talking. So much that they didn't notice the Chevy Cavalier coming full speed around the corner towards them.

Unfortunately the car made it's round right after Scoop and Tony had stepped into the street. The driver came to a screeching halt as soon as humanly possible, but not until after clipping Tony on the left thigh and making him fall back into the right side of the windshield. Tony turned in the same motion and his face and left hand dragged down the windshield before he finally fell back down into the street. The car screeched off down the street.

"Tony! Tony, you alright man!?" Scoop yelled leaning down

to help his friend and trying to turn to get a look at the license plate of the car. But it was too late, the driver was already making a right down Market Street.

Tony had gotten hit, for sure, but not to the point where he was dying. He slowly leaned back up to a sitting position, and then grabbed Scoops arm as he helped him up. A girl driving one of the cars on the other side of the street was holding her mouth and bobbing back and forth in hysterical laughter along with her friend in the passenger seat.

"Yea, I guess I'm alright. Damn. That muthafucka hit me!" he yelled, looking around and becoming extremely embarrassed at the stares he was getting from people on the sidewalk who had witnessed everything. A few young boys had started to giggle. He suddenly wished he had stayed on the ground and faked paralysis or death.

"Shit man, I couldn't even get a plate number. I'm sorry dude," Scoop said patting his friend on the back and leading him back towards the store while walking slightly behind. Scoop turned to the right and closed his eyes as he held his lips together with his other hand and fought back a chuckle with every ounce of restraint in his body.

It was 8:14pm that same day. Quanisha reached down to pick up the quarter she had just dropped. She was standing at the payphone at the Acme Supermarket where she worked trying to call home. After trying several times in vain to pick the quarter up from the dusty white floor, she finally managed to grab a corner and lift it up with her to the phone again. She became lightheaded from getting up too fast and reeled for a few seconds before being able to see the buttons of the payphone clearly again. She resumed chewing her gum loudly as she put the coin into the payslot.

Quanisha was born and raised in West Philadelphia. As a teen she regularly brawled with the other girls on her block and at school, mostly over boys and gossip. Of course because of this, she had a snap's worth of hair, almost two inches, from it constantly being pulled out. She, like a lot of her peers, was forced to wear weaves and braids on a regular basis to cover her wild hair. The complexion of Tamyra Gray from American Idol, Quanisha wasn't fat, but had wide hips, a thick behind and thighs choking beneath a tight pair of jeans underneath her Acme smock. She punched the numbers to her house phone to check her messages or talk to Tony and leaned her elbow on top of the phone while she played with one of her long brown braids. The phone rang once. Then again. Then for a third time. And just as Quanisha was shifting her weight and waiting for her voicemail to pick up she was nearly floored by the sound of a female's voice on the other line.

"Hello?" the girl asked as if she was answering the phone at her own house.

Quanisha was silent as the blood again rushed to her head and her heart began thumping against her chest in anger.

"Who the FUCK is this??" she finally screamed into the phone, startling a few nearby customers who were leaving the store with their wagons.

"What? This Keisha bitch, who dis?" the animated female voice snarled back.

"Who—" before the frazzled Quanisha could complete her sentence she heard a dial tone. She looked at the phone like it was starting to sprout sunflowers right before her eyes.

"Oh fuck nawl," she said and slammed the phone down on

the receiver with all her might. She undid her smock and threw it off angrily to the side, grabbed her purse off the window ledge and left the store in a huff without saying a word to her boss or co-workers.

Tony stood stationary in the bedroom holding Quanisha's phone in his hand as he glared dead into Keisha's eyes. He was still dripping from his shower and holding onto the towel around his waist. He was half trying to figure out what he was going to do about Quanisha, and half brainstorming on which ditch was deep enough to bury Keisha's body in.

"What the fuck is wrong with you?" he finally screamed as he slammed the phone down, almost breaking its flimsy red base.

"I thought—" was all the now scared Keisha managed to whimper out before Tony gripped her up with both hands, letting his towel fall to the floor and literally threw her into the closet door. Keisha hit her head back against the door and slid down to the floor. She shook her head side to side to stay conscious. Tony wasn't finished though.

He rushed over to her before she had a chance to get up from her seated position and slapped her hard across the face with his open palm.

"Tony, please! NO. I'm sorry. I'm sorry!" she pleaded as he leaned down and gripped her by the cut-off T-shirt she was wearing.

"Bitch! I should choke your stupid ass to death right now!! You tryin' to fuck with my situation?" He shook her violently, ripping the cheap shirt slightly at the seams. "What the fuck is wrong with you answering my girl's phone! That's my place to sleep you messin' with right there!"

Keisha was crying by then. She whispered: "Tony I'm so so sorry. It'll never happen again…"

"You damn right it won't happen again. Cuz I'm done with your ass," Tony growled at her and finally let her go. He walked over to the towel on the floor and started drying himself off quickly. He scoured the floor for his underclothes.

"Tony no baby. I swear to you I'll never do nothin' like that again. I promise." Keisha gathered herself and attempted to get up from the floor.

"Get dressed and get the fuck out. NOW," Tony yelled as he pulled on his boxers and a wife beater. He hustled over to the closet where Keisha now stood clutching her shirt together and pushed her aside roughly to find a pair of jeans. Keisha nearly hit the corner of the bedroom door from the force, but recovered just in time.

"No! Tony don't do this to me, I said I was sorry!" she continued pleading as Tony pulled on a pair of blue jeans and a black t-shirt from the top shelf of the closet. He looked at Keisha as if she were crazy for still being there, but then had a second thought.

"Give me some money," he demanded. Keisha just looked at him for a moment, partially shocked at his quick change of tune. He ignored her and walked over to bed to start fixing the sheets. He reached underneath the bed to retrieve the Febreze he kept there specifically for situations such as these.

"How much do you need?" Keisha said as she quickly walked over to her bag, which was still laying on the floor along with her gray jean skirt. She pulled out her change purse but before she could even open it, Tony grabbed it out of her hand. He pulled out all the bills he could find, about 80 dollars, and shoved it in his pocket. Keisha stood by silently. He then grabbed Keisha's jean skirt off the floor and shoved it and the change purse at her before pulling her by the arm out of the bedroom and towards the front door.

"I'll call you aiight? DON'T call me," Tony instructed as he unlatched the door and opened it.

"When?" Keisha said, suddenly getting a backbone. Tony pushed her out the door, even though she was still dressed in her T-shirt and panties.

"I said I will CALL YOU. Damn! You stand outside there for long like that and I won't be responsible for what happens to your ass when Quanisha show up," he warned and slammed the door in her face. Tony was starting to think maybe it wasn't such a good idea to have women over Quanisha's house when she wasn't at home. It was too risky.

Tony rushed to the back and scanned Quanisha's bedroom once more. He squeezed a few more sprays of Febreze out around the room, picked up his black pants and shirt from the floor and threw them in her hamper. Pleased with the look of the room, he went into the bathroom and shaved as quickly as he could. He splashed aftershave on and headed down the hall to the living room where he leaned over and switched on the TV. As he was finally sitting down, he heard keys jingling aggressively at the door. He lounged back on the couch as if he had been sitting there all day, watching Punk'd on MTV.

Quanisha flew through the door and rushed at Tony. She threw the hand up that was holding her bag and brought it down hard on Tony's head before he could react. She got him. The blow shook Tony and gave her the opportunity to get in a few punches to his chest and neck before he finally regained his composure and managed to grab her hands and hold her back as he got up from the couch.

"Baby! Baby what the hell is wrong with you? Calm down," he tried to persuade her.

"Where the fuck is she?? Where is that bitch. Imma kill that bitch!" she screamed obscenities as she struggled wildly to break loose from Tony's grip.

"What? What the hell are you talking about she?"

"Nigga don't play dumb with me! I heard that bitch. She got the nerve to be in my house and put her hands on my phone?!?! Imma kill the ho!" she spat and finally got away from Tony. She ran into the back room and searched for Keisha, but didn't find anything, but a fresh smelling bedroom, and no sign of a woman in the bathroom. Tony followed behind her.

"'Nish, I really don't know what you talkin' about right now, but you need to calm the fuck down," Tony said through clenched teeth, feigning anger.

"Nigga that bitch answered my phone. How you gonna try to tell me different? Where is she?" she said, walking right up to within an inch from his face and throwing her finger up towards his head. She stood only two inches shorter than Tony.

"Nish, I'm telling you, I don't know what you talkin' about. I only *been* here for a half hour, I was watching Punk'd on TV!"

"Then who the fuck just answered my phone earlier. Some bitch Keisha answered my phone! Explain that shit!" she pushed her finger into the side of his face. Tony grit his teeth before continuing with his lies.

"Girl that phone ain't ring since I been here. You probably called the wrong number. Ever think of that?"

Quanisha huffed, out of breath, and looked around, then at the floor and finally back up to Tony, still seemingly unconvinced. She cocked her head to the side and listened.

"Nish, alright, peep this," Tony said, confident that he was getting through to her. "Punk'd about to go off TV right now. This was the one where they punked Omarion, Ashanti and that dude, uh, Bro-man. Tell me how I know that if I wasn't watching it since I came home? Huh?"

Quanisha leaned forward past Tony's frame and looked at the TV, then stood back with her weight on one leg and her arms crossed.

"You gotta stop this shit. Always trynna accuse me of some shit. I'm out there trynna make a couple dollars to help you with the bills and I gotta come home to this. Look, I even got something for you." He reached into his pocket for the $80 he had taken from Keisha. He counted off $50 and waved it in her face. "I helped Jimmy out today and was *gonna* go get you that designer perfume shit you was bitchin' about this morning, but since you wanna *keep* bitchin'..."

A smile grew across Quanisha's face and she snatched the $50 out of his hand.

"Tony, you was gonna go get me my perfume? That is soooo sweet," she said, melting to the gesture. She opened her arms and embraced Tony in a long hug. Tony smiled a devious smile mixed with both relief and the satisfaction of knowing that for the 3rd time that day, he was going to have sex.

* * *

Later that night, after a long session with Quanisha, Tony suddenly awoke from his sleep and had the overwhelming urge to pee. He eased himself out of the bed from underneath Quanisha, who only shifted slightly before resuming her loud snores.

Tony made his way to the bathroom and lifted the toilet seat cover quickly, without bothering to even shut the door or cut the light on. He was still half asleep, and he had to go badly.

Surpisingly, at first nothing came out, so he had to jingle and shake a little. Finally a stream came.

"Ow!" he shrieked and winced in pain at the burning sensation he felt. 'Half asleep' changed to 'fully awake' real fast. He held it in again and stood in confusion and disbelief. Still having to go, he reached over, closed the bathroom door and switched on the light which was also wired to the fan causing a whirring sound to fill the bathroom. He let loose again and felt the same horrible feeling.

"Owwwwwwwwwww shit!" he squealed like a girl as quietly as possible and endured the pain that seemed to last an eternity. Once finally drained, he looked down at his penis which was red and swollen at the tip with wide eyes.

"Oh fuck no! I got burnt!" he groaned. After a long inspection of his private area, he closed the toilet seat cover and sat down. *How could I let this happen?* he thought as he looked back down at his opening, which was now secreting a yellow puss-like fluid. "NO!" he half whispered, half yelled, as he swiped all of the products from the sink onto the floor angrily.

"That bitch! Keisha! Dammit, I knew I shoulda cut her ass loose. Long time ago!" he hissed and shook his head, not even considering the fact that he had slept with at least two other women that week alone before her. Michelle, and Zora…. one of which he hadn't even used a condom with.

"Tony? You alright in there?" Quanisha said sleepily in her normal loud voice from the bedroom. Tony quickly reached for the toilet paper and wiped his penis off, then put it back in his shorts.

"Yea, I'm fine. Go back to sleep," he said, slowly remembering that he hadn't used a condom with Quanisha that night, either.

chapter 2

That next day, Tony managed to pull himself out of the bed and out the door at the wee hour of 12 in the afternoon. He was headed to Upper Darby to consult with his boy Terrance. Tony had grown up with Terrance from the age of nine years old when they met in elementary school. Tony was a hard headed young boy who was constantly making appearances in the principal's office, and Terrance was a promising young athlete who managed to make the varsity high school basketball while still in junior high. They complemented each other in a way. Terrance had high hopes of making it to the NBA, and was shuttled off to Duke immediately upon graduating from high school with a full athletic scholarship. Terrance always had a good head on his shoulders, and knew the importance of getting some experience and higher education under his belt before making an attempt at the NBA draft.

Unfortunately, before the beginning of Terrance's senior year in college, Terrance's left knee completely gave out on him, an injury that ran in his family. His father had had very bad knees, as well as two of his cousins and his great-grandfather, as he was told. His play was very spotty his last year of college, and no recruiter would even look his way after a while – he was too big a risk. Terrance's good sense saved his ass, as he had gotten a free college education, graduated with decent grades and managed to get a lucrative job as a junior brand manager at R.K. Watts and Associates, a company owned by the brother of his college assistant coach. The Duke coaches loved and took good care of

Terrance, even after his injury, because they saw that he had vision beyond his career as an athlete, something they rarely saw in any of their other players.

Despite all of Terrance's accomplishments and drive to go forward in life, Tony had successfully prevented his friend's positivity from rubbing off on him in any way, shape, or form.

Terrance had moved back to the Philadelphia area three years earlier after graduating to start his new consulting gig, which was located in Dover, Delaware. His job allowed him a flex schedule; he worked 4 days a week, 10 hours a day, Fridays off. He bought a house in Springfield, PA, far enough from the drama of the actual city, but close enough to see his mother and sister on a regular basis. Tony pulled his light blue Chevy Cavalier up to the brick house on the corner and beeped his horn several times to purposely annoy his long-time friend.

"Yeeee-owww!" Terrance finally came to the door and outside without missing a beat. Tony got out of the car to greet his friend and they met midway with a soul handshake, then a half hug. "I knew that had to be yo ass, leanin' on the horn like that. Excuse me, but this a 'residential community.' You know we can't be having that out here." Terrance said the last part in an official tone with a laugh.

"Yea whatever, what these crackas gonna do? Come whoop my ass? I think not," Tony scoffed as they made their way into Terrance's comfortable house.

"You want something to drink?" Terrance asked walking into the kitchen and opening his refrigerator.

"Yea, a beer if you got it. Yo Ran, I know you be running through these white broads over here. How many you hit so far?" Tony asked mischeviously from his seat on the living room couch, knowing that his friend had done no such thing. Terrance was a little slow when it came to the ladies. He tended to clam up around them, and he had been on a 'black power' kick ever since his second year in college. So Terrance romancing the white women around his way was highly unlikely.

"Man please, you know that ain't me," Terrance responded as he walked into the living room where his friend was already relaxing with his feet up. He handed Tony the beer and flopped into his soft leather loveseat. He had been watching the scores from the previous night on ESPN.

"Dallas beat New York? No way," Tony said as he watched the football scores flash on the screen. He popped open his beer and took a long sip.

"Yup, preseason. Good game too, you missed it."

"Well, Quanisha don't have the satellite channels like you do, just basic cable."

"Damn! Just basic? Why don't you chip in a couple dollars so ya'll can get the Dish? It's only like $40 a month."

Tony was just silent and ignored his friend's question as he eyed the baseball scores. He took another sip of his beer.

"Where you coming from?" Terrance asked after a few minutes.

"From the crib."

"So what brings you over here? No skirts to chase?" Terrance chuckled, but was secretly a little envious of his boy's girl-getting skills.

"Man please, I don't even be all about that no more, I'm focused."

"Focused on what?" Terrance asked incredulously.

"On my rap thing nigga," Tony responded, slightly annoyed, as if Terrance should have already known. "I know some dudes that got a studio down North Philly who said they can get me in there for a couple hours."

"Oh really," Terrance said, disinterested. Tony had been talking about his impending rap career since they were youngsters playing on the monkey bars.

"Yup," Tony responded confidently. "You know I already got two tracks laid, me and Rob gonna try to get at least three more done." Rob, a self-proclaimed genius when it came to beats, was his partner in crime when it came to music. Despite Rob's 'talent' most people laughed off his beats as garbage behind his back. Everybody except Tony who thought they were the best thing since sliced bread.

"Man, when you gonna get a job Tone? You gotta be able to make money in the process of pursuing your dream. You know, so that you can eventually invest in it."

"Yea yea, I'm working on it. I'm trying to get this job at UPS," Tony lied. He still hadn't made so much as a finger lift towards calling the job line at UPS.

"Well that's good. At least you trying, I guess," Terrance said, unsure of the validity of Tony's words. He knew Tony by now, and that most of the time the words that came out of his mouth were pure bullshit. Terrance didn't know why he even tolerated being around Tony anymore; Tony was obviously not on his level of thinking.

"Yea. Listen man. I gotta ask you something in confidence. You my best boy from way back in the day, so I feel like you the only one I can trust with this information. Probably the only one that can help too. This is between us."

Terrance perked up at hearing this and leaned forward in his seat. "Yea man, you know it. What's up?"

Tony let out a long loud sigh before continuing. He let a few more seconds pass, the thought hanging thick in the air. He considered what he was about to reveal to his friend a few more seconds, and then decided this was Terrance, his boy. "I think I caught the clap or something from this hoodrat chick I been messin' with."

"The 'clap'?" Terrance repeated, struggling not to laugh. "What the hell is that?"

"I don't know man. All I know is my shit is burning, bad. I held my pee in this morning til Quanisha left so I could scream in the bathroom. That's how bad this shit is man. I'm not even playing," Tony said shaking his head and looking at the TV.

Terrance looked at his friend and instantly felt sorry for him. "Did you see a discharge?"

"Yeah."

"You might have chlamydia, or gonorrhea. You need to go to a clinic man, they got medicine for that."

"For real? Do it get rid of it?"

"I don't know for sure. But it definitely stops the burning and shit."

"You mean they don't have a pill that cures it? I gotta deal with this shit forever?" Tony asked with a look of incredulity on his face.

"Naw you don't have to deal with the burning sensation forever, but you do have to keep taking that medicine to stop it from coming back. Some of them diseases do stay wit you though."

"You're kidding me right?"

"Naw man, but it ain't the end of the world, you just gotta stay on top of it. That's all," Terrance said, searching for the right words to say at the moment.

Tony was silent for what seemed like an eternity. Terrance was now avoiding him with his eyes and looking in every direction but Tony's. Terrance thought about whether his friend was having unprotected sex with Quanisha, who was also a good friend of his from childhood.

Suddenly Tony shot up from his seat. "Shit!" he yelled, balling his hands into fists and shaking them firmly in front of him. He ran his hand over his spongy hair which was still badly in need of a cut. When he looked out the window his expression seemed to change a bit.

"Aiight man, I gotta be out." Tony headed down the short flight of stairs to the front door without even giving his boy a pound.

"Where you going, bro?" Terrance asked with a confused look on his face at his friend's quick change in demeanor.

"Back to Nisha's. I gotta pee. Unless you wanna hear a grown man scream."

Terrance let out a restrained chuckle, but ended it quickly. He knew the situation was still a sore spot for Tony, despite his humor. Tony stopped and turned back around at the door before leaving.

"Yo, we going to Devilutions tonight, you trying to go?"

"Devilutions? Man you going to that ghetto ass club?" Terrance asked with his nose scrunched up.

"Hell yeah, they having $1 shots and beers before 12. You damn straight Imma be there. Imma drink myself into oblivion over this shit. Are you trying to go or not?" Tony asked impatiently, as he walked back towards the stairs and then back to the door, trying to hold back the urge.

"Man, you need to be heading to that clinic, not the club. But yea I guess I'll roll through. Who else is going?" Terrance asked, curious about the possibility of his getting some that night. The girl's at Devilutions were notoriously easy.

"Probably Scoop, Rob and Belly," Tony said, his voice trailing off as he headed outside, the screen door slamming behind him.

* * *

Devilutions was a night club populated mostly by dirty, grimy thugs and shameless hoodrats, a few decent types thrown here and there. About 30% of the regular crowd had bullet wounds, and it seemed as if the party wasn't really over until somebody started shooting outside.

Tony, Rob, Scoop and Terrance finally walked in at 11:15pm after waiting on line for about a half hour. Belly couldn't make it because of a prior engagement, but everybody knew it was because his possessive baby's mother told him he couldn't go out. They arrived in just enough time to catch the drink specials, and had only paid half-price because Rob's boy worked the door. He of course got in for free. The women who walked in with them could smell the broke nigga scent emanating from these brothas from a mile away, and each took a mental note of their faces for future reference.

Tony swaggered up to the bar, ready to spend up the $25 he had left after paying admission. He hadn't had time to ask his mom for more cash because of procrastinating in the streets too long. The hispanic female bartender came over smiling.

"What can I get you?" she asked leaning over the bar to hear.

"Gimme two shots of Henny, those are a dollar right?"

"No the Hennessey is regular price, $6 a shot. The only dollar shots are …. Smirnoff, Bankers Club, Bacardi Dark…." the bartenders voice came in and out over the noise as she listed a few more cheap brands.

"Damn. Aiight, just give me two shots of Smirnoff. Naw,

make that one shot Smirnoff, one shot of Bacardi."

"Tony, man, you ain't supposed to mix light and dark liquor. You gonna be fucked up if you keep that up," Scoop piped in from behind him. Rob and Terrance flanked him on either side.

"Shut up the hell up man. I'll drink how I want," Tony said as he watched the bartender pour the liquor into little plastic cups.

Scoop ignored him. "Lemme get a Hennessey. I *gots* a job so I can afford the good shit," he joked back at Tony when the bartender got back with Tony's drinks and threw a $20 bill on the bar. The bartender tried to hide a smile as she turned to retrieve the open bottle of Hennessey. Rob yelled out his order of a shot of Bacardi Dark as well.

"Nigga I can afford that shit," Tony said, slightly annoyed and embarrassed. He downed his shots one after the other. Scoop and Terrance shook their heads, watching the bartender ring up Scoop's Hennessey. When she came back, the bartender gave Scoop change, of which he left $2 on the bar as a tip. She asked if Terrance needed anything, but he waved her off.

"Okay then. That'll be...$3 for the other drinks please," the bartender said, looking at Tony, who was sitting closest to the bar, after adding up the amounts in her head.

"What? Oh naw, you gotta separate that. Those are separate orders," Tony specified.

Rob looked at Tony as if he had farted right in his face. "Nigga you can't pay a dollar for my drink? I'll get you later."

"Naw, naw. You know damned well I ain't down for that. Later on yo ass will be running around the club chasing bitches and I can't find you nowheres to pay for *my* drink. Fuck that, pay for own your drink nigga," Tony said throwing a $5 bill on the bar. The bartender turned around and rang up his order.

"You cheap as shit! I cannot believe this nigga's getting

particular over a buck!" Rob complained as he pulled out a $10 bill and threw it on the bar.

"Bucks add up. Quit complaining," Tony sneered. The bartender came back with his change and Tony took two dollars from her. "Let me get a Bud."

Terrance watched as Tony put the $2 dollars in his pocket. "You ain't gonna give her that?"

"Naw! What the hell for, she ain't do nothing but pour some drinks in a cup," he answered rudely. The bartender overheard the last bit of the conversation, and slammed Tony's beer down on the bar before walking away.

"She'll get over it," Tony laughed and walked away from the bar, following Rob.

The club was getting packed, but it was still light enough to easily pass through the crowd. A cute light skinned girl passed by and Tony jumped in front of her. He was moving to the beat of Da Band's *Bad Boy This*, holding his beer high and looking down at the girl like a piece of meat. She followed suit and grabbed onto him, moving in a two step and then finally turning around, dropping to the floor and grinding her way back up.

The night went on and before Tony knew it, it was going on 2:15am. The club wasn't shutting down until 3am though. Tony was lit. And then had the nerve to go to the bar once again and order another shot of Bacardi, which was now $3. The other bartender working the bar, a short pretty chubby-faced brown skinned girl, went to the other side of the bar to get a new bottle of Bacardi Dark. The hispanic bartender, Melinda, pulled her aside as she was pulling the bottle out of the crate.

"You getting that for that broke ass nigga over there? The one with the fake ass Girbaud t-shirt?" she asked.

"Yea, why?" the brown skinned bartender named Brenda

responded and started twisting the bottle cap off.

"Hold up," Melinda said as she held up her hand and walked over to the middle of the bar. She found a double shot glass holding some dirty bar tools. She took the tools out and saw that there was the beginnings of mold on the bottom of the glass. The glass was so dirty and cloudy with specks of grime that she could barely see through it. Requesting the bottle of Bacardi from her bar-mate, she smiled and looked over at Tony, who was looking as if he was about to spin off his seat. Brenda just looked on, knowing that her girlfriend had to have a method to her madness. She watched Melinda turn around and discreetly pour a healthy glass of the Bacardi dark in the dirty glass, and then walk over to the other side of the bar to garnish it with a lime. She smiled and handed the drink to Brenda.

"Here, give him a double shot of this." Melinda threw her head back and laughed as she walked away to help more customers.

Back on the other side of the bar, Brenda handed Tony the drink.

"That'll be $3 please," she said in her sweetest voice. She watched as Tony threw the shot back without hesitation and cringed. He smacked his lips and made a funny face as he pulled what was left of his money out of his pocket. He put $3 on the bar and got up, but before he left he stopped Brenda again.

"Wait, here." He stumbled, and then shoved his hand in his pants pocket coming out with a handful of change. He picked 50 cents out of the pile and placed it on the bar, pushing it forward and smiled as if he were giving her a twenty dollar bill. "That's for you."

Brenda the bartender pushed the two coins back to him. "Keep it. You need it more than me brah," she said and walked off, annoyed. *That's why your ass just drank a Bacardi and Mildew, nigga,* she thought. No wonder Melissa had a vendetta on him. She wanted to flick those coins at his forehead.

Tony turned up his nose and picked his 50 cents right back up off the bar. "Fine, shit that was almost a 20% tip!"

The women sitting at the bar shook their head at his sorry trifling self.

Tony made his way back over to the middle of the dance floor and roughly pulled a girl wearing a bra top which was only hidden by a sheer shirt towards him. They started dancing wildy, not having any type of regard or remorse for who they were pushing out of the way nearby. After a few moments, a brother wearing a pair of authentic Gucci shades balanced on his forehead pushed Tony out of the way and told him to watch himself. Tony ignored him and kept dancing, even more reckless than before. When the Gucci brotha had been hit a couple more times, he again pushed Tony, causing him to fall forward into the girl he was dancing with. Gucci had about four inches on Tony.

"What the fuck?" the ghetto hispanic girl said balancing herself. Tony had some words with Gucci before walking off to find his boys.

He spotted Rob near the bar, and luckily Scoop not far from him dancing with a girl that looked like she needed a shower with a fire hose. He grabbed them both, talking in a tone that let them know he needed their attention immediately, and they followed him back to the middle of the dance floor. Tony pointed out Gucci, like a little girl telling on someone who had bothered her on the bus, and Scoop and Rob, who was officially heavy at 5'9 285 lbs immediately walked up on the dude with Tony close behind. Rob and Scoop then stood on either side of Gucci, while Tony stood in the middle facing him.

"What seems to be the problem?" Scoop inquired.

"There ain't no problem, yo boy just need to learn how to respect people's space," Gucci said, annoyed, but sensing that something was about to go down. Just then out of the blue Tony reached over to mush Gucci in the face, and when Gucci tried to retaliate, Rob and Scoop immediately pounced on him. One of them threw a punch, while the other tried to restrain his hands. Tony stood by and laughed. Gucci's $400 glasses fell off his face, and hit the floor, along with his cell phone, which had been strapped to his belt. Scavengers rushed to pick up the falling items, one of them of course Tony, who managed to scoop up the cellphone, keys and some money that had slipped out of Gucci's pocket as he was struggling to get free. The bouncers finally got over to the scene and grabbed Gucci from Rob and Scoop, carrying Gucci to and out the door.

"Get the fuck off me! How you gonna take me out? They the ones that came at me!..." Gucci could be heard before the bouncers closed the door in his face.

At 3:00 the club let out and Tony and his boys were still falling out laughing about what had happened to Gucci. When they came out they saw that he was still there, arguing with the bouncers and one of the promoters about having been taken out and losing most of his valuable belongings. The promoters were trying to calm him down, but to no avail. It got worse when he spotted Tony and his friends.

"There they go! These the niggas ya'll let stay in the club and steal my shit!" Gucci tried to make a rush at one of them, but the 330 pound bouncer held him back. Gucci looked at him helplessly. "Come on man, they probably got my keys and shit. I can't get home without my damn keys!"

"You just gonna have to calm down, my man. Just go back in

the club, maybe they got your keys at the DJ booth," the bouncer reasoned.

Tony and his boys stifled laughter as they quickly moved towards Scoop's truck. Terrance was thoroughly confused.

"What happened?" he asked, still uninformed.

About 15 minutes into their ride home, Tony felt his phone vibrating in his pocket. He went to the source and saw that it wasn't his phone, but Gucci's. He quickly picked up.

"Yeee-ooww," Tony greeted obnoxiously.

"Who's this?"

"This ya boy, who dis?" Tony chuckled. Rob and Scoop joined in when they realized what was happening.

"Nigga what the fuck you doing with my phone??!!"

"This my phone, whatchu talkin' about man? Go on with that shit."

Gucci continued yelling obscenities through the phone, but Tony, Rob, and Scoop's laughter only grew louder and louder.

"Yea yea yea, I got me a new phone and some new keys. To a shiny new Benz. Hahaha…." Tony laughed and then hung up the phone. The phone rang three more times before Gucci gave up. Tony scanned the keys and wondered if it would be worth trying to find Gucci's Benz out in the parking lot…

"Ya'll took that man's keys for real? How the hell is he supposed to get home and in his house?" Terrance's voice of reason piped in as he slowly caught up with what was going on.

"Man, fuck that nigga. He should have thought about all that before he pushed me," Tony snorted out and then leaned down in the passenger's seat.

"Oh so he just pushed you outta nowhere. Yea, that sounds right," Terrance said sarcastically and thoroughly angry at the situation. How were they going to take the man's cellphone and keys to his house? What did they need the keys for? That was just trifling.

"Yea that's right. And that nigga got his shit rocked." Tony reached his hand over and held it out for Scoop to slap. "Now he'll know, don't fuck with these niggas in the club. That's a bad idea dude."

"So all three of ya'll niggas were involved right? I thought you said he pushed *you*?" Terrance directed at Tony.

"You fuck with my boy, you fucking with me," Rob reasoned as he started chomping on some barbecue potato chips he had grabbed from the vending machine in the club.

"Nigga, I know you ain't eating no chips in my truck!" Scoop yelled at Rob. "You black burnt crispy Pillsbury dough boy lookin' muthafucka! Why you always gotta be eating somethin'? Damn!"

Rob stopped chewing.

"You know, you always doing that shit Tony. Getting other people to fight your battles. I don't think you've ever even got your own hands dirty, not even back in elementary school," Terrance accused.

"Shut the fuck up Terrance, I ain't trying to hear all your whining tonight. Don't be mad at me cause you ain't get no numbers. That nigga deserved what he got," Tony retorted.

"Actually, I did get numbers. Two. And they wasn't no straight up hoochie ass skanks like the ones I seen you with. I guess they can spot a *real* man when they see him," Terrance confirmed. Rob and Scoop ooooohhed at Terrance's comment.

Tony turned around and looked at Terrance as if he were out of his God-given mind. Rob tried to mediate before things got out of hand. The truth was, he respected Terrance despite his tendency to be a square, and would never think of trying to lay a hand on him in defense of Tony of all people. A stranger though, that was no problem. Besides, Terrance would probably whoop his ass.

"Aiight ya'll. What's done is done, that nigga done lost his shit, and he's gonna have to deal with it. That's the risk you take. We probably was fucked up for taking that shit, but what we gonna do now? Nothin'. So just drop it," Rob said, trying to end the conversation. There was quiet for a few moments.

"Alright. But just know that what goes around come around. You don't do people like that and get away with it," Terrance said after thinking over what his friends had done with complete disdain.

"Yea yea, whatever," Tony scoffed. He rolled down the window and threw Gucci's keys out of the window carelessly. The car sat in silence the rest of the ride home.

* * *

It was 5:14am that same morning when Tony got a call on his cellphone. *Who the fuck could this be? It better not be one of these bitches*, he thought to himself as he looked over at Quanisha. She moved a little, but was still fast asleep. Quanisha was a very deep sleeper.

He reached over and clicked the phone's talk button.

"Hello?"

"Tony! Oh Tony, baby, they robbed me…" the familiar voice moaned.

"What? Momma? What are you talking about?" Tony asked frantically. It was his grandmother, who he considered to be his mother since she had raised and taken care of him.

"Baby, they took everything. Both my TVs and my good china… they just cleaned me out…and knocked me over…"

"What? Momma finish what you sayin'????"

"They knocked me over the head with a gun baby, and I'm bleeding. I'm bleeding bad…" Tony's grandmother's voice faded again.

"Momma!! Imma be RIGHT there aiight??" Tony yelled into the phone to make sure she heard him before he ended the call, fingers shaking. He threw the covers back and leapt out of bed.

When Tony finally jumped in his Cavalier it was about three minutes after his grandmother had made the distressed call. It was breaking his heart; Tony's grandmother meant everything to him in the world. Despite how he treated her — always asking her for money, coming into her house at all hours, smoking weed in her basement, yelling at her when things didn't go his way — he loved his Grandma more than anything or anybody. He turned the ignition and sped off down the street into the night towards his grandmother's house in West Philly.

When he reached the red light at the corner of 53th and Baltimore he had to pause. He had run every light from 60th and on, but now there was a cop crossing down 53rd. He had two nick bags of weed on him, and he didn't need that extra added aggravation. He knew that even if he explained what his rush was about, they would tell him to calm down, detain him at first and hold him from seeing to his Grandma. He watched the officer pass, and the officer looked right back at him.

As he finally saw the officer turn the corner out of sight, his car began puttering and jerking violently. He looked down at the dash as if that would stop what was happening. The car finally just shut off completely.

"What the?" Tony tried the ignition, but it only made that grinding noise that tells you it's not planning on starting up any time soon. He tried it again, and again, cursing and screaming as the car behind him finally got the idea and went around him. He tried one more time, pressing the gas pedal all the way down as he turned the key, but still the car didn't turn on.

"Noooo, this cannot happen right now!" Tony screamed and then fumbled for his cellphone in his pocket. He retrieved the cellphone he had taken from Gucci, and dialed the number to Quanisha's, who had barely even stirred when Tony ran out of the door.

At Quanisha's, the phone rang, and rang, and rang. Quanisha, who was still fast asleep, was dreaming about sitting at her big desk, at her own office at the beauty salon she had always wished she could open. She figured the phone sounds were the phones ringing off the hook at her shop, and smiled in her sleep as Tony's call got sent to voicemail.

"Quanisha!" Tony yelled into the voicemail as if Quanisha could hear him. Gucci's cellphone made a loud beeping sound. "What the hell is wrong with you! Pick up the phone!" he hung the phone up angrily. He dialed Terrance's number and the voicemail picked up on the first ring. Terrance had his high tech home phone programmed to go straight to voicemail at night so that he wouldn't be disturbed before he had to go to work. Only his mother and sister's phones could get through at that time of night. Terrance hated cellphones, and the only one he carried was paid for by his job and used for work purposes only. Nobody even had Terrance's cellphone number besides his mother.

Looking down at the phone he noticed that the battery was about to go out. He threw the phone down and pulled out his own phone. He tried to call Quanisha's house again, but this time his phone wouldn't even dial out. The message just kept saying "connecting." Pissed, Tony threw the phone on the seat. He jumped out of the car and searched his pocket for change. All he had was a bunch of pennies, and the two quarters that he was going to give the bartender at Devilutions. Thank God!

He picked up a payphone, threw in the dimes frantically and tried his boy Terrance again in vain. Instead of the voicemail, this time an automated voice came on and said "45 cents please. Please deposit 45 cents to complete this call."

"Shit!" Tony had forgotten that Terrance lived outside of his 215 area code. He clicked the hook to get his change back, but the bootleg payphone ate his quarter. He cursed again and dropped his last quarter into the slot to try Quanisha again, but the phone just kept ringing. The voicemail picked up before he had a chance to hang up, so he lost that quarter too. He banged the receiver of the phone down several times, trying to break it. It had been a total of about ten minutes since his Grandma had called, and he was still a 15 minute run away from her house. It was time to call the paramedics. *What the hell was I gonna do when I got there anyway?* he thought to himself. He had panicked, and wasn't thinking right. He picked the phone back up and dialed 911.

Tony was sprinting down 52nd Street towards Market, but as soon as he turned the corner on 52nd, three blocks away from his Grandma's house, his legs buckled underneath him and he fell to his knees.

"Ssss, owww. Damn," he winced in pain, holding his left hip, the same one that had gotten hit in his accident on the street that day on 69th Street. It had been bothering him ever since, and nobody had seen or reported the guy who hit him. It had been getting so bad that he was starting to think it was necessary to see a doctor about it, but he had no insurance and no money. A bad combination. Any money he needed to spend on medical problems right now would have to be towards his brand new STD, which was still also causing him urgent pain whenever he went to the bathroom. He wished he could use his grandmother's insurance; she was retired but had very good insurance from her days as a Septa driver. But being 25 and never having even seen the inside of a college, Tony couldn't be claimed as a dependent under her medical plan.

Tony set his right foot up in front of him, still grasping his left thigh, and struggled to his feet again. The pain was unbearable. But he had to get to his Grandma's. He slowly put one foot in front of the other, in a slow and painful gait.

When Tony finally arrived at his grandmother's house, he could hear the sirens approaching in the background. It had been almost 25 minutes, and the paramedics were just now coming? He rushed up, pushed open the already ajar door and immediately saw his poor grandmother leaned back on the stairs in her nightgown, passed out. Her hands were strewn across the steps, and her feet were hanging down touching the floor. There was blood coming down the side of her face. He limped quickly to her side.

"Mom!! Mom!! Can you hear me? Ma? Say something!" he demanded, trying to pick her head up and shaking her shoulders intermittently. She started a low moan and slowly opened her eyes. Though she was beginning to suffer from cataracts, she instantly recognized her grandson.

"Baby? I'm so glad you're here...It..." Grandma's voice trailed off again and she looked as if she was about to lose consciousness again. Tony shook her.

"Ma you gotta stay up and talk to me, the doctor's will be here any minute! Tell me what happened??!!" Tony yelled, feeling a lump develop in his throat.

Grandma tried her best to stay alert. She spoke slowly. "Oh. It was horrible, Anthony. They came in here, those thugs. I think through the back. Cuz I thought I heard something in the back.

They had on black…." her voice trailed and she closed her eyes, then they shot open again. Tony listened intently his red eyes nearly bugging out of his head. "They had on black hoodies, I couldn't see their faces…"

"Why did you come downstairs Ma? You should have just stayed upstairs and called the police!" He could see the lights from the ambulance now flashing in front of the house.

A second later the paramedics came through the door and asked Tony to step out of the way.

"It's about time, what took ya'll so damned long!" he let out a frustrated rant, fear evident in his voice from the situation. The paramedics just ignored him.

He looked down at his grandmother again, who had passed out completely again by this time and stroked her wild hair down a bit before finally getting up and letting the paramedics take over. He felt helpless as he watched them load his grandmother onto a gurney. They carried her out of the front door, her head falling lifelessly to the side as Tony followed close behind.

chapter 3

At the hospital emergency waiting room Tony sat, leaning forward and looking down at his hands nervously. Ironically enough, the pain in his upper thigh had ceased as soon as he had arrived at the hospital. There were blood stains on his shirt, and with the expression Tony was wearing you would think *he* was the one that had tried to kill somebody.

Tony was thinking about who could have done this. Could it be? Naw, there was no way. That guy from the club couldn't have had any way of finding out his name, let alone where he lived. But then again, someone from the club could have tipped Gucci off to Tony's whereabouts. He knew a few people there that night, male and female, some that didn't like his ass one bit. Tony's thoughts were interrupted by the emergency room doctor. It was nearly three hours after they had brought his grandmother in.

"Mr. Jackson? Are you the son of Ms. —"

"Yes," Tony interrupted back. "How is she?"

"Well, she's coherent at the moment. But she's suffered a moderate concussion, a very serious trauma to the head for a woman her age. We are going to have to hold her for a while, and do an MRI to understand the extent of the damage. She's been asking for you," the frail looking white doctor said as he looked Tony directly in the eye.

"I want to see her, where's she at?" Tony requested.

"Right through these doors. Follow me."

Tony and the doctor went to the back through the swinging emergency doors. The doctor led him through a front room, and then into the circular emergency room. There were other patients lined along the room, some concealed by their individual curtains. They finally walked up to the area where Tony's Grandma was laying, hooked up to a heart monitor, IV and other various machines. She lay face straight up, her eyes closed. They had wrapped a bandage around her head. Tony walked up to her side.

"Mom? You hear me?" Tony said, not sure of what he should say. He definitely did not like seeing his grandmother, his mom, like this.

Grandma opened her eyes into a squint and looked into her grandson's worried eyes. "Baby."

"Yeah? How you feelin' Ma?" Tony asked her and grabbed her hand.

"Ohhh, my head is hurting." Grandma tried to reach up and touch the side of her head but the IV was restraining her.

"Just relax Ms. Jackson, everything will be fine, we've given you some pain killers that should kick in within the hour," the doctor assured. "I'll leave you two alone for a moment, then I'll need you to fill out some more papers for your grandmother Mr. Jackson. We'll be moving her into a room this morning."

"Fine," Tony said and turned his full attention back to his grandmother after the doctor had left.

"Oh Anthony, they took everything. It was two of 'em. They went in your room. I know because I saw them with your silver box. The one you keep hidden in your closet."

"What?!" Tony yelled just a little too loud, causing the nurses nearby to jerk their heads in his direction and give him dirty looks. But he wasn't paying any attention to them. "They took my box??"

"Yes baby, that's why I came downstairs. I knew they was in your room downstairs. I didn't want them to take your box. I heard them in the living room and knew they was taking the TV, and my china, but when I saw your box in the big one's hand, I ran down the stairs yelling and started swingin' my bat at 'em. I hit the one, but the other one hit me in the head with that gun and I fell to the floor. They left with your box, the trophies and the TV that was in your room. I'm so sorry baby."

Tony flopped down in the seat next to the bed in complete shock. They had taken his box! The box that held every possession he held dear to him. It contained his real mother's high school ring and her picture, the last items he had to remember her by after her death 12 years before. It held some old baseball cards that were valued at over $3,000 in today's terms and a signed baseball by his favorite Phillies pitcher from when he was seven. At the bottom of the box was page after page of rhymes he had written from age 11 and up, at least 80 pages of his masterpieces. His little league trophies were just about the only thing to prove that he had accomplished something in life. Why would they need to take those? They weren't worth anything except to Tony. And what his grandmother didn't know, was that he also had stashed a $9,000 Rolex watch he had stolen in a carjacking with his boy Lamar a month earlier in that box. He had planned to pawn it, put a down payment on a new Lexus and car insurance, and use the rest to press a thousand CDs when his rap album was finished. That way he could project a believable image of a rap star, he couldn't be taken seriously riding around in an old raggedy Cavalier. It was all gone. All of his plans were done with.

"Tony? Are you alright? Sweetie I'm so so sorry. I tried to stop them." His grandmother started crying from seeing the distress and hopelessness in Tony's eyes. She wanted so badly for Tony to do something for himself in life, and she knew that this was the last thing he needed: to lose all of his precious belongings.

"No Mama, don't cry. It's not your fault." Tony struggled his way up out of the seat, feeling as if he were about to faint at any moment. Regaining his balance, he managed to reach over and kiss his grandmother on her forehead. "Get some rest, I'm going to sign those papers."

"Tony, baby, I love you. It will be alright. My insurance might be able to cover some of it," his grandmother pleaded.

"Right mama. Get your rest. I'll be back tomorrow alright?" Tony ran his hand down her leg, still deep in thought and walked off towards the emergency room exit.

As Tony was walking out of the hospital doors, forgetting to sign his grandmother's papers, he suddenly snapped himself back to reality and realized that his car was still parked in the middle of the street on 53rd and Baltimore, the heart of the hood. He needed to get back to it before it got stripped down to its suspension. He reached in his pocket for his cellphone to call Quanisha, but it was no where to be found. He thought back, and remembered that he had left it in the car.

"Ohhh noooo," he complained and lowered his head down once, lifted it in thought, and then dropped it again in defeat. That phone, and his stereo system, was probably long gone by then.

"What the fuck else could go wrong!!!" he screamed out at the top of his lungs in the hospital parking lot. It was after 9am and hospital people were still bustling around the area, just coming into work, looking at Tony as if he were crazy. Tony thought about what he should do. He could call Terrance or Scoop, but they were probably at work already. And Terrance was probably still pissed about what had happened at the club the night before. He had to get in touch with Quanisha somehow.

Tony walked back into the hospital emergency room and immediately spotted an average looking young sister at the desk which was guarded by a bullet proof window. He cleared his throat and put on the saddest, sorriest look he could muster.

"Miss? Miss?" he got her attention, and the young girl looked up. "I need to get in touch with my sister to tell her about my Grandma."

"Your grandma's the one that just came in, a blow to the head right?" the girl, who looked to be in her early twenties, asked.

"Yes, I need to tell my family. But I don't have a cellphone *or* my car," he let out a big sigh and shook his head. "Can I use your phone?"

The girl looked back at him, overcome with pity. "Of course." She took the phone off the receiver and handed it to him underneath the bullet proof glass. "What's the number."

Tony ran off the number and she dialed. This time Quanisha picked up on the first ring.

"Tony! Where the hell are you? Why you leave that message on my voicemail last night??"

"Nish, it's a long story. Mama got robbed, I'm at Mercy Hospital in Darby. I need you to come get me."

"What happened to your car? How did you get there?" she inquired with a tinge of suspicion.

"Look, my car broke down and I rode in the ambulance. Would you quit asking questions and just come get me? This is urgent, my shit could be getting took right now while you speak!" he spit into the phone, his anger at the whole situation finally coming to a head. Quanisha had a way of bringing it out of him.

"Alright, alright. I'll be right there." Quanisha hung up the phone. Tony handed the receiver back to the girl behind the counter, and she in turn handed him a folded piece of paper.

"My name is Jenny. You can call me on my cellphone here. I'll…. personally keep you updated on your grandmother's condition," the girl said and smiled. Damn, she was bold. Tony returned the smile, tucked the paper in his pocket and moved towards the exit.

Quanisha pulled up to the curb of the emergency entrance dressed in her night clothes and a big gray pull over sweater. Tony got in and the inquisition began.

"What the hell happened??" she asked as she pulled off. "Where's your car?"

"I told you, Mama got robbed. They took just about all our shit and hit her over the head with a gun." Tony stuck his fingers in his spongy fro and leaned his elbow on the door-rest, looking out of the window at nothing in particular.

"What!? Oh no, Tony, is she okay?" Quanisha put her hand over her mouth in amazement, genuinely concerned as she slowed down a bit.

"She alright, damn! Just drive, I need to get back to that car," he commanded. "They already took most of my shit, I don't need them taking my car stereo too! Hurry up!"

Quanisha sat up straight, holding onto the wheel as she resumed her speed. She seemed to think carefully before saying her next words. They were already on Baltimore and on their way to Tony's car when she finally spoke up. "You know Tony, I know you goin' through something right now and I'm sorry about your Grandma and all, but you still don't need to be talkin' to me any kinda way. I'm *here*, trying to help your ass and ask about your Grandma and you yellin' at me? What the fuck did I do? You treat me like *I* was the one that took your shit!"

"Nish, just shut the fuck up right now. I do not want to hear it," Tony said firmly.

"No. No. I will not shut the fuck up. You know why? Cuz you in MY car right now, you living in MY house and Imma tell you exactly what the fuck needs to be said. You gonna hear me out—" Her words were muffled. Tony had reached over and violently pushed her face into the window. Her head knocked into the glass.

"I just said to shut the fuck up right!?" he yelled, gesturing wildly in the car. Quanisha swerved the car and came to a screeching halt. She reached under her seat and produced a sharp kitchen knife.

"Get the *fuck* out my car!!" she screamed at the top of her lungs, clutching the knife in Tony's direction. Tears began to run down her face. She had a crazed look in her eyes that said she meant business. "Get OUT!"

Tony, thoroughly shocked, reached for the door latch and let himself out of the car without a second thought. She had caught him by surprise. Quanisha sped off, leaving him standing on the corner of 58th and Baltimore. Tony, still shook, stood in the same spot for a few minutes before finally beginning to put one foot in front of the other and walk the rest of the way towards his car. Five steps later, the piercing pain returned to his left thigh.

At 54th, the limping Tony could see that his car was still at least sitting in the same spot where he had left it hours before. *Thank God*, he thought. Traffic was now navigating around it. He was surprised the cops hadn't tried to have it towed, but not really since they were rarely on top of things as minor as that. Tony pulled his keys out of his pocket.

When he finally reached the car he looked sadly in through the gaping hole that had been busted in his passenger side window. The stereo was long gone, wires hanging out of the dash. It was definitely the work of a quick and skilled crackhead. Tony slammed his hand on top of the car and said curse words that hadn't even been invented yet. He kicked the car and then slowly made his way to the driver's side, getting in. The pain in his leg had magically disappeared again. How convenient. He put the key in the ignition and the thing started right up.

"What the fuck is going on?" he said aloud to himself incredulously. He merged with the cars going around him and headed for his grandmother's house.

While driving he searched for where he had thrown his cellphone. He looked on the floor, under the seat, and between the seats but it was nowhere to be found. They had taken that too. *Why wouldn't they*, he thought. A look of disgust was written all over his face.

When he got home, he didn't even have the heart to look at the rest of the house. He just went straight downstairs to his room, which was situated in the basement. Just for his own knowledge, just to be sure, he looked in the secret place in his closet for the silver box. Nothing. Without a word, he went over to his bed and laid down, staring up at the worn out ceiling of his room for a moment. When he looked back down he saw the empty table where his television had been.

Never moving any other part of his body, except his right arm, Tony reached over and picked up the receiver of his room phone. He dialed his cellphone number, not really thinking anyone would answer. But someone did.

"Yo," the voice said.

"Yo? Who the fuck is this with my phone??" Tony sat up in the bed and demanded.

"What? Man," the voice laughed. "This is my phone nigga." Click.

chapter 4

"Anthonyyyyy," Jenny drawled out from the bathroom to her new man.

Tony rolled his eyes back into his head, and then continued watching his television program as he clutched one of Jenny's down feather pillows.

For the past two weeks, while his grandmother was in the hospital, Tony had been living with Jenny, the young nurse who he had met at the hospital. He had called her the next day to check on his grandmother, went in for a visit, and before the sun had set he was at her house, banging her back out. He had quickly learned that this girl was easy – very easy – in more ways than one.

In the days that followed Jenny allowed Tony to lay up in her house, and even took him shopping for some new clothes and shoes. When Tony told her about how he and his grandmother had been robbed, she immediately felt the obligation to help him out in any way she could. Tony took full advantage of this, getting over $1,000 worth of new stuff on Jenny's credit card after not even having known the girl for a week. In the weeks that followed, Jenny had bought Tony everything from expensive accessories for his car to a brand new cellphone.

Despite being only 22 years old, Jenny seemed to be pretty well off. She didn't just have an apartment – she had a home. Her house was roomy and decorated with a touch of class. Semi-expensive paintings hung on almost every wall. There were fresh new pine hardwood floors downstairs, and plush red carpets covered the floors in her two bedrooms. Her white leather couch and loveseat were so soft that Tony sunk right into the seat cushions. The only problem was that things weren't exactly as they *seemed* with Jenny — most of her belongings were on credit. She was neck-deep in debt.

"Anthonyyy. Do you hear me calling you baby? I need your help."

"Help with what!?" Tony yelled back, annoyed.

"Can you help me get this toilet unclogged? I don't know what happened…" Jenny said, her voice trailing off as she gave the toilet another try with her plunger.

"What? Hell no. I don't do toilets," Tony said matter of factly.

Several minutes later, Jenny came back into the bedroom and looked at Tony. She thought about saying something in reply to his comment, but changed her mind. She didn't want to upset him. Besides, he looked so comfortable sprawled out on the bed.

"Oh well, I guess I'll just have to call a plumber tomorrow. Just don't use that toilet tonight okay, use the one in the basement."

"Whatever."

"What do you think about us going to grab a bite to eat? Since there's no food in the fridge," Jenny asked. *Since you ate it all,* she complained in her mind.

"Yea, where we going?" Tony perked up.

"Uh, I don't know…KFC? McDonald's?" Jenny said as thought about what she felt like eating.

"Naw, I don't want no nasty ass fast food right now," Tony grumbled.

"What about Chinese then? There's a nice place around the corner?"

"I was thinking more of Red Lobster, down in Springfield. My boy Terrance lives out there. Maybe I could stop through."

"Oh, Red Lobster. Uhhh, yea I guess," Jenny said

apprehensively. She noticed that as time went on, Tony was becoming more and more demanding. Now he wanted Red Lobster? Just two days ago they had gone down City Line Avenue to Fridays, and the day before that Jenny had brought home food from a nice restaurant near her job.

"Aiight, let's go," Tony said, hopping out of the bed. The only time Tony moved so quickly was when he was getting some food or some sex.

* * *

Tony cracked open the last snow crab leg on his plate. He sucked the meat out of the middle of one piece, and then finished off the other. He then reached over to his other plate, grabbed three fried shrimp in a row and popped them in his mouth one after the other. Jenny just watched as he signaled for the waitress to come over, again.

"Yo, let me get another one of these frozen margarita things," he said, pointing to the large empty glass in front of him.

"Sure sir, that will be right up. Are you done with those plates? Let me grab that," the waitress said as she reached over to grab two empty plates off of the table. One with remnants of the shrimp pasta Tony had devoured, and another that had Tony's empty crab leg shells on it.

"And you can bring the check please," Jenny said quickly before Tony had an opportunity to order anything else. She was already dreading the figure that this bill had come to.

The waitress came back with Tony's drink and put the check down next to it. Of course he just picked up his drink and ignored the small black book. Jenny reached forward as if by habit, and picked it up.

"$93??" she mumbled to herself. She looked back up at Tony, who was reaching in for a couple more shrimps from his plate. This was his fourth order of fried shrimp, and they weren't even running any endless shrimp specials at Red Lobster at that time. Tony's facial expression showed that he didn't have a care in the world. She wanted so badly to ask him if he had any cash on him to help with the bill, but felt bad about asking him since he had just lost all of his money and possessions. Jenny simply reached into her purse, pulled out her Platinum Mastercard and placed it on the check.

As they were leaving the restaurant, Tony was insisting that Jenny let him drive her brand new white Jetta, since he knew exactly how to get to his friend Terrance's house. Jenny resisted at first, because she knew he was more than tipsy after having six alcoholic drinks at dinner, but relented when Tony leaned down and kissed her on the cheek to thank her for the meal. When they finally did make it to Terrance's house, Jenny was expecting that Tony was going to bring her in to meet his good friend.

"You wait in here aiight? I'll be right back out," Tony said to her as he hopped out of the driver's seat, not even waiting for a response. Jenny looked crushed. He looked back at her in the car before ringing the doorbell. When he didn't hear any movement in the house, he pulled out the Verizon phone Jenny had bought for him just several days before. Before he had a chance to look for Terrance's number, he heard his friend's deep voice call out from inside.

"Who is it?" Terrance demanded.

"It's me nigga, open up!" Tony slurred.

"Tone? What the hell you doin' here?" Terrance asked as he unlocked and opened the door. He gave his boy a pound and they went inside.

"Man, I'm just stoppin' by to say what's up. I was down at the Red Lobster's," Tony said proudly as he flopped down on the couch and threw his hands up behind his head in a relaxing position.

"Red Lobster? Where your broke ass get money to eat out?" Terrance laughed. "What are you fuckin' with one of the waitresses?"

"Uhhhhhh, no," Tony replied sarcastically as he threw his new fitted hat to the side. "I'm fucking with this bitch that got it made! She got a good job, a house almost as big as yours, and mad money dude. She sprung as shit on me too. She'll do anything for a nigga. She lets me stay at her house ever since Grandma went into the hospital."

"Huh? I know you ain't serious man."

"What you mean? Course I'm serious – this the best set up I had in my life. And this jawn don't even ask me no questions, no arguing, none of that. She just gives me what I want, and I can lay all up in the house chillin' all day if I want."

"You're proud to be mooching off a woman, huh?" Terrance said, shaking his head. He got up off the couch and walked into the kitchen to grab a couple of sodas for him and his ill-bred friend.

"It ain't mooching. Look, women do it to niggas all the time. They got they sugar daddies, well I just got me a sugar mommie. And she happy to buy me shit and take care of me at the crib," Tony said, hopping up to grab the remote control off the coffee table. "That's how a woman is supposed to do for a nigga if you ask me. We lay the pipe, and they lay the green."

Tony laughed deviously at his last comment, as Terrance struggled to keep his composure with his shallow, ignorant friend. He put Tony's soda down in front of him and went back to sit down.

"How's your grandmother doing?"

"She aiight, I just went to see her a couple days ago. She should be out soon."

"That's good to hear, let me know when that happens so I can come with you to get her out."

"Aiight, thanks man," Tony said, nodding his head.

"By the way Tone, uhh… did you ever take care of that little situation? Uhh, you know?"

"Yea yea I went to the clinic and got that fixed. No problem. It was just a little gonorrhea."

Terrance jerked his head in his friend's direction. "Just a little gonorrhea?? How can you take it so light like that? What about Nish, do she got it now too?"

"Listen dude, I don't even want this subject to be brought up between us no more. Got me? That's a dead issue aiight?" Tony said, beginning to get offended by Terrance's questions.

Terrance sucked his teeth and leaned back in his loveseat. "Whatever man."

"So anyways, my little sugar mommie name is Jenny. She ain't that good looking, not all the way up on my regular standards. But her money right though, yah mean…" Tony started again, but Terrance cut him off.

"You ain't supposed to be living off no woman Tony, as a man you gotta make a way for yourself." Terrance was annoyed that Tony was so proud of taking money from a woman. But it was the Tony he had always known – dependent on other people, and totally senseless.

"Ran, man you sound like a broke record," Tony said, spitting as he talked. "Just cause you choose to bust your ass for a dollar everyday don't mean it's right for everybody."

Terrance opened his mouth and then shut it back closed. He was so tired of hearing Tony talk, especially since he almost never made any sense. "You just ain't never gonna get it Tone. I ain't gonna waste my breath on you."

"Fuck you nigga, you don't know everything."

I know one thing, Terrance thought. *I need to get this fool out my house before I kick his ass.*

"Yo listen Tone, I gotta be up in the morning for *work* so if you don't mind…" Terrance said, getting up from his seat yet again. Tony sucked his teeth, rolled his eyes and followed suit.

"Yea, I get the message. Anyways, I got the dumb chick waiting in the car for me," Tony snickered. In his near drunken state, he was just letting whatever came to mind roll off of his tongue.

"Wait, hol up. You got this girl sitting outside all this time while you in here with me?" Terrance asked incredulously.

"Yea, I just told you we came back from Red Lobster's," Tony said, screwing up his face as he went down to the door.

"Why didn't you just bring her up here wit you? I wouldn't have minded. That's fucked up for you to be chillin' in here all this time," Terrance said, shaking his head as he opened the door for Tony to leave. He was starting to get more and more relieved each time Tony was leaving. He almost wished that Tony didn't know where he lived so he wouldn't keep popping up at his house unannounced.

"Cause she ain't worth meeting my friends and shit. She more of a side jawn than anything," Tony explained and then gave Terrance a pound. "Aiight man."

A side jawn, and you laying up in her house like you live there, Terrance thought. *What about Quanisha?*

Tony came to the driver's side of the car and saw Jenny sitting there strapped in with her hands on the wheel.

"Move over," he said, signaling to her through the window by pointing to the passenger side.

"No, I'm driving, go ahead to the passenger side. You had too much to drink Tony."

"What? I said I want to drive, now move over," he said in a more agitated tone of voice.

Jenny just sat there and looked forward out of the windshield, hoping that he would just go over to the passenger's seat. Tony was about to grab the door handle, but changed his mind when he got a better idea.

"Oh aiight then. You wanna be like that then fine, I ain't got time for this mess tonight. You go ahead home, I'm stayin' with my boy Ran," he said as he headed back toward the house. Jenny opened the door and flew out of the car.

"No no, I don't want you staying here tonight. Alright, you can drive. Just promise you'll be careful okay?" Jenny asked.

Tony smirked as he slowly turned back around and got into the car. He always got his way with Jenny, and he loved it.

They reached home, just barely since Tony was driving like a fool and Jenny was so sure that they would be pulled over. Tony got out and lit up his last cigarette. He walked up to the house as he was pulling out the key that Jenny had given him to the house.

"Anthony, baby, could you please smoke that out here? I don't want the smoke smell in my house."

"Geez, it's just one cigarette, give me a break!" he said as he fumbled with the keys and held the screen door open. Before he could even put the key in the door, the cigarette slipped out of his fingers and fell behind the bushes.

"Shit!" he exclaimed. "That was my last one!"

Tony jumped down off the stairs and started searching

through the thick bushes for the burning cigarette. Jenny stood behind him watching to make sure nothing caught fire. After several minutes of searching, and being pricked by the harsh brush, he finally saw the cigarette butt, which had miraculously burned up to the filter in that short amount of time, but hadn't burned anything else.

"Damn!" he said, now on edge because he was looking forward to that cigarette. Now on his knees, he picked up the cigarette and tried pitifully to suck a few last puffs of nicotine. Jenny looked at him like he was nuts.

"Fuck it," he said, throwing the butt back down. "Do you have any cash on you so I can run to the corner store?"

"Nope, not a dime," she answered. And she wasn't about to put cigarettes on her credit card. She didn't care what he said.

Tony looked at the time on his cellphone. It read 11:22pm. "Man, and all the stores that accept credit cards is closed. Awww. Fuck!" he yelled, as he got up and headed back towards the house. He tripped on the second step leading up to the porch, and tried to play it off.

"You alright?" Jenny asked, cracking a smile. Tony didn't answer. He just snatched the screen door open and put his key in the lock.

That night Tony put Jenny down on the floor in her living room and banged into her so hard that she thought he was going to pierce her uterus. He was frustrated at missing his cigarette, and needed a release badly. At one point Jenny tried to stop him, because he was really hurting her, but he just ignored her complaints and kept on going. He finally pulled out and came all over her stomach. Tony didn't know for sure about this girl and her birth control habits, so he wasn't going to take any risks of getting her pregnant. Little did he know that a woman could still get pregnant with the 'pull out' method. Jenny was actually hoping to get pregnant by Tony this way, which is why she never complained about him always pulling out. Tony rolled over onto his back and closed his eyes as he tried to catch his breath.

Jenny sat up a little and rested her head in her hand. "I was thinking maybe we could go up to see your grandmother at the hospital tomorrow morning. You know, the doctors say she should be out of the hospital early next week!"

Tony opened one eye and looked at Jenny strangely. He didn't know how she could be thinkiing about his grandmother literally five seconds after they had just finished having sex.

"Yea, whatever," he said, closing his eye back. But he already knew he had no intentions of going anywhere with Jenny that next morning.

"She's been doing so much better as you know. The last time I saw her, she asked me if I was your new girlfriend, since I talk about you so much," Jenny chuckled and reached over to rub Tony on the stomach as she spoke. "I told her that she should really ask *you* that question. I'm sure she'll be glad to see us both tomorrow. I was also thinking that maybe *next* weekend we could make plans to go see my mom in Germantown. She's been asking about you Anthony. Anthony?"

"What the fuck did I tell you about callin' me Anthony? My name's Tony! Damn it I hate that shit!" Tony suddenly burst out. "And I'm trynna sleep, so shut the fuck up!"

Tony was so tired of hearing Jenny's whiny voice that it was starting to make his head hurt just being in her presence. Sometimes it was as if her mouth were running a marathon; she went on and on about subjects that meant absolutely nothing to Tony.

In fact, over the past few days he had been thinking more and more about Quanisha, and how much he missed her. He hadn't seen her since she drew a knife on him in her car the day his grandmother went into the hospital. Quanisha could be very abrasive at times, but at least she was a challenge. Jenny was so easy that it was sickening to Tony. And she was like a cold fish when it came to sex; Tony had to do all the work while she just laid there. He needed his baby Quanisha back – that was his rock. He could have ten women on the side, but he knew that if anybody was going to have his back, it would be Quanisha. He started dozing off with thoughts of running his hand down Quanisha's soft buttery thighs.

Jenny was taken aback by Tony's sudden outburst, and remained speechless for a long time. Why didn't he want her calling him by his God given name? She debated on whether she should continue what she was telling him, or heed his request for silence. The margarita with an extra shot of Cuervo she had at dinner gave her a little confidence, so she decided to just pick up where she left off in the conversation, in a softer tone.

"Well, I've told my mom all about you, and she really wants to meet you. So I'd appreciate it if you cleared next Saturday? I'll drive," Jenny said. She paused to see if Tony would have any objections, but he said nothing.

"Anth- I mean Tony? Did you hear me?" she asked. Before she could say another word, Tony started snoring; he was fast asleep. Jenny sighed and grabbed a pillow off the couch. She laid her head down facing Tony, and for a while she just watched him sleep. She felt as if she were falling in love with Tony, but didn't know exactly why. He treated her like crap, ran through her money like a faucet, and hardly ever even said two words to her. But it was so nice to have a man around the house. It had been so long since she felt the rush of testosterone inside of those four walls.

"I'll just give it some time," she said outloud to herself. "He'll come around. I'll help him to get a job at the hospital, and as time goes on he'll get to know me for the good woman I am. I just have to have patience."

Tony woke up in the middle of the night. The room was dark except for the light of the television. He looked around him to see where Jenny was, but she was no where in sight. He got up from the floor and took a few seconds to stretch his back out. He looked over at the cable box which read 4:13am.

"Damn, I was knocked out," he said, heading towards Jenny's kitchen for something to eat. When he got there he quickly remembered why they had gone out to eat. There was nothing in the refrigerator except a half a bottle of spring water, some onions and a bag of lemons.

"She really need to go shopping," he said outloud and slammed the door back shut. He went back out to the living room and flopped down on the couch. He turned to BET Uncut and could have sworn one of the girls in the video they were playing was Quanisha. She looked just like her; thick, brown skinned, with the long braids. He started rubbing his manhood as he leaned his head back and closed his eyes. He thought about how wild Quanisha could get in bed, and how she could be so gentle at other times when they were together. *Why am I over here thinking about her when she's just ten minutes away?* he thought.

"I'm goin' over there," he said to himself, and then shot up from his seat to go find out where Jenny was at. Before he left the room, he saw one of Jenny's purses sitting underneath her glass top coffee table.

Tony didn't even think twice about searching through Jenny's purse. There was no way he could resist. He found a $20 bill laying on the bottom of the bag. "I thought she said she didn't have any cash," he said as he crumbled up the $20 bill in the palm of his hands and started to go up the stairs.

He peeked into Jenny's master bedroom and saw her sleeping peacefully with her back turned to the door. He shook his head, glad that he wouldn't have to speak to her again that night. Maybe not anymore at all.

When he reached the bathroom he lifted the toilet seat quietly as he looked back at the door to make sure Jenny wasn't behind him. She could be sneaky like that sometimes. He closed his eyes and shook his head from side to side as he relieved himself. When he finally looked down at the toilet to flush he was startled when he saw that there was feces in there. Jenny had told him earlier that the toilet was stopped up.

"Ewww," he said as he tried to flush again and again unsuccessfully. Forgetting what he had in his hand, he accidentally let the twenty that he had balled up in his fist fall out into the toilet, right in the middle of two turds.

"Shit!" Tony exclaimed under his breath. He looked in the toilet, as the bill became submerged in the toilet water filled with urine and feces. He considered grabbing the money, but it was so disgusting. He was squeamish about things like this.

"Man. I need that twenty," he mumbled to himself as he ran the palm of his hand down over his face. He finally just counted to three in his head and started picking at the twenty in the toilet. When he grabbed hold of it he threw it in the sink immediately. Running the water over the dirty twenty, he washed his hands five times in a row and then squirted some of Jenny's liquid soap all over the bill.

Tony exited Jenny's house holding the corner of the wet twenty dollar bill. It was still dirty as far as he was concerned. He hopped in his car and headed for Quanisha's house. He decided to hold the money near the open window so that it would dry in the wind as he drove.

He was passing Baltimore Avenue and swerved to miss hitting a crackhead, who was only wearing flip flops and sweatpants. The crackhead was walking against the light, and apparently was not at all concerned about any cars that may have been coming down the street towards him. Cursing the crackhead in his rear view mirror, Tony saw a cop headed down Baltimore Avenue towards his direction. As he kept his eyes glued to the cop, an unusually strong wind whipped through the car. He lost his grip on the $20 bill. It flew out of the window and down the street. He hit the brakes on his car and was about to back up, but being that the cop was sitting there at the light he couldn't. He continued on and made a U-Turn as quickly as humanly possible, heading back down the street where the $20 had flown. As he eased down the street looking for the green bill, he saw the crackhead he had just swerved to miss leaning down to pick something up. Before Tony could even stop the car and hop out, the crackhead had dipped out of sight. There was no doubt in Tony's mind that he had found the money and ran.

"I can't believe this shit!" he exclaimed angrily. He couldn't believe that he had just lost the $20 like that, especially after what he had to go through to get it in the first place. Now he couldn't get his Newports, or anything to eat from the 24 hour McDonald's. Furious, he got back into his car and slammed the door. "I can't keep no money for nothing!"

When he finally rolled up to Quanisha's house, Tony was thoroughly pissed. He had wanted to stop at the gas station near her house to get his pack of cigarettes with the money he had just lost. At that point he was feening for a cigarette. But he knew he had to get his mind right before going in there to see Quanisha. He just hoped with all of his being that she didn't have some dude up there with her, because then he was going to truly lose it.

Tony found himself standing in front of Quanisha's door staring at the peephole. He hesitated, and then finally brought his fist up to knock on the door. He didn't know what she might have in store for him.

When she didn't respond to the knock, he pressed the loud, annoying buzzer for her apartment a few times. She still didn't come, so he laid on the buzzer for at least 10 seconds, showing absolutely no respect for any of her neighbors who could probably hear it too.

"Who the hell is that?" Quanisha finally yelled from inside the apartment. She had the revolver her uncle had given her for her birthday by her side.

"It's me. It's Tony."

"What? What the hell do you want?" Quanisha said, grabbing her robe together tightly. Despite all of the hatred she had for Tony at that moment, the sound of his famililar voice was a great relief to her.

"I want to talk. Can you let me in baby? I just want to talk," he said in the most sincere voice he could muster. Quanisha snatched open the door, gun still at her side.

"If you come in here I just might kill your ass. Where have you been?? Do you know what I've been going through!!" Quanisha screamed like a crazed woman. "You gave me gonorrhea you dumb fuck!!"

Tony just stood there and closed his eyes. He had been hoping that somehow Quanisha didn't get it too. His worst case scenario was coming true. Only now he wondered if he should have called Quanisha first.

"Do you know what it feels like, sitting up in that fucking STD clinic alone with all those other infected mutherfuckers looking at you? Do you know how embarrassing that shit is, walking out of there looking around to see who saw you come out?? How could you do that to me Tony, and then leave me by myself to deal with that shit?" Quanisha raged on, not caring about who may have heard her. "I hate your ass!! I hate you!"

Tony came inside and grabbed hold of Quanisha in a hug. He tried his best to conjure up some tears. "Come on Nish, I'm sorry baby. I would never purposely do this to you."

"Then why did you do it! You sorry muthafucka! You couldn't even call a bitch, in two damn weeks?" she asked incredulously as she struggled to break free from his hug. Tony grabbed the gun out of her hand and placed in the back of his jeans.

"I said I'm sorry Nish. I wanted to call you, but I thought you were mad at me. And I been dealin' with all that shit with my mom, I just didn't know what to do. I been wanting to come over all this time. I missed you baby. Please, please forgive me," Tony begged. "Please baby?"

"I ain't tryin' to hear all that shit! You left me! I hate you you stupid *bitch*!" Quanisha screamed. Tony kicked her door closed and picked Quanisha up, carrying her into the bedroom.

"No! I ain't having sex with you! Get the fuck off of me!" Quanisha protested and started slapping and scratching at Tony's face. Tony became enraged when she slapped him across the sides of his face so sharply that it stung, but he kept his composure.

"I ain't having sex with you Nish, I just want you to calm down okay? We can talk about this!" Tony pleaded as he flopped her down on the bed.

"I don't give a fuck what you got to say, you ain't got shit to tell me!" Quanisha responded, rolling over on the bed violently until her back was to Tony. She was infuriated with him, but she didn't want him to leave. She had missed him so badly. Besides her shallow friends and selfish mother, she didn't really have anybody in the world. While Tony was gone she had felt incomplete.

Tony was about to go around the other side of the bed and try to talk to her, but instead he decided it was best to just be there. He knew that she would talk to him when she was ready. He lingered over the bed for a long time, watching Quanisha. She never moved an inch. He admired the trace of her figure inside of her pink robe. She was a sight for sore eyes, even in the midst of her anger. Quanisha was so much better than Jenny, even on her worst day. It was a relief to be back with someone he knew and was comfortable with, even if it meant conflict was in his future.

Tony simply sat down on the bed and took off his shoes and jeans. He laid back on the bed besides his woman and sighed a long sigh of relief.

"Nish… I love you girl," Tony said very softly. He couldn't even believe he had just said those words out of his mouth, but they had just flowed out. He expected some kind of response from Quanisha, but there was none.

"Nish?" Tony asked a little louder. "You up?"

The silence on the other end was interrupted by Quanisha's heavy breathing, which eventually led to heavy snoring.

chapter 5

It was 5:30 in the evening when Tony stepped out of Quanisha's apartment. He looked back in the apartment once more, then finally allowed the self-locking door to close.

Quanisha had since left for work, leavng him in her apartment to sleep. She had slept an uninterrupted and peaceful sleep until 11am that morning. Finally jumping up from the comfort of her bed, Quanisha showered and threw on some jeans and her smock. She had had to be at the grocery store for work at 10:30am, but didn't walk out of the door until 11:22. She was in for some drama at work. She was already treading on thin ice after walking out on her shift when she thought there was a woman at her house all those weeks ago. She looked over at Tony before leaving, but didn't have any time to say or do anything about his presence, so she had just left.

Tony was on his way to the corner deli to pick up a sandwich when the cellphone that Jenny had bought for him started vibrating in his pocket. It was no surprise who the caller was. Jenny had been calling him every hour on the hour since he had arrived at Quanisha's the previous night, finally causing him to have to put the phone in vibrate mode so that he wouldn't wake Quanisha or hear the ringing himself. He was starting to get sick of the very idea of Jenny. She was too clingy. He needed a woman with a little more fight in her. He clicked the 'talk' button to get this conversation over with. He was back with his baby, and he didn't need Jenny's services any longer.

"Yo."

"Anth—Tony? Where have you been?" Jenny asked into the phone sounding as meek as a mouse.

"I been out. What you want?" Tony demanded.

"What do I want? I want to know why you left me last night like that!" Jenny whined and raised her tone a notch. "Why haven't you answered my calls? And why is twenty dollars missing out of my purse?"

"I don't know nothin' about no twenty dollars, so don't even go there. Besides, I thought you didn't have no cash on you?" Tony said, turning the tables on Jenny.

"Well I—" Jenny started, but was interrupted by Tony's commanding voice.

"And I left because I felt like it, I'm my own man. Yah mean? You don't own me or tell me what to do or where to go."

"I never said I did? I just wanted to know—"

"Look Jenny, you got a point to this call? Because I got shit to do."

There was silence.

"Hellooooo," Tony said in a very obnoxious, patronizing tone.

"Tony why are you acting like this?" Jenny asked, near tears.

"Acting like what? Didn't I just tell you I have something to do? And here you go talkin' that shit again. Man!"

"Talking what? How do you mean? I'm just trying to find out what the problem is!"

"Jenny, you know what? I'm gonna make this shit real clear to you right now, so you don't never ask me again. We ain't together no more. We ain't never have been together to tell you the truth! So quit calling my phone bothering me, and I mean it," Tony said, gesturing wildly as he walked down the street.

"Your phone? I—" Jenny was cut off by the sound of Tony

hanging up in her face.

Over at the hospital, Jenny sat in the back area of the break room where the employees' coats hung, with her mouth hanging wide open at her cellphone. A familiar rage started to make its way up her back, simultaneously up her chest and landed on the area surrounding her heart. The rage hugged her heart, softly at first as an old friend would, but then slowly tightened its grip. Jenny frowned hard at the numbers on her phone. Her lip twitched involuntarily as she pressed 'phone' twice to redial the last number.

Tony picked the phone up on the fifth ring. This girl was relentless. "What??? What the fuck do you want??" he screamed.

"Who the hell do you think you are hanging up the phone on me?" Jenny's tiny voice yelled back.

"This the bul Tony, and I'll hang up on whoever the fuck I choose, anytime I wish," Tony said casually and then chuckled as he stepped down off the curb and crossed the street, dodging a few cars as they passed. He never stopped for a red light at a crosswalk. When he made it across the street he pulled his scully cap down low on his head.

"You think this is a joke? Tony we were doing so good! Why do you have to go and mess all that up?"

"What? How do you figure we were doing good? Was you listening? I said we was never really together to begin with! We was just kickin' it, aiight!" Tony said impatiently as he walked into the small arab owned grocery store a block down from Quanisha's apartment building.

"Just 'kickin' it?? I bought you new rims for your car, the car stereo system and not to mention the phone you're talking on. I pay the bills on that phone! I did all of that for you! How is all that just 'kickin' it?"

"Girl please, you buyin' a few things don't mean nothin' at all. Nothin' at all." Tony thought for a second before saying his next words. *Fuck her feelings*, he resolved, *What's this bitch gonna do to or for me in this lifetime that she ain't do already?* "Jenny Imma be straight with you, you ain't my type. I was down on my luck for a bit, and you helped. Thanks, but now I'm aiight okay? I don't need—"

"Anthony Jackson, don't you dare say what you're about to say," Jenny said serenely, shivering in the cold iron folding chair she was sitting in. Beyond the wall separating the coat room from the main break room, several of her fellow employees sat listening to every word being said in her conversation.

"What the hell did I tell you about calling me Anthony! Damn! I hate that shit." Hearing Jenny call him by his broke sorry father's name put Tony over the edge, and he no longer minced his words. "Listen! Your skinny ass just ain't that fine to me, the pussy is wack and I'm *all* the way through with you. I don't need your ass anymore, period!" Click. Tony ended the call and shut off the phone. He didn't want to hear one more word out of Jenny's whiny mouth.

"Tony? Tony??!!" Jenny stood up out of her chair and screamed at the top of her lungs into her phone. "Tony!!!" Jenny's scream was so blood curdling that it made her co-workers shake with a mixture of fear, incredulity and fascination at having the pleasure to have heard the entire conversation. The inside joke around the hospital was that they called Jenny "Lil Penny" after the little girl played by Janet Jackson on Good Times, because on more than one occasion in the past she had shown up for work with black eyes, bruised cheeks and bandages on her arms. The other nurses were going to have a lot to talk about that night.

Jenny redialed Tony's number over and over, only to be greeted repeatedly by the white lady that said the recording for his voicemail. $200 dollars she paid every month on his cellphone bill alone, and was greeted by his voicemail all of the time. He can't even do his damn greeting on his own, she thought to herself. Furious, she threw her phone down on the carpeted floor hard enough to break it, but it didn't break. It just bounced over to the opening that lead to the main break room area. She sat back down in the chair holding her arms crossed close to her body and rocking in place. After a few more seconds she bolted up out of her chair and rushed to the phone on the floor. Snatching it up, she looked to her left and saw four of her co-workers staring right back at her curiously. She stood straight up and frowned her brow up at them.

"What the fuck are ya'll looking at!!" she screamed and then ran full speed out of the break room to make her call in private. The giggles ensued soon thereafter.

Jenny made her way to the X-ray room, which was fortunately unoccupied at the time. She sat down on a chair next to the door and dialed Tony's number again. Again, she got the voicemail. Instead of leaving a message as she usually did, she closed her phone and put her head in her hands. Her body shook as she started to cry softly.

A few minutes later she lifted her head and wiped her eyes clean. Her demeanor changed, and then almost immediately Jenny began to laugh hysterically. When she stopped laughing she was still smiling.

"What am I crying about? Anthony Jackson, you think we're through, but you just don't know. Our love has just begun."

Tony continued stepping around the grocery store, his scully low over his eyes, picking up a few things here and there. He went to the back of the store and ordered a large sub with ham, cheese, tomato, mayonnaise and ranch dressing – his favorite. When it was finished Tony grabbed the sandwich, not so much as thanking the man who had prepared it. The arab deli clerk, who seemed as if he were looking forward to a tip for his tip jar, cursed Tony under his breath and snatched his pack of Marlboros off the counter so that he could go to the back and take a smoke. Tony headed straight for the front door, all of his other items in hand.

"Ay, budd-y," the arab looking man behind the counter looked over and said in a heavy accent as he saw Tony within 10 steps of leaving the store completely without having paid for anything. "Where you going? You paid?" Tony kept stepping, not paying him any mind.

"Ay, budd-y. You didn't pay for that!" the arab man yelled loudly grabbing his bat from behind the counter and quickly making his way around the counter and towards Tony with it. In what seemed like a millisecond, Tony pulled his ski mask down completely over his face, and adjusted his eyes to look through the two peep holes as he pulled Quanisha's half-loaded gun out of his waist and pointed it at the clerk.

"See, if you would have just shut the fuck up! Now I want all your money," Tony demanded. He took the door wedge out from underneath the open door and allowed the glass door to slam shut.

"Hey, hey look budd-y, no problems okay? Go ahead and take it, the stuff you got. I don't want any problems," the store clerk began pleading.

"Too late. Go over there and empty out your drawer," Tony instructed as he nudged the clerk back towards the counter. He leaned his head over to look at the lotto sign. The Powerball jackpot was $92 million. "And give me like 50 lotto tickets. Do it random, quick pick. And hurry the fuck up you greedy sand nigga! Damn, couldn't even let me go for a damn sandwich."

The arab clerk dropped the bat and reached into his pocket for his wallet, never fully going behind the counter. "There is not much in the drawer. I give you what I have here, 10, 20, 40…" the clerk said, counting off his bills.

Tony took three swift and long steps towards the clerk and smacked him hard across the face with Quanisha's gun. "I said open the fucking drawer! What do you think I'm stupid?"

The Arab clerk listened this time, hustling back over to the register and pressing a button to release the drawer. Before he grabbed the money, he tried once more to reason with Tony. "Mister, please I don't have any insurance! My wife is getting the insurance tomorrow morning! Please don't—"

"Man I ain't trynna hear all that," Tony said, stepping forward slightly towards the man he now knew as the store owner. He held the lightweight Glock directly against the Arab man's sweating temple with his right hand, and grabbed the money out of the drawer with his left. He stuffed the money in his jacket pocket, one stack at a time. It looked as if there was more than $500 in the drawer. *What a dumb ass*, he thought of the store owner for keeping so much cash in a store that was located in one of the worst hoods in the city. Tony watched the door as the arab man pressed the lotto machine over and over again.

"Aiight, that's enough," Tony told him, getting nervous about the lotto tickets taking too much time.

When the store owner handed him the tickets, Tony told him to turn around and snatched his still-open wallet from him. He then hit the store owner on the area between his shoulder blade and neck with the gun, instantly causing the man to fall to the ground. Tony jogged a little towards the entrance, pulled his mask up and eased his way out of the store. As he left he could hear the store owner weakly trying to call for the deli clerk to come and help him, but the deli guy was still in the back alley taking his smoke break. Tony made a sharp left after leaving, choosing to take a detour to his car so that no one would see him coming from the direction of the store.

* * *

"Damn man, where you get this haze from?" Scoop asked Tony as they sat in his car smoking the last of a perfectly rolled blunt.

"This bul down Southwest off Kingsessing. He always got the good shit, long as I been knowin' 'im," Tony replied, leaning his head back into the head rest.

"This that fire dawg, I need to get some of this shit tonight for me and Quita. How much for that bag?"

"Twenty."

"Twenty?? For that little bag of shit? You kiddin' me right?" Scoop laughed.

"Nawl man, that's his best stuff. I asked for it in particular," Tony replied, taking the roach from Scoop and straining to take a few more puffs before putting it out in the ash tray.

"Where in the hell did you get $20 to spend on one bag of weed man?" Scoop eyed Tony curiously. "From that little nut broad you messin' with?"

"Don't worry about it. All you need to know is I got it, yah mean?"

Scoop was quiet for a few moments. He knew his best friend had been up to something that day from his demeanor, he just didn't know what. "So that chick was trippin' on you huh?"

"Hell yea, I'm starting to think she really crazy man. She left 15 fucking messages on my voicemail today. Talking about how she will see me soon. That I do need her and she'll show me why soon enough. I'm like, get the fuck outta here. She better chill with all that fatal attraction shit."

"Yea and you better be careful. Don't take that shit lightly. I know you remember that crazy bitch Sheila I used to fuck with. Her ass started trippin' the fuck out, and I was only seeing her for like four days! Showing up at my girl house and shit."

"Yea, well I ain't worrying about that little bitch Jenny like that, she know better," Tony said, reaching forward to change the CD on the new three disc changer Jenny had bought for his raggedy car. A Jadakiss track, *Knock Yourself Out*, started blasting through the car.

"Yo, take me down Kingsessing, I wanna see the bul and get a couple bags of that shit," Scoop said over the music.

"You wanna go down there, this time of night?" Tony asked skeptically. "Yea I guess. Yea let's go, but I gotta be home by 2am so Nish don't be trippin'."

Tony put the car in gear and started out towards Kingsessing, which wasn't very far. When he turned up on the narrow block where he always met his connect, Lou, he turned off his lights and eased up, looking. Lou spotted him, recognizing the car and made his way over to the driver's side. Tony rolled down the window half way.

"What you need?" Lou asked. Scoop had already told Tony he wanted three bags.

"Give me three, that good stuff again," Tony said. His eyes were nearly slitted closed, indicating that he was still high off what he smoked earlier.

"You need three more dawg? Damn you ballin'. Hol' up a

second, I gotta get it."

Lou disappeared into a house for what seemed like ages. More time went on and he still hadn't emerged.

"What the hell is taking him so long?" Tony complained, looking at his watch, which now read 2:11am, more than 15 minutes after they had arrived. He was started to become suspicious. A car came up behind them on the one-way block, so Tony had to manuever out of the main street and to the right side, one wheel on the curb. The driver of the car behind him slowly passed, looking into their car, and then pulled up into a space a little farther up the block.

"What the fuck they lookin' at?" Scoop asked, annoyed, but had a tugging feeling that something wasn't quite right.

Lou came to the passenger's side door and put his hand up to get Tony's attention. He put one finger up as if to tell him "one more minute" then disappeared back into the house before Tony had a chance to fully roll his window back down. Tony leaned over Scoop and looked curiously back in the direction where Lou had just vanished. He figured maybe he didn't have enough to cover their order.

"Damn, he still ain't got that shit? What the—" Tony and Scoop heard the click of a gun cocking.

"Empty your pockets," a harsh voice commanded from behind Tony's head. Tony slowly leaned back in his seat and turned his head, his line of vision greeting the barrel of a gun. "You heard me nigga."

"Fuck!" Tony clenched his teeth and yelled, banging his fist on the steering wheel. Scoop just looked over at the window with his mouth wide open. He was about to shit in his pants because he had about $680 cash on him that he was supposed to give his girlfriend for shopping that weekend. He finally sat back in his seat and sighed.

"Did ya'll motherfuckers hear? Know what, get the fuck out the car," the short, ugly, stocky light skinned brother said, lifting the door handle on the car just as his taller, leaner boy came around to Scoop's side of the car on the sidewalk holding a pistol close by his side which was aimed down at the ground and commanded Scoop to get out also, which he did without much protest. 'Short and Stocky' opened Tony's door and snatched him out of the driver's seat. Holding the gun into Tony's neck, he searched all of Tony's pockets with his other hand. He produced a stack of bills from Tony's right pocket and stuffed it in his jacket pocket without even flinching, as if he already knew what he was going to find. He found the lotto tickets in Tony's back pocket.

Tony instantly began protesting. "Man what the fuck? This is some bullshit. Come on now, how you gonna just take all my—"

"Fuck youuu. Stop whining you lil bitch," 'Short and Stocky' said and bitch-smacked Tony with his free hand, causing Tony's face to flush red with anger. 'Short and Stocky' just laughed and started backing away towards his car with his gun still pointed towards Tony's head. His partner in crime finished taking every last red cent from Scoop on the sidewalk, and then pushed Scoop down onto the car. He chuckled as he started to back away with his friend. It all happened so fast, in a matter of a few seconds Tony and Scoop had been robbed blind.

"Ay ya'll have a good night aiight?" 'Shorty and Stocky' taunted, chuckling as he reached his car and put the gun in his waist.

"Yea whatever, shut your motherfucking midget ass up. You wouldn't be doing shit without that gun in ya hand."

As a child, Tony just could never learn to hold his tongue. It had cost him many an ass whooping courtesy his grandmother. But what was about to happen due to this latest infraction was going to be far worse than a little bruise on his leg from a leather belt.

Scoop slowly looked over at Tony as if he was seeing a ghost. He twisted his face at Tony as if to say, "Are you crazy??"

'Short and Stocky' was halfway sitting down in his driver's seat when he heard the last of Tony's comment and froze. He slowly stood back up and turned around. "What did you say?"

Tony hesitated, but then recovered. He was still refusing to back down. "You heard me," he said in a slightly lower voice.

"Oh you wanna get gully now huh. Okay, okay." 'Short and Stocky' muscle-walked back towards Tony and pulled the gun back out mid stroll. His boy came back out of the car and followed. Tony looked over at Scoop who was still looking stunned and stuck in place as if he were about to witness a murder right before his eyes. Again Tony hesitated, quickly wondering in his mind if he should make a run for it, but figuring it wouldn't matter at that point. He finally made a quick decision in his mind to run and take his chances, but 'Short and Stocky' had already descended on him. He struck Tony's right temple with the gun so hard that Tony fell back-first against the car and slid down in excruciating pain, holding onto his head.

"Get up!" 'Short and Stocky' commanded, furious. "Yo Poo, this nigga think I need this gun to whoop his scrawny ass up. Take this, I'm about to show him something," he snarled as he looked over at his boy and threw the gun, which Poo caught with ease and put in his large pants pocket. 'Short and Stocky' then reached down and grabbed Tony by the collars of the new button down shirt Jenny had bought for him the week before. He snatched

Tony up, while blood dripped down the right side of Tony's face. Tony grasped onto 'Short and Stocky's wrists trying to pry himself free but with no luck. Once Tony was up on his feet, 'Short and Stocky' pushed him back against the car and threw a right upper cut so fast and clean on Tony that it would have put Joe Louis to shame. Blood splattered in the air and along the hood of the car. Tony reeled and his head sagged to the side.

"Tone!" Instinctually, Scoop ran around the front of the car towards his friend to try to defend him, but Poo stopped him in his tracks and punched Scoop in the stomach. When Scoop tried to fight back by hitting Poo in the chin, Poo stunned Scoop with a hard left hook causing him to fall face forward on the hood of Tony's car. Poo pulled out the gun his boy had thrown him and pinned Scoop down on the hood with it. Scoop could only watch as he saw Tony continue to get punched, elbowed, kicked and beaten relentlessly by the short brother. He was short but unhumanly powerful.

"Come on ya'll, I think he got the point... Come on man!" Scoop tried to reason with them as he saw Tony fall to the ground on his knees, his entire face soaked with blood, trying to crawl away. 'Short and Stocky' booted him in the side and then kicked him in the face as if he were kicking a soccer ball. Tony fell to the side, staining the street with his blood.

"Shut the hell up and be the fuck happy you ain't the one catchin' this ass whoopin'," Poo answered Scoop, who was making all kinds of grunting and gasping sounds as he tried to free himself. "Ya boy a real dumb ass you know?" Poo asked rhetorically.

By then Tony was getting stomped in the face by a size 10 black Timberland boot. 'Short and Stocky' was jeering at Tony between stomps. "You wanna be callin' somebody a midget huh?...I'll show you a motherfucking midget...bitch. How 'bout I pound ya pussy ass into the ground!"

"Yo Trek, I think I hear 5-0, let's go," Poo said, finally releasing Scoop a little. Trek stopped stomping on Tony and looked over at his friend for a moment. Tony was no longer moving but Trek could still see his chest moving in and out. Remembering in his mind again how Tony had had the nerve to call him a "bitch ass," Trek leaned forward and grabbed Tony by his shoulders to balance him up on his knees. Holding Tony up by the collar with his left hand, Trek reached his bloody fist high into the air and struck Tony across his cheek bone so hard that Scoop heard something 'crack.'

"No!! Tone! Awwww, come on ya'll he's dying!" Almost wanting to shed tears for his boy, Scoop's voice trailed off as he finally stood all the way up and witnessed his best friend slump back down on the concrete in a pile. Trek let him fall, and shook his own hand a few times to recover from the impact on his knuckles as he walked back towards his car.

"Aiight, let's go," he said as Poo shoved Scoop one last time and then followed Trek back to the car. Scoop immediately ran over to his friend on the ground. Tony wasn't moving and Scoop wasn't even sure that he was breathing. He stood back up and looked around, watching as Trek and Poo drove off with their money and possibly Tony's life. Poo had taken Scoop's cellphone, but he remembered that Tony usually left his cellphone in the car instead of on his body. He stepped over his friend and quickly opened the driver's side door to retrieve Tony's cellphone from the seat. But it wasn't there – Trek must have taken it.

Thankfully Scoop didn't need the phone. Less than a minute later, he watched two police cars pull up on the narrow block and stop in front of Tony's body.

chapter 6

Quanisha sat in the house watching the Maury show on her barely functional television. It was her day off and she would normally have her feet up relaxing, but instead she was uptight and disturbed.

For one, she was upset because she had been getting a series of hang-up calls on her home phone ever since Tony had come back. The day before when she came home from work, she checked her voicemail and heard 12 hangup clicks. Her caller ID read 18 new callers, one of which was from her mother, one from her friend Saria, and the others were all private calls. She figured it was just a telemarketer.

The previous night, Tony had left her a note on her dresser saying he loved her, was committed to making things work, and promised on his heart to be back by 2:30am that night if she wanted to talk. Quanisha had waited up all night for him to arrive, giddy about the fact that Tony had finally said the words she had been waiting for him to say for over six years. *Well, he didn't actually say it out of his mouth yet, but he did write it in so many words*, she reasoned. She loved Tony too, despite all of his faults.

But when the clock struck 3:10am Tony still wasn't home. So being that she didn't know how to get in touch with Tony besides at his Grandma's house, she had gone and found Scoop's number from the black address book she kept in her panty drawer.

She had listened to Scoop's phone ring four times before she heard someone pick up and fumble with the phone. She heard some male voices in the background that didn't sound familiar and someone referred to as "Poo." *Who the hell is Poo?* she thought to herself as she repeatedly said "hello" into the phone before the line was finally hung up by whoever was on the other end. She tried to call back but Scoop's voicemail picked up from then on. She left a message for Scoop and considered going out on the block to see if she could find Tony herself. She had stayed up until 5:00am, when sleep had finally gotten the best of her.

"In regards to Talisha Evans, Tyrone, you are NOT the father," Maury said as Tyrone leapt from his chair almost breaking his neck on stage. The mother of the child ran off the stage crying.

"Yea, yea! I told you!! Didn't I tell you!?!" Tyrone yelled at the cheering audience, who just minutes before were booing him. He did his ghetto dance on stage, a combination of the chicken dance and the perkulator before 'peacing' everybody and walking off stage to go taunt the mother.

"I *knew* that bitch was suspect," Quanisha said to no one in particular. "See that's why I can't be going through all that, uh uh. I'm just not ready to be dealing with all that bullshit," she said as she rubbed her tummy and looked down sadly. She shook her head at herself, because she couldn't even be honest talking to her own self. The truth was, the three abortions Quanisha had in her teens had caused her to be unable to bear children, or at least carry them to term. She had been pregnant twice after the abortions and miscarried on both. The doctors were telling her that it was very unlikely that she would be able to have a child. It tore her up inside, and she would never admit it to her family and friends.

Just as she was becoming more involved in her sad thoughts, her phone started ringing. Making a beeline for the cordless in her bedroom, she picked up on the middle of the second ring.

"Hello!" she yelled into the phone, thinking it was Tony.

The person on the other line hesitated, so she said 'hello' again, even angrier this time, and finally the person spoke. "Uh yea Nish? This Scoop."

"Scoop? Scoop, where's Tony, he didn't come home last night..." her voice trailed off as she realized that something must be wrong if Scoop was calling her instead of Tony.

"Yea, listen, don't go all crazy on me aiight? But something bad happened to Tony and me last night..."

"What?!?" Quanisha half asked for an answer, half screamed.

"We got robbed, and it was bad Nish." Scoop paused for a few moments trying to collect himself. "Tony was running off at the mouth and they beat him up, real bad Nish. Real bad."

"So... huh? What... Where is he Scoop? Scoop. Please. Don't tell me—"

"No, no Nish, he's not gone but he don't look good. He got some broken ribs, his face is really fucked up, and his eyes are sealed shut. He even lost some teeth they said. He's at the Mercy hospital in Darby. It just crossed my mind to call you as soon as I got home and remembered I had his phone—"

"It JUST NOW crosses your mind? What if he woulda died overnight or something and you're just calling me now!!" Quanisha screamed into the phone and then immediately hung it up. "Dumb ass niggas!! He knows my motherfucking number! Shit!" she said to herself as she grabbed some clothes out of her drawer. She threw them on, grabbed her car keys and ran out of the door.

Tony was laid up, with half of his torso, as well as his entire head, bandaged in thick white gauze. The doctors had him restrained on the bed so that he wouldn't attempt to move around and do more damage to his rib cage. He couldn't open his eyes past a thin slit and was in excruciating pain until the doctors knocked him out with several doses of very strong muscle relaxers. They had him in the intensive care wing of the hospital until he finished going through some tests.

When they brought him in the night before, he was still unresponsive. He hadn't finally fluttered his eyelids a little until 8am that morning. The doctors took that as a very good sign, but were still unsure of Tony's condition. In addition to losing a lot of blood and a few broken ribs, Tony had been hit in the head so many times that they were concerned about brain injury and were almost positive that he may have lost some of the hearing in his left ear.

The cops had questioned Scoop about what went down, but all he could say was that they had gotten robbed, and that the thieves had beat up Tony. He gave descriptions of Trek and Poo, but knew in his heart that there was no chance that the cops were going to track down those two and hold them accountable for this crime.

Tony's door creaked open and in walked Jenny, bubbly as ever, with her hands in the pockets of her nurse uniform. She had asked to be specifically assigned to Tony's room during his stay, claiming that he was her fiance. She was in bliss at the thought of personally nursing Tony back to health. She figured that when he did get on his feet they could be back together again.

Jenny walked over to the side of Tony's bed nearest the door and sat down. She placed her hand on top of his hand, which was restrained at the wrist by his sides. Tony stirred a bit.

"Baby, how are you feeling?" Jenny asked, trying to sound like a mother. Of course, there was no audible response.

"Do you like the flowers I got you honey?" she asked, pointing up at the vase of flowers she had brought in for him early that morning. "Let me read the message I wrote to you."

Jenny stood up and reached for the vase, grabbing a small card out of the top. She stood, leaning over his bed and began reading the card. " 'Anthony: They say that everything happens for a reason. Whether you're well or whether you're sneezing, you're the reason for my breathing. And now that God has brought you to me again, I promise to love you like this paper loves my pen. Together with you forever; Love Jen.' So poetic. I can hardly believe *I* wrote this! Even my name rhymes!"

Tony stirred again, and almost seemed to shake his head 'no.' Jenny continued talking.

"Baby, I mean what I said on this card. I love you, and I promise I'll never let anything bad happen to you ever again. Once you are back to good health, which the doctors say could be a few weeks, you'll move back into my house and I'll get you a job here at the hospital. That way you can stay off the streets. You shouldn't be among all that violence. Maybe we can get married. That way I can really take care of you the way you need me to, and then I can put you on my health insurance to help cover the doctor bills from this stay."

Tony moved slightly and his eyes fluttered a bit. He mumbled something under his breath and then whined something out a little louder. To Jenny's ears, it sounded as if he said the word 'yes.'

"What was that baby? Did you just say yes?" Jenny's heart jumped and she gasped as she threw her hand with the card still clenched in it up to her chest. "Oh baby, you want to marry me! I do too! I mean, no I want to marry you too!"

Tony tried to lift his head to make it easier to speak, but it only caused an excruciating pain in the back of his neck. When he dropped his head back down quickly, it looked as if he had nodded. Tony just closed his eyes and groaned in pain.

"Ooohh baby, do you need some more morphine?" Jenny asked as she upped his dosage. She reeled again at the thought of getting married. She was too far gone now – lost in her newfound fantasy. Reason and common sense were no longer playing a part in this situation. Jenny had been wanting to get married for too long to pass up this opportunity. Once she finished helping Tony, she started pacing the room as the thoughts raced through her mind.

"Wow Tony, I can't believe this is actually happening so fast. So I guess I've got to get a dress, and book a church and tell the pastor at my church. I'll get you the best tux out there Anthony, I promise you. The best money can buy. We've got to go get the marriage license first, and I need to do an invitee list. It can be something small and quaint." She looked over at Tony with pure admiration in her eyes.

"Baby, you won't regret this. I promise, I'm going to make you the happiest man in the world," Jenny placed the card on Tony's bandaged chest, closed her eyes and leaned over to kiss him on his bruised eyelids.

"What the fuck is this?" Jenny heard an annoyed female voice ask from the doorway. She jerked up and met eyes with an angry face. Jenny did a quick analysis of the woman. She was pretty in the face, wasn't fat, but was about two McDonald's quarter pounders from busting the seams on the tight white t-shirt and grey sweat pants she was wearing. She had long micro braids and looked like she was about to flip out.

Quanisha held her ghetto stance, crossed arms and all of her weight on one foot as she stared down the rail thin nurse that had just been kissing on Tony. "Just what the fuck kind of 'service' do ya'll nurses be giving here? Why you got your lips on my man bitch?"

"Your man? I don't think so. This is my man, we've been together for over six months. And I don't appreciate you calling me a bitch, you don't know me." Jenny frowned and tilted her head to the side for effect. She lied about how long she had known Tony, knowing now for sure that this woman was in fact Tony's ex-girlfriend Quanisha. She was willing to do whatever was necessary to get Quanisha completely out of the picture while she had the chance. Tony had told Jenny a few things about his ex-girlfriend during their short time together. Jenny had been afraid that Tony had gone back to Quanisha when he left.

"What? Bitch, you trynna catch a thumpin' up in here! What the hell you mean that's yo man?" Quanisha made her way over to the side of the bed Jenny was standing on. She pushed Jenny back towards the wall and glared her down. "You better get your little Mary Poppin's ass away from my man, I know that."

She looked down on the bed and saw the card Jenny had placed there not five minutes before.

"What the hell is this?" Quanisha asked.

"That's not yours!! Give me that!" Jenny protested as Quanisha held her back with one hand and read the card with the other.

"Whether you're well or whether you're sneezing, you're the reason for my breathing'? Girl what the hell is this?" Quanisha couldn't help laughing.

"Stop it, that's for Tony!" Jenny protested, but Quanisha just crumpled up the card and threw it in the corner.

"Look little girl, I don't know what kind of fantasy world you're living in, but this is MY man. He don't deal with no Sally

Sunshine bitches like you. He need a real bitch in his life and that's me. Only me. Got it? Now get the fuck out of here, and get me some of those sweet hospital peaches or somethin.' I love those things," Quanisha sneered as she pushed Jenny roughly towards the door. She then pulled up one of the hospital chairs and sat down next to Tony. She had already prepared herself for this sight, and he actually didn't look as bad as she first thought he would.

"Tony baby, I'm here," she said as she tried to grab his hand. Tony's morphine had kicked in, and he was now completely unconscious.

All of a sudden out of nowhere, Quanisha felt a hard blow to her back and she leaned forward to recover. She turned around and there was Jenny, holding a heavy hospital phone.

"Bitch is you crazy!!!" Quanisha yelled at the top of her lungs. She put her hands up in just enough time to shield herself from Jenny's second attack.

Quanisha grabbed the phone and threw it against the wall. She stood up and slammed Jenny back against the same wall. Just as Quanisha was about to rear back and smack the shit out of Jenny, a husky black hospital security guard ran through the door and got between the two, pushing Quanisha backwards onto the bed.

"What in the hell is going on in here? Nurse Storms?" he said in reference to Jenny. "There is a patient in critical condition here!"

"This nurse bitch just tried to attack me with a phone that's what!" Quanisha yelled, furious. She still had some blows to get in.

"Is that true Nurse Storms?" the security guard asked. When Jenny, who was looking like a mad woman by then with her hair flying out of the bun in her hair, didn't answer, the security guard instructed them both to follow him to his office.

"But I'm here to see my man!" Quanisha protested, looking and pointing back at Tony, who was still slightly moving around on the bed.

"Ma'am I said follow me!" the security guard commanded and started walking towards the door.

chapter 7

"What the hell do you mean you don't got no money!??" Scoop's wifey Shaquita screamed at the top of her lungs. She was definitely heard in the next apartment over.

"Baby...I... you don't... listen—" Scoop struggled to find the words to put together. He was terrified of his girlfriend. At 5'11 with a solid stature, Shaquita could go toe to toe with most men. She could get very violent at times, and had a hair thin temper.

Once when she and Scoop first started dating, Scoop made the mistake of pushing her out of the way and telling her to "go on with that" when she innocently asked where he was headed. Before he could reach Shaquita's doorknob, she had snatched him up from behind and slammed his face into the door so hard that his nose broke. Scoop learned soon after that that even though Shaquita could be the sweetest, quietest, most mild mannered woman at times, when you made her mad she came out of her shell swinging. Scoop worried that she might be bipolar or manic depressive.

"I don't want to hear nothing you got to say out your slimy lying ass mouth! You know I was supposed to go shopping today!! I got Camille waiting at her house for me to pick her up! Now what am I gonna tell her!" Shaquita ranted. She was so close up on Scoop that he could see her tonsils as she yelled directly at his nose.

"Quita please, you ain't giving me a chance to tell you what happened! I got robbed!" Scoop said as he backed up two steps.

"Oh is this your story? This is what you're gonna tell me!! Camille is gonna be laughin' at my ass, and the only story you can make up is that you got robbed!! Aaaaaahhh!!!" Shaquita lunged forward suddenly and pushed Scoop down into the arm of a nearby sofa chair. She caught him offguard. Before he had a chance to recover, she reared back and slapped Scoop so hard that he bit his tongue. Scoop hopped back up with his eyes watering and his face stinging around the outline of where Shaquita's hand just was. He grabbed Shaquita by the arms to stop her from any more of the abuse. She writhed wildly in his grip, trying her best to reach her fingernails up to his face to scratch him. When that didn't work, she stretched her neck forward and bit down on his nose with all of her power.

"Owwwwwwww!!" Scoop yelped as he finally let her go and got free of her teeth. He couldn't believe that she had just bit him on the nose! When he grabbed it, he already knew it was bleeding, because he felt the blood droplets running down into his nostrils.

"That's what you get motherfucker! Don't you ever put your hands on me!" Shaquita ranted.

"You bitch! What the fuck is wrong with you! I was trying to explain, it wasn't my fault! Some niggas robbed me and Tony!"

"Bitch? Oh I'll show you a bitch, wait right there," Shaquita said as she turned on her heel and headed for the kitchen. Scoop didn't know what she was going in the kitchen to get—a knife, a pot, or the big turkey fork – but he wasn't waiting around to find out. He hustled his way to the front door and shot out before Shaquita had a chance to reappear. As he ran down the steps of the apartment building he heard Shaquita yelling in the hallway.

"Scoop get your black ass back here! I swear if you don't come back here right now Imma fuck you up real good when you come home! You better have my money!"

Scoop shivered a little as he finally emerged from the building and headed to his truck. He thought about why in the world was he still with this crazy female – he had over 10 women that thought he was *their* man running around the city. This type of violent episode happened way too often in their relationship. As soon as he climbed into his truck, he reached under the back seat to grab an old t-shirt he kept there and used it to stop his nose from bleeding. He hated to admit it to himself, but he was the victim of an abusive relationship that he just wouldn't leave. He had battered man syndrome.

Scoop was aware that Shaquita knew all about his hoing around. There were way too many hang up calls at her house and short conversations when Scoop answered his cell phone for her to not be suspicious. But she hardly ever brought it up. She was one of those women that really didn't care about her man cheating, as long as he was lining her pockets on a regular basis. But it was an unwritten rule that Scoop was never to bring any of his other women around Shaquita or stay out overnight. Those were the rules.

After three of Scoop's other women got stomped in broad daylight from trying to approach Shaquita on the street about 'their' man Scoop, the word got around; 'don't mess with Quita.' It wasn't so much about a love thing for Shaquita as it was about flossing in front of her broke friends. She drove a white 2003 Infiniti Q45 courtesy of Scoop, who could barely afford the payments. She wore all of the top designers, and refused to put on anything that didn't have an authentic brand name etched across the label. She owned over $10,000 worth of purses that she collected over the years from Scoop ranging from Gucci to Gharani Strok. Shaquita's sole purpose for living was shopping, and if she went a week without going to her favorite mall, she went through withdrawal, usually at Scoop's expense.

The problem was this. Scoop was going broke because of Shaquita and her habit. He could hardly afford to pay attention, and spent every moment outside of his flings working overtime to satisfy all of Shaquita's desires. His job paid well, but not enough for Shaquita. So he had started selling drugs on the side. He had worked his way up to distributing to the lesser dealers on the block, and was trying to move up his position with the help of a dude he ran with on the streets who they called Rock. Rock was one of the only Puerto Ricans who had lived in the heart of that black neighborhood in Southwest Philly all his life. As a team they were doing enough sales to give the major players confidence in consigning them more and more weight at a time, but still only just enough to meet Shaquita's needs. Scoop felt good about his current position on the streets, but was wary of Rock. Sometimes he didn't trust him, and feared that Rock would get sick of splitting their profits two ways, especially since Scoop spent a lot less time on the block. It was no secret that Rock did more work than Scoop, and had even suggested on one drunken St. Ides Malt Liquored up occasion that Scoop should only get a 30% cut. That suggestion ended up in a brawl between them at the bar where they were drinking, and a night in lock up at the local police station. However, after sobering up they worked out the disagreement and the profits continued to be split in half for each of them. But now Scoop knew exactly what was really going on in Rock's mind – a drunk mouth tells no lies.

Scoop's mind wandered back to why he was still dealing with Shaquita as he drove past the Sunoco station at 45th and Baltimore Avenue. Why? She wasn't even the best looking out of all the women he messed with.

The truth was, he had found a comfort level with Shaquita

that he just couldn't achieve with any of his other chicks. With them it was all about the wild sex, but he loved to curl up in a warm bed with his Quita and just hold her. They had been together for eight years and there was no turning back now for Scoop. Shaquita's presence filled a need within him that he didn't even know he had. He was in love with her, and didn't even know exactly why. She was both the poison and the cure.

Scoop had been headed to his number four girl, LaToya's, house before he had those thoughts about Shaquita. Even though his nose was killing him, he softened as he thought about his wifey, and decided that instead of going to LaToya's, he was going to go visit Tony in the hospital. It was only right. How could he even consider going to get some quick ass, when his best friend was laid up in the hospital. As he approached the threshold between Philadelphia and Lansdowne where his favorite Jamaican restaurant was located, he decided to stop there and get a large Jerk Chicken platter to bring in the hospital. He was tired, hungry and frustrated, and could only hope that Quanisha was not sitting by Tony's bed. He didn't need anymore drama from women that day.

When he finally reached Tony's room, he peeked inside first, to see if Quanisha was anywhere in sight. When he didn't see anyone, he breathed a sigh of relief and looked around behind him before finally going inside.

"Tone!" he said excitedly, as if Tony was going to respond the same way. Tony was barely able to open his eyes, but he definitely looked better than he did two nights ago. They had patched up most of the wounds on his face and head, and had him drugged up on painkillers, so he looked alright, but was very unresponsive. Scoop already figured that much. He pulled the curtain separating Tony from his roommate, who was fast asleep as well, and sat down on a chair that was already pulled up next to Tony's bed. He then started to pull out his food so that he could dig in.

Before he had a chance to eat the first bite of the steaming hot chicken and rice, a middle aged black male doctor came to the already open door and knocked lightly.

"Oh, come in," Scoop said, putting his fork back in the box and closing it up. "What's up Doc, you here to do some tests or something?"

"No, actually, I came in because the nurse paged me to let me know that the brother to this patient came in. I'm Doctor Stephens. I've been trying to talk to one of his family members, but I haven't been available over the last couple of days when his wife came in. You are his brother, correct?"

"Oh, yea, Scoo - I mean my name is Eric. So what's going on?" Scoop said, getting up from his chair and reaching his hand out to shake the doctor's. Seeing the distinguished black doctor in his crisp white coat gave Scoop an instant level of respect for the man. He immediately tried to talk more formally with the doctor, instead of his usual slang and colloquialisms.

"Well, things could have really been worse for this young brother. We feared brain damage when he first came in. We did a Cat Scan, and the results were good. He only suffered a mild concussion, he has some broken ribs, and we're hoping it's only a *temporary* hearing loss in his left ear. We won't know if it's temporary or not until about two months from now. Let's just pray for the best."

"Oh damn. When do you think he'll be getting out of here?"

"I'd say about another week or two. He has to fully heal. He's gonna be out of it for a couple of days. We might be moving him out of intensive care to a regular room the day after tomorrow."

"Okay. Well I'll definitely be here when he gets better."

"But that's not the only reason I wanted to speak with you Eric. One of the security personnel told me that the patient's wife came in here and assaulted one of my younger nurses. I don't know if she thought my Nurse was too close in handling the patient, and I really don't want to get into the semantics of the whole situation. All that I know is she came in here and caused a big commotion, and that's something that the patient really doesn't need at this time. He needs peace and quiet as he heals. So, if you can, I'd appreciate it if you would personally notify his wife that she has been excluded from the restricted list of visitors to this patient's room, until she comes and speaks with me directly. Can you do that?"

"Uh, sure. You say she attacked somebody?"

"When the security officer came in the room she had Nurse Storms pinned on the wall. In the interest of my patient, and the safety of my nurses, I can't allow her back. Also, now that Mr. Jackson has a roommate, he needs his peace too."

"Alright, I got you," Scoop said as he thought about how crazy Quanisha could get. She must have been really distressed about Tony being in the hospital.

"Great, I'll be going now. Enjoy your visit, but just so you know, visiting hours are over at 4pm," Doctor Stephens said as he took a few steps towards Tony's bed to check his vital signs.

"Okay, thanks Doc," Scoop said as he turned back to the chair where his food was sitting. He sat down just as the doctor left the room.

"Whoa Tone, what the hell is goin' on with these women. They straight trippin'." Scoop paused as if Tony would respond.

When he didn't, Scoop just shook his head and started eating.

chapter 8

"Ma I don't know what the hell is going on! All I know is Tony is fucked up in the hospital, and some crazy nurse is thinking that that's *her* man! She hit me in the head with a phone, but they gonna take *me* out like I'm some criminal and tell me not to come back. Ain't that some shit!? I can't even get in touch with Scoop, and he's the only person that knows anything!"

"That's what you get for messin' with that knucklehead. I told you a long time ago to leave that fool alone. But here you go, still supporting his sorry black ass..." Quanisha's mother Netta said in a monotone voice through the phone.

"Ma don't even go there, cuz you didn't do much better with that bag of bones so called father of mine. He ain't paid a dime of child support in 22 years but you still letting him lay up in *your* bed— " Before Quanisha could finish her statement, there was a click and a dial tone.

"Stupid bitch," she said, cursing her mother. "I'm tired of her ass, gonna tell me about my relationship. She ain't never had a good nigga in her lifetime."

Then her subconsious kicked in and a thought crossed her mind that made her even angrier. *Trifling niggas or not, at least she got some kids out of the deal.* The truth was Quanisha couldn't relate or talk to her mother, on any level. Especially since her mother had done everything wrong in her life. She had lived on welfare all her life, getting pregnant for the first time at age 14. At one point she had abandoned all of her five kids when she was strung out, and wasn't sure who the father of three out of five of her children were.

Quanisha strived everyday to be the exact opposite of her mother. It was the reason she had all of those abortions when she was young, because she didn't want to be a teenage welfare mother like Netta. But as soon as she entered her twenties she wanted to have kids. It was more of a mental thing than a common sense thing for her. Being a teenage mother was repulsive to her, but having a baby at age 20 would have been okay.

Quanisha also refused to be on welfare, no matter what her situation was. She worked over 45 hours a week to pay her rent, her car payment and all of her other bills. She earned an honest living, but unfortunately most of her leftover cash went to helping out Tony.

Tony always had some catastrophe going on. One time it was his grandmother's 61st birthday, he was dead broke, and she had supposedly been begging him to get her a new microwave. Another time his car broke down and he needed a new muffler. Not to mention all the times he had a big money scheme, where he was supposedly guaranteed to make three times his investment in a matter of days, but of course it fell through and Quanisha was the only loser.

The cordless phone next to her started ringing again. "Oh Lord, now I bet she wanna apologize or somethin'," Quanisha said, rolling her eyes as she grabbed the phone.

"Hello?" she said with an attitude.

"Nish, it's Scoop."

"Scoop? Man what the hell is going on, why ain't you—"

"Nish, what happened at the hospital? They came in there tellin' me you beat some nurse up or something."

"What? Hell no I ain't beat nobody up!" Quanisha yelled as she stood up from the couch. "That bitch got me with a phone!!"

"What?"

"I went in there to see Tony, and this nurse bitch is all kissing up on Tony! She hit me over the head with a phone, but when I grabbed her ass up the security guard came in. They told me I can't go back there!"

"That's what I was callin' to tell you. I went by there today, they said you can't go back up to see Tony 'til you go talk to his doctor. Ummm. Man I forgot his name?"

"What? What the hell I got to speak to some doctor for, it wasn't my fault! He need to go talk to that loony ass nurse they got working there. I swear if I see her little skinny ass again Imma fuck her up real right this time!"

"You can't do that Nish, don't you want to see Tone?"

"Yea. But…"

"Go back up there, and ask to speak to Tony's doctor. Matter fact, call them before you go in to make sure he gonna be there," Scoop told her.

"Aiight, but I swear if I see that bitch…"

"Just tell the Doc what's up aiight? He'll handle that. Right now they thinkin' you a nut, so you gotta clear that up, yah mean?"

"Aiight, Scoop, could you please tell me what happened?? Who did that to him?" Quanisha asked, softening up now that someone was finally talking to her about Tony.

Scoop and Nisha talked about everything that happened that night, but Scoop conveniently left out the part about it all starting because they were doing a weed run. Nisha immediately realized now how everything had went down. Scoop gave her his new cellphone number, and she promised to call and update Scoop on Tony's condition.

chapter 9

It was Jenny's day off from the hospital. She normally would have still gone in to check on Tony, but today she had some very important plans. It was a perfect 70 degree day, not a cloud in the sky – no better afternoon to do some very special shopping for her special day.

She walked into the small quaint shop, and heard the bells ring, signaling the sales woman that someone had entered her store.

"Hello ma'am, how are you doing this beautiful day?" the pretty young saleswoman asked Jenny.

"Oh I'm doing so well. Thank you so much."

"My name is Sarah, and I'll be helping you today. So, you're looking for a dress huh? What is your style?" the sales lady began. "Wait, let me guess."

Sarah hustled over to a beautiful dress in the corner near the register. It was strapless and had sequins covering the front. The lower part of the gown was full and perfectly satin. "Classic and elegant. Am I right?"

"Uhhh, no. Actually, I was looking for something more along these lines," Jenny said as she opened up a *Today's Bride* magazine and pointed to a more simple chiffon sleeved dress with a well defined torso wrapped in lace, a straight gown with a long train running behind.

"Oh now that is absolutely gorgeous. Hmmm," Sarah put her finger on her chin and thought about what she had in stock. "You know I think I might have something with a lace torso. When is your date?"

She guided Jenny over to an area at the center of the store. She showed her several dresses of that style and let her know that as a dressmaker she could tailor the dress Jenny chose to look almost exactly like the picture within a week. Jenny put her hand on her stomach and rubbed it affectionately.

"What if I needed a last minute modification to the abdomen area? Woud you be able to do that?" she asked.

"Ummm, yes I can do that." Sarah's eyes roamed down to Jenny's hand, and she immediately knew what Jenny was talking about. "And you know what? I would even do that at no extra charge."

Jenny left the store less than an hour later having bought a $2,000 wedding dress on her credit card. Ecstatic at her purchase, she got in her car and headed to the jewelry store to pick up the two carat engagement ring she saw on sale for $2,500 at the Jewelry Factory in Norristown.

She only hoped that by the time the wedding happened, she wouldn't be needing that last minute dress modification.

* * *

Quanisha didn't know why she was so nervous as she walked through the automatic sliding hospital doors and headed to the front desk. She had rumbled with the worst and argued with the best over her 22 years. But something about Dr. Stephen's voice over the phone made her feel anxious about this meeting. Fortunately he was in that day, and had a free appointment at 10:30am. He said that their discussion shouldn't take more than a few minutes, so she would be in time for work at 12 noon.

"Can I help you miss?" the receptionist asked as Quanisha approached her desk.

"Ummm, yea. I'm supposed to be meeting with Dr. Stephens at 10:30. I'm a little early."

"And what is your name?" the receptionist said, eyeing Quanisha as if she were there to blow up the building or something.

"It's Quanisha," she replied with a slight attitude with an accent on the 'ish' part of her name. She was tired of people judging her as some type of hoodrat whenever she walked into a professional atmosphere. She was working a steady job just like this receptionist.

"Dr. Stephens to the front waiting area. Dr. Stephens, please come to the front waiting area."

Quanisha sat down without another word to the receptionist. About five minutes later, a good looking older black gentleman with salt and pepper hair stepped up to the front desk and said something to the receptionist. She pointed over to Quanisha and he looked over at her with a smile. Quanisha stood up as the doctor approached and saw the warmest look in his eyes.

"Mrs. Jackson?"

"Uh, yea. That's me," Quanisha said. She had lied to the hospital about being Tony's wife, which is why this doctor was referring to her by his last name.

"Come this way."

The doctor led Quanisha down the hall to a row of small offices, until he reached the one with his name on the door. She felt like she was going to the principal's office.

"So Mrs. Jackson, sit down." He didn't waste any time getting to the point. "I've been told that you were involved with an incident with one of my nurses—"

"It wasn't no incident! Your nurse attacked me with a phone! When I came in there she was kissing Tony and I told her to get out. Then she came from behind me and bashed me in the head with a phone! I'm still gettin' headaches from it. I should sue this hospital!" Quanisha lost control over herself and became agitated.

"Okay, slow down Mrs. Jackson. So you say she hit you with a phone?" Dr. Stephens asked. This was new information for him. The security guard had only told him that Quanisha had Jenny pinned on the wall.

"Yes! Listen, doctor, I don't got no reason to be coming in your hospital and fighting folks. I do what I'm supposed to do. I work hard at my job and I take care of my business. Now, I come in here to see my man, I get attacked by Nurse Ratchet in there, and *I'm* getting punished? I can't see my man now? I'm just now hearing about why he's here in the first place! And he's the only family I got!"

Suddenly Quanisha put her head down in her hand and broke down in tears. She looked as if the weight of the world was on her shoulders.

"Mrs. Jackson. Mrs. Jackson, it's gonna be alright." The doctor looked at Quanisha with compassion. Then he finally got up; he couldn't stand to see a young sister in distress.

"Come here," the doctor commanded as he walked over to her and opened his arms to give her a hug. Quanisha hesitated for a minute, but then found herself melting in this stranger's arms. He reached over to grab a tissue off of his desk and gave it to Quanisha.

"Thank you," she said as she finally let go of the doctor to blow her nose. She didn't want to leave the doctor's embrace. His presence was so warm and loving. She could feel the positivity, compassion and genuineness oozing from him. He had an almost fatherly presence. A father figure was something that Quanisha had never had in her life.

"Now look, I'm going to talk to Nurse Storms and sort all of this drama out. I know that there are always two sides of a story, and I'll get to the bottom of this Mrs. Jackson. I promise you that. But as far as the visitation situation, you can feel free to visit your husband now. Just try not to get into any other confrontations like before. If you are having any type of problem with a nurse, or any other personnel, just come right here to my office and talk to me directly. Matter of fact, let me give you my pager number," the doctor said as he grabbed a card from the small holder on his desk. He handed the card to Quanisha and smiled.

"Thank you Dr. Stephens, Imma definitely call you if that happens, cuz I'm telling you the truth. That nurse is crazy, and somebody needs to put her in her place," Quanisha said.

Something about what Quanisha had just said made Dr. Stephens think back to a bit of office gossip he heard while eating lunch in the cafeteria about a year before. Someone had told him that Nurse Storms was off from work that day because she was going to court to fight a restraining order that someone had put against her. He thought nothing of it at the time, but now he was analyzing that information with the story that Quanisha had just told him.

"I will look into it Mrs. Jackson. Would you like to go in to see Tony now? I'll take you in," he offered.

"Yes, I would, but only for a little while. I gotta be at work by noon. My boss be trippin'. Just so you know if you need any new employees in here, I'm available!"

The doctor chuckled as he opened the door. "I'll keep that in mind. Alright, come on then Mrs. Jackson."

Quanisha stood up slowly and turned to the doctor. "Wait. I

gotta tell you something."

"Huh? What's that?" the doctor asked as he shut the door back, thinking that it was something personal.

"I gotta tell you… My last name isn't Jackson, it's Williams. I ain't married to Tony, I just said that to get to see him. They wouldn't have let me up to see him in intensive care if they knew I was just his girlfriend," Quanisha admitted and looked down at the floor.

The doctor folded his arms and looked at her sternly. One would think by the expression on his face that he was upset, but really he was impressed with Quanisha. Here she was, this passionate hard working young lady, admitting a lie to a complete stranger. She didn't have to tell him the truth about not being married to the patient, and he would have never known either way.

"Young lady, don't worry. We'll keep that between you and me okay? Let's just go in to see Mr. Jackson," the doctor reassured as he opened the door again and led her out of his office.

chapter 10

The real Mrs. Jackson, Tony's grandmother, was being released that day. To her surprise, instead of her son coming to pick her up, the thin light skinned nurse who claimed to be Tony's new girlfriend was taking her home. Jenny had only told her that Tony was unavailable, and that he had asked her to take care of things for him.

Only one of Mrs. Jackson's so called friends had come to see her the whole time she had been in the hospital, even though they had made an announcement about it in church. She was really feeling some kind of way about that. They were always the first to call when they needed something from Mrs. Jackson or wanted to gossip, but didn't even care to visit her when she was laid up.

Now, Mrs. Jackson couldn't believe that her own grandson wouldn't make the time to come pick her up from the hospital himself. And even worse, he hadn't come to see her in over a week. Even worse than *that*, he had sent this annoying girl Jenny to handle her. Jenny had been coming in there to see her almost every day since she was admitted, and she wasn't even her assigned nurse. She wanted to tell her to leave her alone so many times, but the God in her just wouldn't let her hurt the girl's feelings. Still, there was something about Jenny that just didn't sit well with Mrs. Jackson.

"Are you doing okay Mrs. Jackson?" Jenny asked for the sixth time as she wheeled Tony's grandmother down the hospital hallway. Tony's grandmother only nodded as she leaned her elbow on the arm of the wheelchair and put her head in her hand.

On the ride home, Jenny had to ask Mrs. Jackson for directions to her house.

"Tony didn't tell you where to drop me off child?" she asked curiously.

"No, he was in such a rush that he didn't have a chance to write down the directions for me," Jenny explained quickly.

"Oh, well. I guess. The directions are so easy though. Why couldn't he come pick me up from the hospital again?"

"Um, I think he said he had to go see a friend of his about some business. Maybe he is going to get a job?" Jenny mused.

"Hmmph. Maybe," Mrs. Jackson said skeptically. The last time Tony had a job was when he was 21, helping with newspaper sales on the street. That job had only lasted for three days, because Tony started complaining that his feet were hurting him from standing up for so long. Her grandson would much rather lay down on someone's couch and live for free.

"Tony and I are really getting along well. He is such a loving man. I see great things for his future," Jenny gushed.

Tony's grandmother looked over at Jenny for a long while. She examined this young woman closely, and wondered if they were talking about the same Tony. She loved her grandson to death, but had never thought of him as a 'loving' man, especially not to a female who he had just met. *What could Tony possibly see in this girl*, she thought. Jenny was… indescribable. She just wasn't Tony's type. She was meek and average looking. Her eyes were dark and untrustworthy. She didn't have any fire in her belly. She was just… there. Yes, Jenny and Tony had come into her room to visit on several occasions, but it never came off to her the way that Jenny was describing. Most of the time Tony seemed very unconcerned about Jenny's presence; it was almost as if Jenny wasn't even in the room. Mrs. Jackson wondered if anything Jenny was telling her about their relationship was the truth.

When they finally pulled up in front of Mrs. Jackson's rowhome, Jenny helped Mrs. Jackson up the stairs and into the door. As soon as Tony's grandmother stepped foot in the door she was waving Jenny off.

"Go ahead chile, don't let me hold you up," she told Jenny as she turned around to get ready to close the door shut in her face.

"Are you sure Mrs. Jackson? I can go get you some new food, and cook you a nice lunch?"

"No don't worry about that, I can go shopping for myself a little later. All I want to do now is just rest," Mrs. Jackson reassured.

"Oh. Okay, well you have my phone number now, so feel free to give me a call if you need anything," Jenny replied as she backed up a few steps.

"I surely will, you take care of yourself," Mrs. Jackson said as she shut the door promptly.

"That girl is a pain in the ass," she mumbled to herself as she shuffled her way over to the kitchen so that she could set her bag down and call Tony. She looked up at the ceiling. "Forgive me Lord."

The phone just kept ringing and ringing as Mrs. Jackson sat at her kitchen table and attempted to call Tony. She tried again and got the same result.

"What in the world is going on with that boy," she said to herself. She rubbed her forehead in distress. She tried to remember Quanisha's phone number off the top of her head, but her memory was suffering after the blow to her head that caused her to be in the hospital for all that time. At least Quanisha would be able to tell her more of what was really going on. She was going to get to the bottom of what was really up with Jenny and this whole Tony situation, one way or another.

* * *

Quanisha sat in Tony's hospital room reading the latest issue of her favorite gossip magazine, which she had picked up from the gift shop. She loved reading about all of the celebrity news, real or fake. Tony was finally wide awake. He was staring up at the ceiling in deep thought and memory. It was obvious that he had a lot on his mind, in particular his near fatal encounter with Trek's boot. He and Quanisha had been fighting non stop ever since Tony became conscious and started speaking to folks again, which was only two days before. This was a rare moment when neither of them were speaking. Quanisha just sat by with him for support before she had to go to work at noon.

"Where's this doctor at?" Tony asked as he turned his neck to Quanisha. He was still in a lot of pain.

"I don't know, he busy. He got shit to do," Quanisha answered without ever looking up at Tony. She was still highly pissed and confused about the whole Nurse Storms confrontation. She still wanted answers from Tony about why that nurse thought she was his woman. Tony was pretending as if he didn't know what she was talking about, and Jenny hadn't shown up again at a time when Quanisha was visiting. Lucky for Jenny, because regardless of what the doctor had said, Quanisha probably would have descended upon her on sight. After years of being with Tony, Quanisha knew he wasn't telling her the whole truth about this nurse girl.

Quanisha had come to see Tony everyday since Dr. Stephens had given her the okay to come visit again. He had asked

Quanisha to give him at least a week to talk to Nurse Storms himself. It was a beautiful fall Friday afternoon, almost a week since she and the doctor had spoken so she was hoping he had an update. Maybe he could tell her the things that Tony wasn't. She had checked Dr. Stephens office earlier, but he wasn't in until later on in the afternoon.

"Well I wish somebody would tell me what the hell is going on with my moms! Jen— the nurse told me she was still in this hospital, but that they wasn't letting anybody see her right now. What the hell is goin' on!?"

Quanisha looked up from her magazine and looked at Tony curiously. "I told you I don't know Tony, but I'll go try to check out her room myself before I leave. What room she in?"

"Ummm. What was it… I think it's room 503? On the fifth floor."

"Aiight, but if they ain't lettin' nobody in there I doubt they gonna let my ghetto ass in. And who the hell is 'Jen the nurse'?" Quanisha asked, not missing a beat as she looked at Tony with her nose scrunched up.

"Nobody," Tony said as he turned his head away from Quanisha and scratched at his balls. Quanisha hopped up from her chair and threw her magazine on the floor.

"You know what nigga, you ain't foolin' nobody! I'm gonna get to the bottom of all this shit one way or the other. So you gonna either tell me now, or you're gonna pay out your ass later. What's it gonna be?"

"There ain't nothing to tell Nish! I don't know what the fuck you tryin' to figure out!" Tony tried to sit up and argue with Quanisha, but he became lightheaded and had to lay back down.

"You know I'm sick of your lyin' ass! You know what I had to go through just to see your dumb ass? And you still ain't bein' upfront about this shit? That nurse bitch said you was her man!"

"Baby, I'm telling you. I ain't dealin' with no nurse. I don't know what that girl told you, but it ain't true."

"Yea whateva nigga," Quanisha said, getting her stuff together. "I ain't never comin' back here. Fuck you. After all this, and you still treatin' me like shit."

"Nish, come on Nish. Baby don't leave," Tony pleaded as he watched Quanisha bustle her way out of the room. "Quanisha!"

Quanisha looked at her watch and saw that it was only 11:10am. She wanted to stop and talk to Dr. Stephens, but she was so furious that she couldn't even bear to look at him at that moment. She was afraid he might peg her as some out of control hood rat chick that was always angry. She just wanted to go about her day and forget that Tony had ever existed.

Driving to work, Quanisha got a call on her cellphone. It was her friend Trina, who was just coming out of the beauty salon.

"Hey girl what you doin'?" Trina asked in a huff.

"Nothin', what's up with you," Quanisha said, not really wanting an answer. She was trying to calm herself down after dealing with Tony.

"Girl, I just left Shakira chair, so you know my weave is bangin'. This shit looks real! All 'dem at the salon said it looked just like my own hair. I told them they need to stop sweatin' me," Trina laughed. "Now all I need is to get my nails did up at Kim's and then I'll be ready to go. I'm gonna shake my ass all over the club tonight. You still goin' right?"

"Tonight? Man I don't know. Where you goin', Palmers?"

"Hell yea, girl you better be going. I got this new 'fit just for tonight, and I ain't lettin' it go to waste."

"Ain't Tahira goin'?"

"Naw. She backed out at the last minute, like she always do.

Girl I ain't focused on her anyway. You know she still owe me money from the last time we went out, buying her all them drinks. How the hell you gonna come to the club with $10 in your pocket? Then we gotta leave when she wanna leave. Fuck that," Trina ranted.

"Okay, aiight. I'll guess I'll roll through there. I need somethin' to get my mind off this nigga girl. I swear once I find out what's goin' on with this Nurse Storms bitch Imma snatch *somebody* head off."

"You still on that? Girl you got to be kidding me. If I hear one more thing about that broke ass nigga Tony I think Imma tear this fresh new weave out of my head! Girl leave that nigga alone! He all up in the hospital, pitiful as shit," Trina paused to laugh at the image in her mind. "There ain't no better time to leave his ass. Everybody in the hood talkin' bout how he got his ass whooped up and down Kingsessing Ave. Personally, I wouldn't worry about his ass no more if I was you," Trina went on.

"Well you ain't me, so don't be tryin' to tell me about my man," Quanisha went into defense mode. Trina had a bad habit of running her mouth too much, and it drove Quanisha crazy.

"You the one always bringing his ass up! Don't be talking about the nigga every second of the day if you ain't trynna hear nobody opinion about 'im," Trina spat back.

"Fuck you bitch. Yo Imma get off this phone before I end up cursin' yo ass out for real. What time tonight? You comin' to get me right?" Quanisha said, getting ready to get off the phone. She wasn't even totally sure she was going, but if she was going she damn sure wasn't driving.

"I gotta come get you?" Trina thought about that for a while. "Aiight, whatever nigga, I gotchu. Be ready at like 10:30. We might be able to catch the ladies night thing and get in for free."

"Aiight, call me before you head out."

* * *

By the time Quanisha and Trina got to the club at around 12 midnight, the line was wrapped around the corner. Trina began bitching almost instantly.

"Oh hell naw. I ain't waiting on this line," she said, gesturing to Quanisha with her head as she began walking straight up to the door. All the women waiting on line looked her and Quanisha up and down as if they were the most audacious bitches that ever walked the face of the earth.

Quanisha was dressed in a black leather bustier with a tight short jean skirt and some black boots that looked like sandals at the bottom with their open toes. Trina was dressed even more scandalously in a see through pink top held up by spaghetti straps that kept slipping down her shoulders and revealed her white 36 DD bra underneath. She had on a pair of tight white jeans that were ripped strategically, showing various parts of her body, including the sides of her larger than life butt cheeks. The word around town was that Trina was dipping and dabbling in the stripper scene around North Philly, and even doing some whoring in the Atlantic City area on weekends. That was why she always had money on her. She did her dirt away from her home in West Philly in the hopes that nobody in her hood would find out, but of course they did.

"Yo, I know the dudes that's throwin' this party. They told me to come and ask for 'im," Trina said confidently to the bouncer.

"What's your name?" he asked as he stared at Trina's double D's.

"Trina, but my buls call me NaNa," she answered with a smile and a wink. She licked her lips with her pierced tongue to entice the bouncer even more. Quanisha folded her arms and leaned back in her ghetto stance. She rolled her eyes at Trina's antics, and hoped that everybody else at the club didn't think she was some kind of stripper ho like her friend.

The bouncer smiled and gestured Trina in. "They can go ahead," he said to the lady collecting money behind the booth, and they strolled right into the club. Some of the women waiting on line started talking about "how did those hos get in like that," jealous at the fact that Quanisha and Trina were let in without having to wait, and without having to be searched by the burly female bouncer.

"Yo go get us some drinks, Imma go to the bathroom," Quanisha told Trina as she headed towards the back of the lobby area. She wanted to check her makeup, but also wanted to go in separately to the main party area in an attempt to disassociate herself from Trina. Trina was way too hoish for her taste, which is why she didn't really like going to the club with her. But Quanisha needed a release that night. Maybe she could meet a baller that night who would sweep her off her feet and take her away from Tony for good. She needed a brother that was paying all his own bills, had money, his own place to live, and knew how to treat a lady. He also most definitely had to be faithful and trustworthy.

Quanisha snapped out of her daydream as two loud women brushed past her and into the bathroom before her. She stopped and looked in the direction where they just went and tried to compose herself. Quanisha had a short fuse that was usually lit by ignorant project bitches that showed no respect to anyone or anything. But she was trying to have a peaceful night tonight, so she decided to brush it off and continue on.

"Nish you know you gotta chill," she said to herself and chuckled as she headed into the bathroom.

When Quanisha walked up the stairs to the first floor of the party at Palmer's Night Club, it was packed out. She was kind of glad though, because that way she had an excuse to not find Trina so quickly and man-watch instead. She grabbed an apple martini from the bar, and then posted up a few steps away from the door in her best model stance. She was trying to attract the attention of any one of the dudes standing by with their clean cut Freeway beards, throwbacks and fitted hats. She was hoping one of these dudes were ballers, not just fake wannabe's that came to the club with $5 in their pocket. Her theory was that if they didn't buy you a drink, they were broke, hands down. Any true baller wasn't going to sweat over an $8 drink.

After a few minutes, Quanisha glanced over and saw a tall dark skinned brother with a red hat on over his eyes looking her way with a smirk on his face. He looked interested in what he saw, and was holding a half full bottle of Moet in one hand. Those bottles cost at least $100 each at that club, so she knew this dude was balling something terrible. She smiled deviously and rolled her eyes at him playfully. Before she had a chance to turn back and take another look, Trina came barrelling her way and put her hand on Quanisha's shoulder to hold herself up. Quanisha knew Trina was showing off when she looked down at the ground and started shaking her head.

"Girl, these niggas is wearing a sista OUT!" Trina exclaimed as she finally lifted her head and nearly spit in Quanisha's face as she spoke. Quanisha moved out of the way.

"Bitch, stop trippin'," Quanisha said seriously as she rolled her neck to the opposite direction, looking around for the guy that was just grilling her. This was just the scenario that she was afraid of. Now all the brothers in the club were going to think she was a nasty stripper ho too.

"Ewww, look at you trynna be cute. Well fuck you too," Trina said as she positioned herself to stand right next to Quanisha. Quanisha's heart was sinking into her stomach. She could feel the stares in her direction now that her outlandish friend was standing right there. Hardly anyone was even looking in her direction before, but now they couldn't help but notice them both. It was unwanted attention in Quanisha's opinion. Trina was gyrating to the beat seductively. *Probably the same way she do to the pole*, Quanisha thought.

"Let me go get another drink," Quanisha said, making an excuse to get away from Trina.

"Oh let me go get one too," Trina said. She stopped dancing and downed her Tequila Sunrise in less than three gulps. Before Quanisha could protest, a short husky light skinned brother came up on Trina and grabbed her, pulling her close by the waist. Even though he was pretty rough, Trina didn't complain. She just moved her body to the beat and ground her pelvis into his crotch.

Quanisha quickly made her way to the bar and asked the bartender for another drink. She then eased her way past Trina and her new man. She made her way to the staircase so that she could visit the next level. But before she had a chance to make it up the first two steps, someone grabbed her hand from behind.

"Where you going baby doll?" the brother with the red hat asked her.

"I'm goin' about my business," Quanisha said with an attitude. She was really beaming at the fact that he had followed her outside of the main party room, but was trying to play hard to get. "Why, what's that to you?"

"Yo cuz, what's all that attitude about. I'm just trynna see what's up wit your fine ass, yah mean?" he replied cockily.

"Ain't nuffin'," Quanisha said as she folded her arms and looked at him smugly.

"Aiight, never mind then. Go 'head upstairs," he said, waving her off and heading back towards the party room.

Quanisha was about to call after him, but didn't want to play herself. Even though she was crushed, she brushed it off and continued on up the stairs. There were plenty more fish in that sea of clubgoers.

When she hit the upstairs room there was reggae music playing, and most of the people up there were dancing so dirty that they might as well have been having sex. Reggae music was her favorite, so Quanisha moved slowly and nodded her head to the beat. Almost instantly, some guy came up behind her and started grinding his hard penis on her behind. She backed up into him and leaned over to give him the full feel of her soft round behind. When the song changed, she stood straight up and turned around to look at the guy but he was long gone. Quanisha felt stupid and desperate for assuming he was interested in more than a dance.

It went on like that for Quanisha pretty much the whole night. She even hit the last floor of the club to no avail. Nobody seemed to be really interested, and her confidence was shot. She felt unattractive. Not even one brother had asked for her number. Finally giving up on finding her baller at around 3:30am, let out time, Quanisha decided to go back downstairs and look for Trina. She was ready to go.

When she got there, Trina was putting her number in some guy's phone and falling all over him drunk.

"Here she go lookin' like a straight up dirty coochie having hoochie gettin' all the play," Quanisha mumbled under her breath jealously.

"There you go!" Trina yelled. "I was looking all over for you."

They went outside together and Quanisha had to endure Trina's chatter about all the brothers who she had snagged, and how some guy had grabbed her breast right out of her shirt. Trina laughed about that incident; apparently she thought it was cute. Quanisha was boiling inside.

They stood outside for a while as Quanisha hoped for a last minute baller to notice her cute facial features in the street light outside. When Trina was getting too much attention from one of the guys that she had been dancing with inside the club, Quanisha started hating and told Trina that she was ready to go. Trina gave her male friend a long kiss on the lips and then told him to call her. He begged her to leave with him, but she declined. There was no way that Trina was going over some dude's house and he hadn't even bought her something or taken her out to eat first. Her love wasn't free.

As they started towards the car, to Quanisha's surprise someone grabbed her hand again. It was the same guy with the red baseball cap that had blown her off inside the club.

"You adjust your attitude yet?" he asked, grilling her intensely. Quanisha loved his gangster, and wasn't about to let him get away again. She was much nicer this time.

"I didn't have no attitude, I'm just sayin'. Some of these niggas out here ain't about shit, so I had to feel you out first," she explained with a smile.

"Yea, whatever," he replied with a knowing smirk. Some of his boys were calling him from the crowd to come on with them. "Listen, I gotta bounce, so let me get your number and I'll call you."

"Where's your phone?"

Quanisha put her number into his phone without hesitation. When he turned around without even saying goodbye, she felt as if she had already given him a lot of power. She was desperate for some attention, and was ashamed of herself for being so easy about giving up her number. She didn't even get his name or tell him hers so that he would be able to distinguish who she was in his phone. Still she hoped that he would give her a call.

"Girl he was hittin', that's a good look," Trina said, nodding at Quanisha.

Quanisha looked back at her friend and then started walking to the car again, this time with a little more pep in her step.

"This'll teach Tony's ass. Two can play this game," she said under her breath.

chapter 11

It was Wednesday, and the doctor had told Tony that he would finally be getting out of the hospital in two days. His recovery was very progressive, and the only catch was that once he was released he would have to keep his ribs wrapped in bandages for support for another week or so. His hearing was slightly off, but the doctor was hopeful that it would be 100% again soon. He had long since been moved out of the intensive care unit to a regular floor.

Tony was getting stir crazy in that hospital, and he wanted out. Quanisha hadn't come by to see him since that previous Friday, and he was starting to feel some kind of way about it. She didn't even answer her cellphone when he called.

Even more, he wanted to finally find out what was going on with his grandmother. Jenny had come in several more times, and was telling him again and again that his grandmother was in a room that accepted no visitors at the time. He didn't know why, being that at that point in time his grandmother should have been doing well. Jenny told him that she was doing fine, but that the doctors wanted to keep her under observation. But when he asked another nurse she checked the hospital computer and told him that no woman by the name of Teresa Jackson was currently registered.

Tony was sitting on the side of the high hospital bed with his legs hanging over the edge. His hospital robe barely covered his thighs; it was so short that you could almost see his balls hanging out. He looked around the room for something to put on, but nobody had brought over any clothes for him, not even Jenny. He remembered the jeans that they had brought him in had to be somewhere in the room. He opened a few drawers but didn't find them in there.

"They must've thrown them out," he mumbled under his breath as he leaned back up slowly to steady himself. His head was still hurting badly, and whenever he moved too quickly or got up from the bed too fast he felt lightheaded. On one occasion while Quanisha was visiting, he had gotten up without even thinking and fainted right in the middle of the floor in his room.

"Fuck this, I'm going outside or somethin'," Tony said. He slipped into some slippers one of the nurses had given him, grabbed a big towel out of the bathroom, and peeked out of the door. His roommate peered over right before Tony left the room.

Easing his way down the hallway slowly, he made a quick turn down another hallway and was happy when he saw the signs for a staircase not far away. He headed up the stairs to the fifth floor, hoping that he was remembering his grandmother's room number correctly.

Everybody was looking at him funny as he passed them in the halls, holding the towel close to his private parts. He was glad the 'Nazi Nurse,' Nurse Johnson wasn't working that shift because she surely would have given him a tongue lashing for this. Room 503 was all the way on the other side of the hospital so he had a long walk.

When he finally got there, he glanced around as if he were up to no good and looked into the room expecting to see his grandmother laying there. But all he saw was an empty bed. He walked to the other side of the curtain, and was taken aback when he saw a frail old white lady looking back up at him with the most frightened look on her face that he had ever seen.

"What do you want!" she screamed and pressed the button for her nurse immediately.

"Nothing, nothing. I thought you was somebody else," Tony said, backing up slowly and holding his forehead. His head started to hurt and he felt light-headed as if he were about to faint.

"Can I help you?" a nurse said with an attitude from behind, startling Tony and causing him to jump a little.

"Oh, uh… yea. My grandmother was in this room. She's supposed to be in this room," he said with a confused look on his face.

"Unless you half-white, your grandma ain't in here," the young Latina nurse said, peeking over at the old white lady, who was still looking terrified.

"Teresa Jackson. She wasn't supposed to be in here?"

"Who, that nice old black lady Mrs. Jackson? They let her out like a week ago. She ain't here no more. Who you to her?" the nurse asked, questioning Tony now and becoming defensive. Mrs. Jackson had been so nice to her during her whole stay and didn't cause any problems.

"Tell this boy to leave my room!" the old white lady said angrily. It was apparent that this lady didn't like black people around her.

"Boy? Who you callin' a boy?" Tony responded as he turned back around to look at the white lady. The lady was now quiet and the nurse rolled her eyes at the fact that these two were eating into her time playing solitaire on the computer.

"Yea, that's what I thought. You stupid white bitch!" Tony spat at the lady nastily as he brushed by the nurse and stormed out of the room. He vaguely heard the old white lady bitching and moaning about how she wanted a lock on her door from now on, and that she wanted to call her son. When he got two doors down, he started to feel the effects of his quick movements and had to lean back against the wall.

What did they mean his grandmother had been out for a week? Jenny had told him that she was still there and under close watch by the doctors. Why did she lie about that? His anger at Jenny grew with each moment that passed. He couldn't wait to see Jenny again so that he could strangle her.

When he regained his composure, he walked further down the hall and the smell of food caught his nose. He had eaten two hours ago, but his stomach was grumbling again from hunger. His grandmother and Quanisha were always pissed at him for eating so much food, even after he had already eaten a full meal. He regularly emptied out their fridges and never bought any groceries to replace the food he ate.

He wandered down another hall and saw that there was a small room with a couple of trays of food laid out. Both plates were some kind of beef dish with macaroni and cheese on the side. They smelled so good, he just couldn't resist, even though he knew deep down that this was probably somebody else's dinner. He glanced around nonchalantly and then sauntered into the room. He snatched both of the plates off of the tray and grabbed a fork. Plates in hand, he rushed out of the room and hustled to a nearby men's bathroom made for one occupant at a time. He sat down on the toilet and started grubbing.

Only 20 minutes later, Tony emerged from the bathroom with his stomach full and satisfied. He had eaten both full course meals in no time because he had been shoveling the food down his throat and barely even tasting it. He had been laughing as he ate, at the patients who were probably mad and hungry somewhere on that floor. He got an excitement from doing things he had no business doing. That excitement made his loins tingle with delight. He had forgotten all about his grandmother while he was tearing into the warm food.

Tony quickly made his way back around the corner and into a nearby elevator going down that was just about to close.

Back where Tony had found the food trays, the orderly walked into the room where he had put the dinner rejects. The cafeteria had already notified him that the Beef Carrington trays were to be pulled because the macaroni and cheese was bad. He looked down at the trays that were missing plates for a long while, and then just assumed that someone had come behind him and chucked them as he was about to do himself. The orderly shrugged his shoulders and grabbed one of the jello bowls to eat before emptying the rest of the trays in the garbage.

By the time Jenny came into Tony's room to visit that evening, Tony's stomach was doing flip flops, he was dizzy and his head was sweating. He looked up at Jenny and saw a woman's face that he wanted to rearrange, but he could hardly move.

"Tony? What's wrong?" Jenny said, immediately noticing that Tony was out of it. He had been fine when she came in to see him the day before.

"Ugghh. I don't feel good," he said, shaking his head from side to side.

Jenny sat on the side of the bed and put the back of her hand on his forehead. "Baby, when did you start feeling like this?"

"I don't know, like an hour ago," he said weakly. His stomach turned even more when he heard her call him 'baby.'

"What hurts?"

"My stomach, I feel like I wanna throw upppp," he

complained and tried to get up. Jenny helped him up and then followed him into the bathroom where almostly instantly, Tony started throwing up violently into the cold white bowl. The force behind the food that was flying out of his mouth was so strong that he felt as if his eyes were going to bug out of his head.

"Oh my goodness Tony, what did you eat?"

"Nothin'… just that hospital food," he answered as he took a pause between spewing his guts. *It must have been that beef,* he thought to himself. He knew something didn't taste quite right in those plates of food.

"I think you got food poisoning. I've got to talk to the cafeteria," she said, nodding her head as she rubbed his back. Tony burped in response and another long round of food came flying out of his mouth into the toilet as Jenny turned her head and scrunched up her nose in disgust.

* * *

Quanisha was in a daze as she stood at her register swiping item after item to close out a customer. She was supposed to be working the Express Lane that night, ten items or less. But of course the lady she was ringing up either didn't read or didn't care, because she was still piling stuff up on the conveyor belt. Quanisha would have normally told the lady about herself, but she was too caught up in her own thoughts.

Why hadn't the guy she met at the club called her yet? It had been almost a week now, and Quanisha still didn't see an unfamiliar number pop up on her phone. No messages, no missed calls, nothing. She was discouraged, because she had honestly thought that this guy was her opportunity to break free from Tony for good. He must have just been playing with her, just to get another number that night and look good in front of his boys. She wished she could go back to that night and take back her number. He deserved to be the one that got played.

One thing was for sure, Quanisha didn't want to be at work that night. It had been her day off, but she ended up having to not only come in, but do a double shift that night. She was pissed, tired, and feeling down on herself; a bad combination for someone like Quanisha who had a temper like a killer bee.

"Wait, that rang up wrong," the 40ish woman in her line said all of a sudden as she examined the screen.

Quanisha sighed, rolled her eyes, and kept ringing up the items.

"Excuseee me," the woman said obnoxiously as she rolled her head. "Did you hear me? I said that bag of Fritos rang up wrong. It's supposed to be $1.99, it rang at $2.29."

"Far as I know, there ain't no sale on the Fritos. You probably got the wrong size bag," Quanisha said lazily. She really didn't feel like doing a price check.

"No, I know what size I got. Get somebody to do a price check," the woman insisted.

Quanisha was put off by the woman's demanding tone. "I just said, I saw the aisle earlier today and there wasn't no sale on Fritos."

The woman looked at Quanisha menacingly and put her hand on her hip. "Girl if you don't get on that little phone and call somebody to do a price check Imma get ghetto up in here."

"Lady, you half past ghetto crying over 30 cents that's gonna go on some damn food stamps. You betta get out my face with that," Quanisha said loudly, as she continued to ring up the lady's order as if nothing had happened. The people standing in line behind the lady were amused, and they covered their mouths to hide their smiles. One older black man threw his head back and laughed, not even attempting to cover his amusement.

"Oh shit," he said when he finally recovered from his laughter.

The woman gasped. Now she was embarrassed. "Come from behind that register and I'll show you just how ghetto my black ass can really get," she threatened. Quanisha stopped ringing up the items and squared up behind the register.

"Bitch, if I have to come from behind this register you gonna be coughin' up those Fritos. You don't want none of this," Quanisha responded, as serious as a heart attack. Nothing could have made her feel better at that moment more than beating this woman's ass.

The two women argued back and forth for some time before Quanisha's assistant manager came over and broke it up.

"What the hell is going on Quanisha?" she asked. The assistant manager, Sharon, was a young sister, only a few years older than Quanisha. Sharon was going to school at Temple University in North Philadelphia part time to get her degree. Everybody at the job knew that Sharon was a lesbian, and she didn't do much to hide that fact – she was glad they knew. Sharon and Quanisha usually got along, and she was a big reason why Quanisha still had her job. Quanisha respected Sharon's confidence and drive to succeed, and aspired to be like her in a lot of ways.

"This chick just threatened me, talkin' bout she gonna get ghetto on somebody," Quanisha answered without hesitation.

"This girl got too much attitude! Everytime I come in here she throwin' nasty looks at everybody. I asked her to do a damn price check and she won't do it!" the lady screamed.

"You ain't even supposed to be in my line, don't you read? It says 'Express' E X P R E S S, ten items or less. You got like 50 things in your cart!" Quanisha said angrily.

"Yes I read, you little bitch. I can read the 'Thriftway' stamped on your shirt. You working at a damn supermarket and tryin' to get cute with folks," the woman scoffed, trying to get back at Quanisha for her earlier comment. But her comeback was no match for Quanisha's sharp tongue.

"At least I work for a living instead of living on welfare you stupid stamp-swiping bitch!" Quanisha shot back.

"Quanisha!" the assistant manager Sharon called out to stop the back and forth. She called one of the people working the floor up front to handle Quanisha's register and took her to the back room. When they got there, Sharon grabbed her by the arms and laid into her.

"Quanisha you can't talk to the customers like that. I know some of them are annoying as hell, but you still can't talk to them that way!" she exclaimed.

"Sharon I ain't about to let some tired old raggedy bitch talk to me however she want!" Quanisha cried out, trying to regain her composure. Her blood was surging through her veins with a vengeance. She knew she had to calm down; she had had problems in the past with high blood pressure and mild heart palpitations.

"Nish, I don't know what is wrong with you, but you are going to have to adjust your attitude. I can't keep covering for you! One of these days these incidents are going to get to Roger, and you know he ain't having it."

Quanisha opened her mouth to say something, but instead put her hands up to her face and rubbed her temples. "I know, I know. I'm just having a bad day. I wasn't even supposed to be here today Sharon! I'm just... I don't know I'm just tired. I'm sorry girl, I just…"

"I get it Nish, but you can't do this anymore babe. You know what?" Sharon said, looking up at the clock on the wall. "Go ahead and finish out this shift on the floor, I think you got another 40 minutes, then go ahead home. I'll cover your second shift, alright? Go home and get your head straight."

Quanisha sighed and looked at her assistant manager. "Thanks Sharon."

"You're welcome girl, I just want you to be alright," Sharon replied and pulled Quanisha into a warm embrace. She was a good friend and Quanisha really needed one of those at that time in her life.

When Quanisha got back out into the store, the rude lady was long gone. She was relieved that for the rest of the night she could just stay in the aisles and help stock the shelves because she didn't feel like dealing with people. For some reason she thought about Tony for the whole 40 minutes she remained at her job.

On her ride home, Quanisha listened to the Hot Boys on Power 99 talking about the party at Palmer's that was being thrown that next night. She considered giving Trina a call to see if she wanted to go to the party again for Round Two. Just as she was turning at a major intersection, her cellphone started ringing in her pocketbook. She nearly ran over the curb trying to see who it was. A 267 number flashed across her screen and her eyes lit up.

"Hello?" she asked, trying not to sound desperate.

"Yea, who dis?" the voice asked.

"Uh, you callin' me right, so who dis?" Quanisha said, twisting up her face.

"This Randy, who this? Quanisha?"

"Yea, how do I know you?" Quanisha asked, already having an idea of where he knew her from.

"I met you up at… up what's that club name…" Rob said, trying to recall.

"Up at Palmer's?"

"Yea, up there. What's goin' on?" Rob asked, settling into the conversation.

Quanisha had butterflies fluttering in her stomach as she drove down her street towards her apartment building. "Not much, what about you."

"I'm trynna see you. Where you at?" Randy said urgently. Quanisha could hear a lot of people talking in the background.

"I'm just getting home from work," Quanisha said as she got out of her car and slammed the door. "Why?"

"I was gonna come scoop you. But if you busy…" Randy said, leaving his sentence open ended.

Quanisha sensed that he was trying to bait her. As badly as she wanted him to come over, she resisted. She had already given him the advantage that night at the club, she didn't want him thinking she was easy. "Yea, I'm tired. I need to go lay down."

"Lay down?" Randy asked, surprised that she was turning him down. "You'd rather lay down then go sit down at *Fridays*?"

Quanisha smirked at his comment. He was doing exactly what she wanted. "I don't know, I gotta get up early tomorrow for work…"

"Girl come on and stop playin'. I wanna see you tonight. It'll be worth your while."

"Uh, hold on." Quanisha pretended to think as she pulled the phone away from her face and walked up the stairs to her apartment slowly. Her whole attitude had changed since leaving her job, and she was now floating on air. "I guess I can come out for a couple hours."

* * *

Randy and Quanisha sat across from each other at the booth in *Fridays*. Randy had been staring at Quanisha, for more than a few minutes, as if he had never seen a woman before. But it wasn't really flattering; it just made Quanisha uncomfortable. But Quanisha continued to be her usual boisterous self, and was trying at the same time to be as reserved and proper as possible. She didn't want this guy to think she was just another chick that he could get quick sex from. She wanted him to know that she was the relationship type. And she wanted him to replace Tony.

"You don't talk a lot," Quanisha said to Randy as they ate.

"That's cuz I got a lot to think about instead, yah mean?" Randy answered.

"Like what?"

"Like… private shit," Randy said seriously.

"Oh. Well my bad. I thought you might have been thinking about me or somethin'," Quanisha said as she twirled one of her braids around her finger. She was trying to make the conversation fun and light, but it wasn't working out that way.

Randy just looked at her and lifted his head to acknowledge her comment before digging back into his food.

"So where you live at?" Quanisha asked innocently.

"Damn you nosey," Randy said rudely. "I stay down North, but I be out West too."

"Asking you where you live is nosey? I ain't gonna ask you nothin' else then, damn." Quanisha was becoming annoyed at his arrogance. What bothered her even more was that he balanced it off just enough to make it seem as if she was overreacting when she called him out about it.

"Naw, I'm just cautious about who I let into my B-I baby," he said, cocking his head to the side briefly. "You know, like how you cautious about 'some of these niggas out here'."

Quanisha remembered what she told Randy that night at Palmer's. "Well you know, it's the truth. You can't trust every nigga that come your way. Some of them is just out for the coochie, you know?"

"Me? I don't deal with niggas like that so I don't know what the hell you talkin' about," Randy said sarcastically.

"You know what I mean," Quanisha said, getting slightly annoyed again.

"Naw I don't, but whatever," Randy said flippantly and waved his hand at Quanisha dismissively.

"You know, I don't know if you're big-headed or just an asshole," Quanisha said, screwing up her face. She was just about done with this date.

"I'm both, and the quicker you realize that the better we'll get along aiight?" Randy replied, not missing a beat.

Quanisha looked up at him and knew deep down that she should make up an excuse to end the date and keep moving, but something about his overconfidence was very attractive. It didn't help that he was good looking and well groomed, with narrow sleek features that came together to give his face an edgy, mysterious feel. His dark brown skin was smooth and even, and his hair was trimmed to perfection. He was the best looking guy she'd gone out with, probably ever in her life.

"Listen baby doll, I ain't trynna scare you off. I just stay real eight days a week. I don't candy coat shit. Love me or hate me, but most bitches love me. Now if you want, we can go see that flick and continue this little date, or you can be out. It's up to you."

"So what, you classifying me as just some bitch now?" Quanisha asked, totally blocking out everything Randy had said after the word 'bitches.'

Randy sighed. "You know what ma, I don't got no patience for these little kids' games. You wanna go or not?"

Quanisha was grinding her teeth as she mulled over what she wanted to do. She was fuming at this brother, but was still curious about him. He seemed like a complex person who most people probably had a hard time understanding. Quanisha decided that she would take some more time to get to know who he was. She nodded her head and took a sip of her drink.

"Aiight, that's more like it," Randy said. He pulled a wad of money out of his pocket and paid for the meal.

When Randy pulled around Quanisha's block, she was surpised when he passed right by her front door and pulled into a spot down the street. They had just finished seeing a really boring movie that Quanisha almost fell asleep on, and she was so ready to climb under her sheets.

"What you parking for?" Quanisha asked as he backed in.

"I'm coming up. Is that aiight wit you?" Randy said, putting the car into park.

"Uh, I never invited you in."

"I'm inviting myself. Yo, what's your problem? I spent up all that loot out there trynna show you a real good time, and all you do is run your mouth. Do you want me or not?"

"I do like you Randy, but man! You are a little too much. What makes you think you can just talk to me anyway you like? This is a first date, you gotta show some respect," Quanisha spoke up.

"Listen Quanisha, I been with a lot of bitches. Most of them think they can come at me anyway they want but then they get that rude awakening. I ain't lettin' no woman tell me what to do, or try to take my money like these schemin' ass bitches out here. So I establish shit from the gate so there won't be no confusion, feel me? This is how I am and if you don't like it then that's cool, but we can't be cool."

"And I ain't trynna take your money or none of that. I got my own job, my own place and I take care of my own shit. I ain't got no reason to scheme on you."

"You right, I feel you baby doll. Maybe I came off a little strong, my fault. I never met no female that had a job. That's real," Randy said as he turned in his seat to look Quanisha right into her eyes.

"Exactly, I ain't like all these other gold digging bitches out here. I don't even got no kids."

"No kids? You ain't tell me that."

"That's right. You ain't give me a chance to tell you," Quanisha said with a smirk as she folded her arms and rolled her eyes. This was one of those moments when she was truly proud of herself for not having kids like all of her peers.

"True. Well, we gonna go upstairs and you can tell me all about it. Oh yea, and we can puff on this while we at it," Randy said as he pulled an already rolled blunt out of a compartment under his driver's seat.

"What's that? Oh shit," Quanisha said, nodding her head with a smile.

"That's that purest of the pure, you can't get no better haze than this right here," Randy said as he waved the tightly rolled blunt in her face.

"Well damn, what we waiting for?" Quanisha said, opening the car door and getting out.

When Randy rolled off of Quanisha's back they were both sweating heavily. He smacked her behind one more time and then dropped his head back on her pillow. Quanisha collapsed onto the bed as well. She couldn't remember ever coming three times in a row in less than an hour.

"Damn Randy, you just don't even know," she said breathlessly. She couldn't open her eyes or stop grinning for a long time.

Randy didn't respond. He just removed the condom from his now limp member and threw it on the floor. Quanisha had begged him not to use a condom, insisting that she had gotten her tubes tied and could not have kids. Of course, Randy didn't believe her and wasn't about to take the risk of getting some chick he just met pregnant. Besides, Randy was also extremely cautious about the STDs that were going around the hood like an epidemic. He had gotten burned once, luckily with something that was curable, but he had seen one of his best boys get herpes from one of his baby's mothers. Another close friend of his had gotten a real nasty case of crabs from his cheating girlfriend. One of his cousins had even contracted the monster, HIV, several years before, from a one night stand. Not one of them had been using condoms. So Randy wasn't taking any chances – he was strapping up every time.

"Randy, how you gonna throw that condom on my floor like that," Quanisha complained. She had opened her eyes and gazed in his direction just in time to see him do it.

Oh boy, here this bitch already go nagging at me and I ain't even her man, Randy thought. "I'll pick it up later," he lied. *She* was going to pick it up later.

"So what did you want to do tomorrow? I got off of work," Quanisha asked, jumping the gun.

"Girl, go to sleep," Randy said as he rubbed his balls and got ready to take a nap.

"What? I'll go to sleep when I feel like it!" Quanisha said, getting an attitude.

Randy didn't respond again.

"Randy? Randy, nigga did you hear me?" Quanisha asked a few times before she realized that his heavy breathing had turned into snoring.

* * *

Quanisha was awakened by someone slamming a door in the next apartment. She jumped and sat straight up in bed. She came to her senses when she realized that Randy was no where to be found.

"Randy!" she yelled out, even though she knew that he was long gone. "Randy you here?"

When she got up and looked around the apartment her earlier thoughts were confirmed. She looked for any trace that Randy was around, or that he planned to come back. When she finally accepted that he had left without a word, she sat down butt naked on her raggedy old couch and cried. For some reason, she had never felt more alone in her life than at that moment. Randy didn't even leave her a note to say 'thanks' or anything. Quanisha was becoming an emotional wreck, and being used for sex by a guy that she really liked wasn't making things any better.

"What is my problem," Quanisha said, rubbing at her eyes. *I'm probably jumping to conclusions. Maybe he'll give me a call later today,* she thought hopefully as she got up and grabbed her pocketbook to search for her phone.

Then, as if God had read her thoughts, her cellphone started ringing on queue. However, it wasn't a 267 number. It was the phone number to her job calling, probably wanting her to come in to work on her day off again. They were the last people she wanted to talk to right now.

chapter 12

"You ain't my woman, so you don't got no say in what I plan to do," Scoop yelled, five inches from Shellie's face.

"Nigga you don't know who you fuckin' with. I will cut your ass while you sleep!" Shellie threatened.

"Bitch you won't do such a thing, cuz you sprung," Scoop said confidently. "You know if I ever catch you so much as looking at me wrong in my sleep, you cut off."

"That's what you think. I don't need you nigga. The only thing you got going for you is your dick game," Shellie scoffed. "And even that needs work."

"Yea, whatever. If that's so, then how 'bout I ain't coming to see your stupid ass no more," Scoop said, grabbing his baseball cap off of Shellie's kitchen table.

"Fine then, bye," Shellie said and waved him off as she stomped to the bathroom. Scoop wasted no time taking this opportunity to hustle to the front door and leave out.

"Scoop!" Shellie yelled out after him, coming back out of the bathroom. He closed the door before she could say anything else. She couldn't believe he had actually left.

Scoop didn't even have a chance to step up into his truck before his cellphone was ringing. The name 'Shemar' came flashing on the screen, his code for 'Shellie.' He wasn't trying to talk to her, so he put her number on block and started up his car.

He had to think up a good lie to tell his girlfriend Shaquita this time. He had gone over Shellie's house after a long shift at work, and ended up falling asleep by accident. That was against the rules.

Shaquita was going to trip, but if he thought up a good reason to tell her why he stayed out and couldn't call, the blow would be easier.

It didn't help that Scoop hadn't been feeling well for almost a week. He was tired and weak all of the time, falling asleep at work, throwing up and feeling like crap. He didn't know what was wrong with him, but his boss had told him to take the next couple of days off. They couldn't risk having Scoop at work spreading something contagious to the other workers.

He pulled up in front of Shaquita's house and saw one of her girlfriends, Lisa, coming out of the apartment complex.

"What's going on Lis," Scoop said, acknowledging her.

"Ain't nuffin'," she replied. "But I do know that Quita 'bout to be going up in your ass. She in there trippin'. She talkin' 'bout how she bought a Nina to handle yo ass."

Scoop's gulp could be heard down the block. "She bought a gun?"

"Nigga I don't know if she was lying or not, but if I was you, I would turn your ass around and get the hell out of here," Lisa warned before walking on down the path towards her car. Normally, Scoop would have asked Lisa when he would see her again, but he was too shook by what she had just told him. He had been having an ongoing affair with Lisa, and two other girlfriends of Shaquita's on the side. They had all been really good about keeping their mouths shut, and Lisa especially, with her thick caramel thighs, kept him having wet dreams. It was exciting for Scoop to be doing Shaquita's girlfriends without her knowing, and he was going to keep it going for as long as possible.

Scoop thought about going to the store first and grabbing a

dozen pink roses, but knew that wouldn't fly with Shaquita. He pulled out his wallet and counted off $300. *It's not much, but this is the only thing that's going to make her happy*, he thought as he rolled up the money and placed it in his fist.

Scoop made it upstairs and turned the key in the lock slowly and quietly. He didn't know what was awaiting him behind that door, but he had to face the music. He became dizzy and shook his head a few times before walking into the apartment.

"Quita baby? I'm home. I got a surprise for youuu," Scoop called out as he walked towards the bedroom in the back of the apartment.

He only had one foot in the room when Shaquita jumped out from behind the door and hit him with a heavy right jab to the jaw. Scoop went flying and hit his stomach on the corner of the nearby dresser. The money fell out of his hand onto the floor.

"Yea I got a surprise for you too bitch," Shaquita said, rolling up her sleeves and squaring up. She was ready to fight. Something in Scoop flared up. He made a charge for Shaquita, body slamming her on the bed with all of his might.

"Nigga if you don't get the fuck up off of me!" Shaquita hollered in a voice that was probably deeper than Scoop could ever achieve. She punched and slapped at Scoop mercilessly. He grabbed her hands, finally getting hold of her. He reared back and slapped the taste out of her mouth.

"Don't you ever *ever* punch me like that again. I don't care what the hell you going through!" Scoop yelled at her. He didn't know what had come over him, but something about the way she hit him out of nowhere and sent him flying like that made him furious. But once he regained his senses, he regretted what he had done.

Shaquita laid there on the bed holding her cheek with a look of astonishment on her face. She couldn't believe that Scoop had actually put his hands on her, let alone on her face. Nobody touched Shaquita's face and got away with it.

"Nigga! You 'bout to die!" Shaquita let out a chilling yell and bucked wildly, finally freeing herself from Scoop's hold. She stomped out of the bedroom and headed for the living room. Scoop looked around the bedroom helplessly and thought of what he should do. Should he stay there and fight off whatever Shaquita had in store, or high tail it?

When he finally came scurring out of the bedroom, it was too late. Shaquita was posted up on the wall near the kitchen holding a dusty, old looking gun near her crotch, looking like a character straight out of *Boys in the Hood*. The gun was probably something she had bought on the street. Scoop saw her and said to himself that now she had gone too far. He had to stop this craziness.

"Girl what the hell are you doing with that gun?" Scoop said, approaching Shaquita with caution. "You actin' real dumb right now."

"Huh? You gonna call me dumb, and here I am holding the end of your life? You better think about what you gonna say before you say it nigga," Shaquita said ominously and then lifted the gun up to point it directly at Scoop's head.

"Quita, I ain't playin' around wit you right now. You don't pull no weapon on your man, I don't care what you goin' through," Scoop said as he moved even closer.

"And you don't roll up in here the next fucking day like it's all good neither! You lost your damn mind!" Shaquita screamed at the top of her lungs.

"Mommy!"

Shaquita and Scoop both jerked their heads in the direction

of the hallway and saw their young son Yusef standing there with his head low down on his chest and his eyes looking up at his mom with the gun in her hand. She looked like a mad woman with her hair all over her head and her eyes glimmering with hate. Shaquita lowered the gun a little when she saw her son standing there looking forlorn.

"Sef, go play your Playstation little man. Everything's alright," Scoop assured his son.

"Yusef baby, go to your room! Now!" Shaquita screamed madly, and Yusef scurried to the back.

"You see that? Your son was asking for you all day yesterday, and meanwhile your stupid ass is out there in some other bitch's house fucking! You don't care about your family!" Shaquita continued yelling.

She cocked back the hammer on the gun and started to point it at Scoop again, but before she could lift it all the way, Scoop charged at her and grabbed hold of it just in time. He tackled Shaquita down to the floor, took the gun and smacked Shaquita hard across the face with it, several times.

"Bitch you must be crazy! I give you everything!! And all you do is complain! I'm tired of this shit! I'm a muthafucking gangsta, don't you know? You take my kindness for weakness. I do everything for your ass and you gonna point a fucking gun at me? *Fuck* you you stupid whore!" Scoop shouted and then jumped back up off of Shaquita, who looked as if she were about to lose consciousness. But Scoop didn't care, because he was seeing red.

"I work damn near 80 hours a week so you can have Louis Vuitton, Gucci and that brand new car outside! You ain't never happy. You always tryin' to hurt me. You ain't no better than my mom! I'm sick of this shit man. I'm out!" Scoop yelled before he stepped over Shaquita and headed for the door. He still had her gun in his hand.

"Scoop, Scoop baby come back," Shaquita said feebly as she tried to get up from the floor.

"Don't fucking say nothin' to me! I'm through wit your crazy ass!" Scoop yelled. He looked back and saw his son Yusef peeking out from the hallway at him. He had probably seen everything. Shaquita was now crying on the floor looking helpless.

Scoop finally just shook his head at the scene and slammed the door behind him.

chapter 13

"What in the hell is going on with me?" Tony asked himself as he sat on the corner of the hospital bed.

For the past couple of days leading up to his release from the hospital, he had been sick from some kind of food poisoning, and he was still feeling like he wanted to throw up some more. And he had to assume that it was all because he had stolen that hospital food. The time he spent laying up in that hospital room gave him a lot of time to think about what had been happening to him lately. Was God trying to punish him or something?

Jenny was on her way to pick him up from the hospital. The wheelchair was already waiting in the room for him, and he was just waiting for his ride. The day before, after an entire day of uninterrupted sleep the day he got the poisoning, Tony had gathered the strength to dial his grandmother's home number. The phone rang and rang and rang off the hook. Even though he didn't trust Jenny one bit, he had to assume for the time being that what Jenny told him about his grandmother being transferred to another hospital was true. What else could explain the nurse upstairs telling him that she had been released, and no answer at her home phone number?

"Hey baby!" Jenny walked into the room and said happily, just as Tony was reaching for his hospital phone again.

"Stop calling me baby, damn," Tony said, immediately becoming annoyed. There was something about Jenny that just made his skin crawl. But she was the only person that was there to take him home. He didn't even know where his own car was at, but assumed that Scoop had it.

He hadn't heard from Scoop or Quanisha in the longest time, and Terrance wasn't answering his phone. Terrance had told Tony a while ago that he was going away on a business trip to California soon, which was probably where he was now. In fact, Terrance didn't even know yet that Tony had been in the hospital. So Tony would just have to put up with Jenny for a little while longer.

"Did you have a good day?" Jenny said, unphased by what Tony had said.

"I'm gonna have a great day once I get out this damn hospital. I ain't never coming here again. Next time just let me die," he said flippantly.

"Anthony, don't say things like that," Jenny said as she helped load him into his wheelchair.

Tony looked up at Jenny as if she was deaf, dumb and blind. "Are you retarded or something? Be honest, because I don't know how many times I got to tell your ass! My name is TONY, not Anthony!" Tony said through his teeth as he threw his hands up in frustration.

"Uhh, excuse me." They both heard a knock at the door, and saw that it was Doctor Stephens.

"Oh, hey Doc," Tony said as he reached forward to give the doctor a handshake. He and Doctor Stephens had gotten pretty close during his stay at the hospital. They talked all the time about life stuff, man stuff, and women. Tony told him all about how his mother had died, and how his father abandoned them a long time ago. The doctor gave Tony advice on mundane issues, and Tony caught the doctor up on the new things that were happening in the hood. Doctor Stephens was the one bright light to Tony's stay at that boring hospital.

"Heyyy, Tony. So you're getting out today huh?" the doctor asked with a big smile.

"Yea, no offense, but I'm ready to get the hell up outta here Doc," Tony said with certainty.

"I feel you youngblood. And you had better heed what I told you, about that uhhh…" Doctor Stephens looked over at Jenny and hesitated. "Well you know, I don't want to embarrass you in front of the lady. Listen Nurse Storms, do you have a minute before you go? I wanted to talk to you."

"Sure Doctor Stephens," Jenny said, following the doctor's lead out of the room to the hallway. When they were there, Doctor Stephens' smile turned to a more serious look.

"Nurse Storms, I've been made aware of what happened a few weeks ago when Tony was admitted between you and—"

"You mean that crazy woman that attacked me in his room," Jenny said, jumping on the offensive.

"Uh, yes. Well I wanted to hear your side of what happened," Doctor Stephens said, looking intentionally in Jenny's eyes to gauge whether she would be telling the truth.

Jenny looked away towards Tony's room and instead of answering Dr. Stephens she said, almost in a whisper, "Did you say something to Tony about that?"

"No I didn't, why?"

Jenny looked relieved. "Well it was really crazy. His ex-girlfriend came in the room while I was talking to Tony, and didn't like what she saw. She was jealous that he chose me over her. So she attacked me."

"So, not to pry into your business, but you are dating Mr. Jackson now?" Dr. Stephens asked.

"Yes, actually, we are engaged to be married. See?" Jenny said, flashing her shiny brand new three carat diamond engagement ring.

"Oh! Wow, would you look at that. Tony didn't tell me anything about being engaged," the doctor said curiously.

"Yup, we've been talking about it for a few weeks now," Jenny said, smiling from ear to ear.

"Well, congratulations Nurse Storms. I wish you all the happiness and luck," Dr. Stephens said sincerely. But he couldn't help but wonder about this engagement. How did she get engaged while Tony was in the hospital? And he knew that Tony had no job and no place to live, so how in the world was this boy able to afford an engagment ring? How could he be ready to get married?

"Thank you. Well, I'd better get back in there to my fiance!" Jenny said and went back into the room before Dr. Stephens had a chance to ask any more questions.

When Jenny rolled Tony out of the hospital, he sighed at the feeling of being outside for the first time in weeks. The wind felt so good against his skin.

"I'm going to take good care of you Anth—I mean Tony. The doctor said you need at least another week for your rib cage to heal."

"Yea whatever, I'll be fine," Tony answered. He didn't like the idea of going to stay at Jenny's house, but he didn't know where else to go.

"Yo, can you take me to see my grandma? You said they transferred her right?" Tony asked Jenny for the umpteenth time. But he never got an answer he liked.

Jenny thought for a while before answering.

"Did you hear me? Take me to go see my moms," Tony said again.

"I don't know where your grandmother was transferred to," Jenny finally said. "I can find out for you."

"You always sayin' that shit! You told me you were gonna find out two days ago. What the fuck is going on Jenny? Where's my grandmother?"

"I don't know Tony! I got a lot going on myself, I didn't have time to find out just yet. I promise you, I'll find your grandmother for you," Jenny lied. She didn't even really know exactly why she wasn't telling Tony that his grandmother was home already. But if she wanted to be honest with herself, she was doing it because she knew that Tony's grandmother didn't like her. She didn't want anyone throwing negative ideas in Tony's head about her, and messing up their plans to get married. Jenny wished he would stop bringing up his grandmother's name everytime he saw her, but no such luck.

"You better get on that shit ASAP, and stop playin' Jenny. I want to talk to my mom," Tony said seriously. Jenny just wheeled him to the car and thought more about how things were going to be now that she had her man back.

* * *

"Hello, is Quanisha Williams there?" Dr. Stephens asked into the phone.

"Yea, this her," Quanisha said skeptically. "Who dis?"

"Hi Ms. Williams, this is Dr. Stephens, from the hospital, where Tony Jackson is registered?"

"Oh yea, how you doin' Doctor," Quanisha replied. "I was looking for you the last time I was in the hospital, but I haven't been back in a while…"

"I know. I wanted to get back with you and touch bases about our conversation. This might be an old issue at this point for you, but I like to keep my promises. I told you I would speak to Nurse

Storms about your confrontation with her."

"Yea, and what did she say?" Quanisha said, shifting in her seat.

"Ms. Williams, I don't know entirely what is going on, but she says that you attacked her and—"

"*I* attacked *her*?" When Quanisha heard this her blood pressure started to rise.

"But listen first. She also told me that she and Tony were engaged to be married. I don't know how true this is, but I've got to be honest with you Ms. Williams, the whole situation seems a little fishy to me. Tony and I talk all the time and he never told me anything about being engaged. Actually I was surprised because he told me many times that *you* were his girlfriend. I honestly don't know what's going on."

Quanisha became frozen in time when she heard Dr. Stephens say that Tony and the nurse were engaged.

"Ms. Williams?" Dr. Stephens said when Quanisha didn't respond.

"Well do you believe me now then? That she's crazy? There's no way they're engaged!"

"I don't know about crazy but… well all I can tell you is that I will keep my eye on Nurse Storms. My instincts tell me that she's hiding something, or just not being totally truthful about something. She doesn't usually work on my floor but…" The doctor hesitated as he struggled between his human instincts and his need to remain professional. His conscience was winning. "Let's just say I'm going to keep tabs on Nurse Storms. Something's not right. In the meanwhile, Tony was released from the hospital today, and he went home with her. I just hope everything will be okay. Tony reminds me of myself when I was younger, and I'd hate for him to get caught up in some mess."

Quanisha shook her head and felt as if she wanted to start crying again. Tony? Engaged? It couldn't be. Not to that frail shapeless boring nurse! And he was going home with her?

"Doctor, I gotta go."

"Are you going to be okay Ms. Williams?"

"Uh, yea. I don't know. I just need some time by myself."

"Alright. Well, don't hesitate to call me if you ever want to talk. I may be just an old doctor, but I have an ear to listen. I know how it is out here for you young people these days."

"Thanks Doctor. I'll talk to you later," Quanisha said, holding back tears. She hurried up and hung up the phone before the doctor could hear her crying.

Before she could get it out, her home phone started ringing. She wondered if she should even answer it, but something in her was hoping that it was Tony.

"Hello?" she said in a low voice.

"Quanisha! Baby, you don't know how happy I am to hear your voice child," Tony's grandmother said happily as she grasped her chest.

"Miss Teresa?"

"Yes Quanisha. I been tryin' to call you for the longest time. I thought I had the wrong number!"

"I thought you were in the hospital?" Quanisha was confused.

"Girl I've been out that hospital for almost a week now. Where's my son Anthony? Is he there?" Tony's grandmother asked hopefully.

"Miss Teresa, I don't have no idea where Tony is right now. He just got out the hospital today."

"Huh? No I said *I* just got out the hospital baby," Tony's grandmother corrected Quanisha.

Quanisha was quiet for a moment. "Yea, I know. And so did Tony. He just got released from the hospital today, but I don't know where he is though."

"Tony was released from the hospital? What was he in the hospital for??" Tony's grandmother started panicking.

"Miss Teresa, you tellin' me you didn't find out by now that Tony was in the hospital?"

"What hospital is he in child! Speak!" Tony's grandmother said, growing impatient.

"He ain't in the hospital no more. He got released today I think!"

"Oh my God. Oh my God."

"Miss Teresa calm down, he alright. He just got into a little fight," Quanisha said, undervaluing the 'fight' Tony had gotten into. "I went to see him last week."

"Where's he at now??" Tony's grandmother demanded.

"I don't know for sure Miss Teresa, but I was told he went home with some nurse," Quanisha said and choked back her emotions. "I'm not sure what's goin' on."

"Quanisha, what's wrong?" Mrs. Jackson said, sensing that Quanisha was about to cry.

"Nothin' Miss Teresa, I'll be aiight. Listen, let me get you his doctor's phone number." Quanisha retrieved Dr. Stephen's pager number from her purse and read it off. By the time she got off the phone, she was very much affected by Mrs. Jackson's panicked state. She noticed a piece of the blunt that she and Randy had been smoking still sitting in a tray on the coffee table. She immediately picked it up and went to light it on her stove.

She couldn't believe that Mrs. Jackson had no idea what had happened to Tony in the past few weeks, and now she and Quanisha couldn't even get in touch with him. Quanisha took a long drag from the blunt and began to feel sorry for herself. Tony was engaged? There was just no way that could be true. He had told her that he loved her. How could he run off with that stupid nurse? Quanisha felt a sharp pain in her chest when she thought about how the nurse had been right, and she had been wrong all along. Maybe Tony really wasn't her man anymore.

chapter 14

"Jenny! Get off my fuckin' back!" Tony yelled as he shook Jenny off of his shoulders. She had been kneeling beside him on the couch and trying to give him a massage, but was annoying the hell out of him instead with just the sound of her voice.

"Fine! I was just trying to give you a massage. You know, I'm getting sick and tired of how you've been treating me. What the hell did I do?" Jenny was willing to accept that her relationship with Tony would not be easy, but she decided that she was going to make the best out of it. Many women had this type of relationship, and they just dealt with the negative side of it. They took the good with the bad, and that was what Jenny was going to do. She was going to do whatever she could to keep her man around so that she could finally walk down that aisle and get married. In the meanwhile, she could take a few insults from him, but once in a while she felt the need to say something back.

"You bother the shit out of me all day long, that's what you do," Tony complained. "Why don't you go the hell to work or somethin'?"

"Because I took off time from work to be with you Anth— Tony. I love you, and I want to make sure you're okay before I go back in," Jenny explained.

"Bitch, you real crazy. Damn, you got me all fucked up!" Tony said and shook his head as he flipped through the channels. "I told you I don't love your ass. Stop sayin' that shit. And go to work, I don't need you here."

Jenny folded her arms and looked at Tony sideways. "You know, that's no way to talk to your future wife. You shouldn't be calling me a bitch."

Tony slowly turned to look at Jenny. But this time he *really* looked at her. A very serious thought ran through his mind and he started to wonder if this woman that stood before him was really mentally challenged. He had done everything in his power to express to her that he wasn't into her, but yet here she was, thinking she was his future wife!

"What did you say?" Tony asked incredulously. He couldn't even bring himself to say the words. Jenny smiled and looked at him with excitement.

"Stop being silly," she said, putting out her hand and gazing at her engagement ring. "I know you've seen the ring, but baby I've got some of the nicest things to show you! I wanted to save the dress for the traditional wedding reveal… but never mind that, I want to show you now."

Jenny got up from the couch and dashed upstairs. Tony could hear her footsteps walking around the room above him. He was sitting back on the couch with his mouth wide open in amazement.

"Yo, this is a bad dream," he said, chuckling to himself nervously. There was no way this chick was serious.

Jenny came back downstairs and all of Tony's fears came true. There she stood with a long white silk wedding gown draped over her arm, a veil on her head, and a small box clenched in her hand.

"Who's that for?" he asked, still in denial.

Jenny looked at him with a peculiar smile on her face. "Uhh, it's for me, duh."

"And, who you getting married to?" Tony was still playing

along. He thought this was some kind of practical joke. He was half expecting a candid camera crew to jump from behind the couch.

"Uhh, baby, hello I'm getting married to youuu," Jenny answered. Her smile was quickly becoming a frown as she saw the expression on Tony's face.

"No you not, you playin' right?" Tony said, laughing.

"Anthony, what are you talking about? We talked about this at the hospital. You said we were getting married!" Jenny said, looking as if her face was going to crack. Her eye began to twitch.

Tony started laughing hysterically. He couldn't even control it. His ribs were killing him, but this laughter he was having was involuntary; he couldn't stop. Jenny just stood there hovering near him, with a fear that her whole world was falling apart.

"Marry you! Girl I must be on drugs if I was talkin' bout marrying you!" Tony cackled at the top of his lungs. "Matter fact *you* must be on drugs!"

The look of distress on Jenny's face at that moment could break a stone cold heart. She couldn't stop her eye from twitching as she spoke. "What are you saying? That you don't want to marry me?"

"Hell no!" Tony said, bolting up from his seat. He went instantly from laughing to dead serious when he finally realized that Jenny was serious. "You musta lost your mind!"

"Tony, you know we love each other despite our differences—" Jenny started, but was interrupted abruptly.

"Bitch you better get out my fucking face with that shit," Tony threatened as he pushed Jenny and the dress aside. "Damnnn you crazy as shit! What the hell would I marry you for?"

"Nooooo," Jenny suddenly started moaning. It grew slowly

from a low moan to a loud groan.

"You ugly, you skinny and you got a negative ass. Your breath stink like dirty chittlins all the time. Your hair is stringy like a dog," Tony said, counting off reasons on his hand. "You broke as shit, you charge everything you own on a credit card, your pussy's wack, your head game is wack. Your eyes are damn near sunken in your head, your teeth are fucked up, you annoying as hell… and you think I wanna marry you??"

"Nooooo!!!!" Jenny let out two piercing screams when she heard what Tony said. "Noooooo!!!!"

Tony was a little taken aback by her screams, but didn't relent in his verbal assault. "And then on top of that, you crazier than a muthafucka. I don't want your ass! Man, I'm gettin' the fuck up out of here before you start trippin' for real."

As Tony started to pull on the jacket he had gotten out of his old closet at Jenny's house, Jenny came over and latched onto him like a leech. Her white veil flailed in the air as she struggled with Tony.

"No baby, don't go. Don't go. Baby you can't leave me again. I need you here with me. I'll give you anything, I'll buy you anything, just don't leave me alone in here again. Please!" Jenny pleaded. "Baby I got you a present. I bought you a ring, it's two whole carats!"

"Bitch get off me!" Tony said, trying to shake her off. All he knew was that he needed to get out of there, fast!

"Tony you promised me. You said we would be together forever. You promised!" she screamed at the top of her lungs. Tony finally pried her loose from his arm. He reached back and slapped Jenny hard right across her lips. She held her face in astonishment as Tony picked back up his jacket and headed towards the door.

Tony was trying to get the top lock undone when he felt a

blow to his head. The last thing he saw was the door fading to black right before he passed out.

* * *

When Tony slowly came back to consciousness he was laying on the floor close to the couch. Jenny had dragged him there after she hit him over the head with a large crystal candy dish.

He heard a lot of commotion coming from the downstairs basement. Remembering his whereabouts, he pulled himself up off of the floor with all of the strength in his body and made his way over to the basement door. He held his ribs, which were hurting so badly that he actually wanted to go back to the hospital now. He could hear the sounds of Jenny cursing and throwing stuff around down there.

"Fucking *asshole*! If he thinks he's leaving me again he's the one that lost his mind!" she alternated between screaming and mumbling. It sounded as if she were looking for something down there.

"Damn, what the fuck is she doing?" Tony said quietly to himself. Instead of sticking around to find out, Tony closed the basement door slowly and locked the door. "That'll teach that crazy bitch. She ain't never gettin' out, with her dumb lonely ass."

Tony grabbed Jenny's cellphone out of her purse and hurried up out the front door. He ran down the block and turned the corner, even though he had no idea where he was going. The one trusty number he remembered was Quanisha's, and he didn't hesitate to dial her number. He rubbed the back of his neck where a stress bump was forming as the phone rang and rang. He prayed that Quanisha would pick up.

Quanisha groggily reached for her phone. She could barely say hello before she heard Tony's deep voice bellowing through the phone.

"Nish! Baby, I need you to come get me," Tony said, sounding as if he was troubled.

"Tony, nigga where you been?" Quanisha said, struggling to wake herself up.

"I'm down in Darby you need to come scoop me baby. I'm in trouble."

Quanisha rubbed her eyes and sat up in bed. "What kind of trouble?"

"What the fuck do it matter—" Tony caught himself before he got disrespectful with Quanisha. She was the only person that was going to get him out of this mess.

"Tony do you know that your mama and everybody been lookin' for you? Where the hell you been at?"

"Nish, seriously, you gotta come get me right now. I'll tell you everything later," Tony promised. He already knew there was no way he was going to tell Quanisha about staying with Jenny. He would just tell her he got into a fight with Terrance, and that he had gotten left in Darby. Little did he know that she already knew everything.

"Aiight, well give me the address then," Quanisha finally replied as she threw the covers back and jumped out of bed. She didn't even care about the nurse, the so-called engagement or where he had been any more. She could put all that behind her. As much as she was pissed at him, and tired of his antics, she needed Tony. She didn't have anybody else. All she cared about was that he was calling her now. All that mattered was that he was coming home.

chapter 15

"Nigga pass the blunt, quit chokin' up all the smoke," Tony commanded Scoop from the passenger's seat of Scoop's truck.

"Nigga you in my car, puffin' my weed. I'll smoke on this shit long as I want," Scoop answered before taking another long draw of smoke into his lips. He held it for too long and started coughing hysterically.

"Man gimme that, talkin' all that shit," Tony said as he snatched the roach away from Scoop.

It had been over a week since Tony had finally realized what was going on with Jenny. She had been lying to everybody. He had finally talked to his grandmother, and she told him all about the fact that Jenny had lied to her about his whereabouts, and that she had been out of the hospital for several days before him. His grandmother explained that some idiots had been pranking her at the house, and she didn't even bother to answer the phone half the time, which is why she probably didn't pick up the couple of times Tony had tried to call from the hospital.

Tony's grandmother said again and again how she knew there was 'something wrong with that girl.' Tony couldn't believe that he had been messing with a real life psycho. He still couldn't believe she actually thought he wanted to marry her. Jenny even showed up at his grandmother's house the day after Tony left her, asking where Tony was. Tony didn't care; he was trying to set up his situation with Quanisha again and didn't want to hear anything else about Jenny. To his great pleasure, Quanisha wasn't asking anymore questions about Jenny, and he wasn't offering any answers.

"Don't you know Quita talkin' bout she need a new ride now?" Scoop started complaining. "She said the car be actin' up. Now she need a new one. Ain't that a bitch?"

"That's a brand new whip dawg. I don't know why you keep puttin' up with that crazy bitch and her bullshit."

"Yo, don't be talkin' bout my lady like that bruh, you crossin' the line," Scoop warned.

"Didn't you tell me that bitch pulled a gun on you?" Tony turned and asked his friend.

"That don't matter nigga, I told you we put that to rest."

"Whatever. I wish Nish would pull a gun on my ass," Tony laughed.

"You watch, the way ya'll shit go, you just might get what you wish for," Scoop replied.

"Yea, whatever nigga. Bitch ass nigga. That's why you broke as shit now, takin' care of that dumb ass girl. She evil as shit."

"You broker than me nigga, I know you ain't one to talk. And your girl the one up at the hospital rammin' on nurses. Check your own girl before you run your fat mouth about mines," Scoop responded in a voice that told Tony he was stepping over the line, and that he was not to go any further with this conversation.

They sat in silence for a while as they both accepted the fact that they both were seriously hurting for money. Ever since they had gotten robbed, neither one of them seemed to be able to get back on track. Tony was so happy when he found out that Scoop had kept his car parked at Shaquita's house the whole time he was at the hospital. It was one thing to be broke, but a much worse thing to be whip-less *and* broke.

"Yo, Lil Joe was tellin' me bout this dude down Germantown

that be dealin' wit that plastic," Tony said out of the blue as he took the last puff from the roach and put it out in the ashtray.

"What? You mean credit cards?" Scoop said, frowning when he saw that Tony had finished off his blunt. *This nigga don't got no manners whatsoever*, he thought.

"Yea." Tony exhaled and took his time to think before continuing. "He said he get them mostly off the connects he got in the restaurants and bars. You know how people get fucked up and be leavin' they shit by accident and don't realize it. Shit like that. Well, he said he can get at least three of them jawns a night."

"Word? Well, how that work? Don't they be reporting them in stolen or somethin'?" Scoop inquired as he put his hand on his chin and rubbed it in deep thought.

"Nawww, not until the next day usually. That's why you gotta get on them things early that night. Go to Best Buy or one of them other high priced stores and buy as much shit as you can fit in your cart," Tony explained as he gestured with his hands.

"Man. So how we get on that?" Scoop said without much hesitation. His dealings with Rock had been going sour lately, and they weren't making much cash. Rock was getting more and more vocal about not getting the right cut, and it was becoming a strain on the business relationship. On top of that, their main supplier had gotten locked up in a raid a few weeks before. His job paid pretty well, but not enough to pay the large bills that Shaquita racked up, on top of his own.

"We gotta give him like, $20 a card? I think… I gotta ask Lil Joe again. But you serious about that dawg?" Tony turned and nodded once at Scoop.

"Hell fucking yea I'm down wit that. What's the worse that could happen?"

"Yea, I know. But yo, on another note. I heard that nigga

Rock been talkin' mad greasy down on the block on your ass. You better handle your business nigga," Tony said, trying to incite his friend.

"Mannn, fuck that nigga. I ain't worried 'bout his retarded ass. He petty as shit talkin' bout that little change," Scoop said as he started up his car.

"That's what you get for fuckin' with a nigga that smoke up the supply. You knew his ass was half crackhead."

"Yea, well you live and learn. Yo let's get outta here." The truth was, Scoop was terrified about what kind of things Rock was spreading around the hood. They actually snorted coke together on a couple of occasions, and there were things Rock knew about Scoop that he never wanted getting out.

* * *

"How much you said?... 40? Man, what the fuck, you told me 20 the other day!" Tony yelled into Jenny's phone. Gullible Jenny had left the phone on for him just so that she could blow it up all day long, trying to get in touch with him. She just wouldn't give up.

"Well never mind then, you trynna rob me nigga... Naw, cause you know you just trynna get your cut off the top...I ain't trynna hear all that man we already discussed this...Aiight well call me back then," Tony said, clicking off the phone finally. He had to keep close tabs on the phone since his voicemail box was full. He left it full just so that Jenny couldn't leave anymore messages.

"Man, that nigga trippin'," Tony said to Scoop as they walked down South Street on a lazy Saturday afternoon. They were reaching out to the connection for the credit card scheme they were trying to get into. "He talkin' bout $40 per card. Man, get the fuck outta here. That ain't worth it."

"Well, you can't get 'im down?" Scoop asked as his eyes became glued to the body of a girl passing by.

"That's jail bait nigga," Tony warned Scoop when he followed his trail of vision. "I don't know, he said he was gonna call me back. You know all I got is $10 right now. My mom's check don't come for two weeks."

"Yea, and I don't have much cash on me either. And I'm tryin' to eat in a little while."

"Man. I wanted to get this shit started *tonight*. This a big bar night. There's probably mad drunk white folks leaving their cards at the bar by accident," Tony complained.

"Oh, I don't know if I can do that tonight. I got an appointment. I gotta let you know."

"Aww man! What kind of appointment?" Tony said, turning to look at Scoop with disgust.

"A 'nonna ya damn business' appointment. I gotta be there at two o'clock sharp or they ain't taking me. They close at three."

"Then what the hell you doin' out here with me nigga? It's almost 1:30 now!" Tony said as he threw his cigarette down on the concrete.

"What? I thought it was closer to twelve… I came down with you cause my appointment's in South Philly," Scoop said as he checked his watch. "Aww man, how I do that? Let me get outta here then man. You gonna be aiight?"

"Yea I'll just take the sub home."

"Appreciate it man, stay up."

"Yo call me later if you still wanna do this thing," Tony said as he gave Scoop a soul handshake. Right after he and Scoop parted ways, Tony got the call from Lil Joe that he was waiting on.

"Ya'll gonna do $20? Aiight, bet."

* * *

As Scoop sat in the chilly doctor's waiting room, wondering when he was going to be called and why they were blasting the air conditioner, he flipped through one of the women's magazines on the table looking for some good looking women. Unfortunately, in the one he was looking at none of the fine women were half naked like in his favorite magazine *King*.

"Uhh, Mr… Boston? Eric Boston?" The receptionist called out the next name on her flip chart.

"That's me," he said as he threw the magazine back on the table and headed straight for the back room. He figured it was about time for a doctor's check up since he hadn't been feeling well lately. He thought it might have been due to inhalation of the tar that they used on his job to fill up the potholes. It was well known at his job that extended exposure to the fumes could cause medical problems.

Thirty long minutes later, the doctor finally came into the room.

"Hello Eric, how are you doing?"

"Fine, now that I don't have to wait no more," he said with slight attitude. He couldn't stand to have to wait. *Why did they even call my name if the doctor wasn't ready yet?* he thought.

"So what are we in here for," the young Italian doctor said cheerily. He was happy that his weekend was almost over, and he could go home to relax with his wife and kids. He remembered Scoop coming in to see him some months ago about an STD problem. He had been shocked when he learned that Scoop was sleeping with at least eight different women every week, and rarely using a condom.

"I don't know Doc, I don't feel too well lately. I think it might be the fumes from my job getting to me."

"Okay, what exactly is giving you problems?"

"Everything," Scoop admitted quickly and then chuckled.

"Okay," the doctor chuckled along with him. "Well let's take a look."

When Scoop emerged from the doctor's office he cursed the doctor for wasting his time.

"What the hell I come all the way down here and pay that co-pay for just so that nigga can tell me to get some rest and take some vitamins," he spoke under his breath. He ripped the bandage off of the inside of his arm where they had stuck him with the needle. Looking at his watch again, he decided to call Tony to find out where he was. They might still be able to do that credit card thing with Lil Joe that night.

"Yo where you at?" Tony asked. He was almost yelling.

"Yo calm down nigga, I'm still down South Philly. Where you?"

"I'm still on South Street. Come scoop me," Tony commanded before hanging up the phone. Scoop hated it when Tony got like this – acting like he was the general and Scoop was his soldier, whenever they had something big planned, even just a party. But he wasn't trying to worry about small issues right now, he was about getting some money.

Tony and Scoop got the credit card from Lil Joe with ease. They even got a few free drinks at the bar that Lil Joe's brother owned in Germantown. Everything was going as planned. It wasn't even nine o'clock and they had a fully loaded credit card, all ready to get swiped at the Wal Mart on Columbus Blvd. When they pulled into the parking lot, they sat in the car to plan what they were getting.

"They got that new Playstation out, and I wanted to get one of them big screened TVs. Naw, two of them jawns. I want one to keep at Quanisha's crib. That's gonna get me some ass for a whole week!" Tony said as he reached over to give Scoop a pound.

"Aiight, so you do the TVs and shit, and I'll go down that expensive computer aisle, grab some of them modems and laptops. Do they got computers down at Wal Mart?"

"All I know is I'm grabbin' everything I see," Tony said as he opened his door to get out of Scoop's truck.

During the next hour Tony and Scoop filled up two carts with high priced merchandise and had two big screen televisions worth over $3,000 being carted out to the front customer service area. Scoop warned Tony that they shouldn't go too overboard with their spending, because someone might get suspicious. But there was no shame in their game as they rolled both of the carts right up to the electronics register in the back of the store.

"Wow, we've got a lot of stuff here..." the red haired female cashier said as she started ringing up the items one by one. "This is only $99.98? I might have to pick up one of these myself," she said outloud to herself. The entire order took close to twenty minutes to ring up. Some of the people waiting behind them decided to go up front to ring their things up.

"Okay, your total is $4,845.19," the young lady said, trying not to sound surprised at the figure. But she was, and her prejudices overwhelmed her despite her self-proclaimed liberalism. *How could these two young black men afford all this stuff?* she thought. Tony smoothly swiped the credit card and wiped his nose. He had studied and practiced the signature on the back of the card several times to be accurate and was sure he had it down pat, but luckily, the cashier didn't even bother to look at the card. Scoop was standing at the far end of the register, shifting his weight from side to side and trying not to look nervous.

Tony signed the signature pad and everything looked like it was going through okay. But it was taking a lot longer than usual for the authorization to go through.

"This never takes this long," he said, trying to fill the silence. The cashier nodded and agreed. Scoop's heart started beating so hard that he was afraid someone might hear it.

Finally the signature pad read 'Approved' and the receipt started printing. It took some time, but finally the cashier ripped the receipt off and gave it to Tony.

"You have a good night," she said and watched as Tony and Scoop rolled their carts away.

When they finally got to the housewares section of the store which was well out of sight of the back register, Tony stopped and gave Scoop a pound. They both could breathe easy now. They were afraid that the card was going to be declined, or even worse, reported stolen.

"Whew. I didn't think it was gonna go through," Scoop said as he wiped some sweat off his brow.

"I don't know about you, but I was gonna haul ass if it didn't," Tony said chuckling.

"Damn. You was gonna leave me wasn't you. We didn't plan that," Scoop said, shaking his head as he began wheeling his cart again.

"I'd think you'd already know that nigga," Tony said as he followed Scoop. "Man, I can't wait to get home and show Quanisha that TV. She gonna love my ass."

On their way out they turned down the aisle where all the

household cleaners were, and Tony stopped again. "Oh hold up, here go them Swiffers. Quanisha always talkin' bout them jawns. I wonder if I can put another couple of these on that card."

"T, come the fuck on. You in here looking at Swiffers, and we gotta get the fuck outta here," Scoop commanded. "And we ain't putting nothin' else on that card."

"Nigga, who the fuck you think you talkin' to? You don't tell me what to do. I'll get a Swiffer if I damn well please!" Tony said as he picked up four Swiffer's and threw them in the cart on top of all the other stuff.

"Nigga you are retarded. I ain't stickin' around here while you fuck us up," Scoop said as Tony started rolling his cart again. Tony threw a few more items on top as he rolled past. Scoop couldn't believe his friend was playing with fire; he was about to go up a second time with the stolen credit card. Scoop considered leaving Tony and getting into his truck with his cart, but knew that at Wal Mart they wanted to see a receipt when you left. Tony had the receipt in his pocket.

When they got up front, Tony put all of his new items on the conveyor belt. Scoop stood on the other side of the register closest to the door waiting for his friend to finish and hoped that everything would be alright. When Tony swiped the card, again it took a very long time to go through.

Scoop heard two beeps from the register signifying that something had gone wrong.

"Ummm, could I see the card? And your driver's license?" the cashier said as he picked up his register phone to call a manager over. Tony handed him the card.

"What for? Is there somethin' wrong? I don't got my license on me," Tony said, getting nervous.

"Man, I don't know. All I know is the computer is telling me it was declined and to call a manager... Roger to register four, Roger to register four," the young cashier said over the loud speaker as he sat up on the edge of the register looking at the card. He was nervous himself, because he was really supposed to ask for a driver's license before processing a credit card.

"Here let me try it again," Tony said as he grabbed for the card. Before he had a chance to swipe the card again, he saw the manager approaching. He was sweating by then. His instincts were telling him to run, but he just couldn't bring himself to leave all of that stuff. Maybe it was something that could be resolved.

"Tony, let's just go. Maybe you're over your limit," Scoop said looking at Tony as if he were crazy for wanting to stay there and still try to get the other items. "Let's go, we'll figure it out later."

Tony looked at his friend Scoop and realized that he was being greedy.

"What's the problem," the manager said as he took a look over the transaction.

"Ain't no problem, I think I just went over my limit today. I'll come get this stuff another time," Tony said as he wheeled his cart away from the register. Scoop followed quickly.

When they got to the door, they saw the two large screen televisions waiting on a special cart near the customer service area. The lady asked for their receipt as Scoop went over to retrieve the televisions. She looked it up and down, alternating between the receipt and their cart for a few minutes, and was about to stamp it, but then she heard a commotion.

"Stop those two!" a voice said from near the register area. It was the manager, Roger. He was signalling to the security guard to follow him. "Don't let them leave with that merchandise!"

Scoop and Tony pushed the carts out of the way and ran full speed out of the doors. Scoop nearly tripped over a little five year old girl who was in his way. Tony pushed people out of the way roughly as he made his way out to the parking lot.

When they got to the truck they could see the security guards standing outside the store looking for where they had gone. Tony and Scoop dove into the truck and screeched out of the lot in no time.

"SHIT SHIT SHIT SHIT!!!" Tony screamed as he punched his fist into Scoop's dashboard.

"Yo, don't be punching my car you stupid motherfucker!" Scoop yelled at Tony. "If your dumb ass didn't go back to buy those motherfucking Swiffers we would have gotten out of there with all that shit!"

"Fuck you nigga!" Tony said as he rolled down his window and spit.

"I can't believe your simple ass. We were home free!"

Tony just left the window open and let the night air blow into his face. He was trying to cool off the deadly anger that was consuming him.

"Damn, I blew it!" he finally admitted to himself. "Five g's…"

"Man, why did you have to get cocky? We woulda sold that shit in a day. Now they gonna be watchin' for us… Fuck it, I ain't doin' that shit again. I ain't goin' to jail for your ass," Scoop said more to himself than to Tony. "And who's to say they ain't got cameras in the parking lot that saw my truck?"

Tony put his head back on the head rest and rolled the window back up. He had nothing to say. He had cameras, DVD players, Playstations and XBOXs, computer equipment, and all kinds of pricey electronic components in his cart, and he gave it all away for a Swiffer. Scoop was right – he had gotten greedy, and cocky. He had never felt so stupid in his life. All that trouble, and he and Scoop were still negative $20. They were worse off than they started. Tony knew that Scoop was telling the truth – Scoop would never try the credit card thing again after this. Scoop or not, Tony was going to have to find a way to get some money, and fast.

chapter 16

Quanisha and her cousin Pamela walked down the stairs of the Gallery Mall, heading for the food court. They had been shopping all day long on Quanisha's day off. Pamela didn't work a steady job, she was doing welfare to work and this was the time in her cycle when she was receiving welfare instead of working.

Pamela had three kids going on four and now lived in the new projects they had built in North Philly. She had been born in Philly originally, but moved to Camden, New Jersey when she had gotten married. The marriage lasted for two and half years. Pamela and her husband James had both been cheating on each other, even before they were married. No one understood why Pamela and James wanted to tie the knot in the first place since neither one of them knew the meaning of monogamy. But no one tried to stop them, not even her mother. After two years in the marriage, James came home early and found Pamela asleep in bed with another man. From that point on James had become very violent with Pamela, despite his own infidelities. Pamela couldn't take the beatings anymore, and moved out with all of her kids in tow, right back to Philly.

"What you eatin'?" Quanisha asked her cousin as they approached the food court.

"I don't know, whatever you eatin'. You know I'm broke," Pamela said as she plopped down at one of the tables.

"What you mean you broke? You just dropped $100 for that 'fit," Quanisha said as she pointed at Pamela's bag.

"That was my last. Come on girl you gotta spot me. Just get me a pizza or somethin'."

"Bitch, you knew we was gonna eat before we left. You shoulda saved some money," Quanisha said as she walked off over to the chinese food area.

Pamela smiled as if she had gotten over. "Good, I wanted some Chinese food. I hope she gets me a Kung Pao Chicken."

When Quanisha came back, Pamela was disappointed to see that she was only carrying one plate on her tray.

"Where's mine?" Pamela said.

"I don't know, where is it?" Quanisha said as she sat down and started wolfing down her food. She hadn't eaten since 10am that morning. All Pamela could do was sit there with her famous boo boo face on. Quanisha wouldn't even let her touch a piece of chicken off her plate. The smell of the General Tso's Chicken with broccoli platter wafted over to Pamela's nose, making her stomach growl. But Quanisha didn't care. She was tired of Pamela always trying to mooch off of people.

When they left the mall, Quanisha's thoughts instantly drifted to what Tony was doing. It was Thursday and she hadn't seen him since Wednesday morning. He had told her that he was staying at his grandmother's house for a few days, to make sure she was okay. Quanisha was already feeling as if Tony was settling right back into his old ways. He had called her that past Saturday to tell her that he had a big surprise for her, but then she didn't hear from him for two straight days. Her instincts told her that he was still messing around with other girls behind her back. She knew he was definitely still lying to her after Tony told her that he had *supposedly* gotten into a fight with Terrance and Terrance *supposedly* had left him in Darby. That didn't even sound like Terrance to her. She knew that Tony was probably in Darby because he had been staying with the nurse girl and she kicked him out. But she wasn't bringing that up so that she could keep the peace.

Quanisha was actively ignoring Pamela's silent treatment as they rode in the El train to Quanisha's car which was parked in West Philly. She knew Pamela had an attitude about dinner, but didn't care. Quanisha's phone started ringing right before they arrived at their stop. It was Trina.

"Hey girl, what you gettin' into tonight?" Trina asked.

"Nothing girl, it's Wednesday," Quanisha said as she walked down the stairs at 63rd Street Station towards her car. Pamela dragged along behind her, thinking that her attitude was actually affecting Quanisha.

"Wednesday nights are hot at Chrome Nish, you know that."

"Oh yea. What, you wanted to do that?" Quanisha said as she turned down the street and saw her car sitting there. She almost forgot that Pamela was with her.

"Yea, I'll meet you down there, at like 11 aiight?" Trina said.

"Aiight, see you down there," Quanisha confirmed and then hung up the phone.

Quanisha got into her car, followed by her cousin, who still had an attitude. But now Pamela wanted to know where Quanisha was going.

"What you just gonna go somewhere and not invite my ass?" she finally said as Quanisha pulled up in front of her building.

"You just said you was broke. I ain't giving you no money to be at the club," Quanisha said, rolling her eyes.

"Why you gotta be like that? You know I'm struggling right now. You supposed to help your family out," Pamela said as she got out of the car. "What was you just gonna drop me home while you go have fun? That's fucked up."

"Girl you know you need to stop. Your ass ain't struggling

after you bought all that shit at the mall—"

"Don't be worryin' about what I buy with my own money," Pamela protested.

"—and you know you need to go home and take care of all them kids. You wrong for wanting to party when they got to get up for school tomorrow," Quanisha finished.

"Oh, see, now you trippin'. Don't you tell me about my kids and what they gotta do. That ain't none of your business. They with they aunt."

"They need to be with their mother, and I'm sure they asses are hungry, but you just gotta have a damn outfit so you can profile in front of those other welfare bitches that don't got shit." The words flew out of Quanisha's mouth so fast that she couldn't catch herself. Right after she said it, she knew she was wrong.

"You dry barren bitch. Who are you tellin' somebody about they kids? Once you pop one out of that dried up pussy of yours you can talk to me about my kids," Pamela hissed back as she walked into the lobby of Quanisha's building.

Quanisha whipped around with her fist clenched and caught Pamela dead in the nose. Pamela stumbled back and couldn't stop herself from falling on her behind.

"Now take your broke ass home then, since you wanna talk all that shit," Quanisha growled at her cousin and tried to hold back her tears. "I don't care if your triflin' ass walks to North Philly!"

Quanisha left Pamela sitting there in shock as she hustled up the stairs to her apartment and slammed the door.

It was an hour later when Quanisha sat on her bed, still listening to her cellphone ring. This was the fifth time it had rung in the hour. She had been bawling her eyes out after Pamela's insensitive comment. How could she be so cruel? Bringing up something that Quanisha had told her in strict confidence was the lowest blow to Quanisha's spirit. Not even Quanisha's mother knew that she couldn't have children.

Now that she had hit Pamela, Quanisha was sure that Pamela was going to go tell her mother all about the abortions. She didn't need this additional stress in her life. Her boyfriend was cheating on her, she had gotten smutted out on the first date by some stranger, her boss had put her on a final warning at her job for her attitude, and now Quanisha was going to have to deal with her evil mother hanging the fact that she couldn't have children over her head. It was way too much to bear.

Quanisha finally snatched her cellphone off of the nightstand.

"What!" she screamed.

"Uh, hello! Who the hell you screaming at?" Trina asked.

Quanisha wiped a tear from her face and took a deep breath. "Nothin', my fault girl."

"You aiight?"

"Yea, I'm fine!" Quanisha said, about to get an attitude again. "What's wrong, didn't you say 11?"

"Yea but—"

"You know what? Listen Trina, I don't think I'm gonna be coming out tonight. I got work in the morning."

"Oh girl, don't start with that shit. You don't work 'til the middle of the day."

"I know, I just wanna get my rest," Quanisha insisted.

"Bitch please, you coming out with me tonight. I called you cuz they got $1 night from 8-11 tonight at Tre's Bar out West. We can get popped for like 10 dollars!" Trina laughed.

Quanisha thought about how fun drowning her problems in cheap alcohol would be. But she really didn't feel like being around Trina, who would be getting all the attention all night. She was sure to be dressed in some kind of ho gear and turning every head in the bar. Then again, Tre's was only down the street and around the corner from her house, so she could leave whenever she wanted.

"Yea, yea. Aiight Trina, I'll meet you down there at 9 o'clock," Quanisha affirmed and then hung up the phone. She was surprised when she learned that it had been Trina calling her all those times; Pamela hadn't even called her once.

* * *

"Girl look at all these niggas up in here," Trina leaned over and whispered to Quanisha momentarily.

Quanisha didn't have an answer. She just walked over to the bar and started ordering shots of Tequila with training wheels. She could already see several men eyeing them, and was getting prepared for all of them to pass her up for Trina.

"Yo ma, I got that," a rough looking bearded brown skinned brother sitting right next to her at the bar said.

"Oh. Thanks." Quanisha was unimpressed. It was only $2. *If he thinks he's getting some ass for some dollar drinks he is severely mistaken*, she thought.

"Where you live at?" he asked.

"South Philly," she answered quickly, lying.

"South? What you doin' all the way up here?"

"I'm just minding my own business, tryin' to get some drinks in," she said snidely as she took her first shot.

"Whoa, take it easy baby," the guy said and chuckled to

himself.

"Whatever," Quanisha said as she grabbed her other shot and moved herself to another part of the bar.

To Quanisha's surprise, she was getting a lot of attention that night. All she had on was a white t-shirt tied to the back and a pair of tight jeans. She didn't even make the effort to go all out that night with her outfit. Trina, in her low cut tight fitting v-necked shirt and cut off cargo shorts was getting guys as usual, but even she was looking over at what Quanisha was doing more often than Quanisha was checking up on her.

After the bar, they left and decided to hit up Chrome as they originally planned. Quanisha was drunk to the point of tripping over her own feet as they made their way to Trina's truck. She had gotten four solid numbers from guys at the bar – one who was really cute – and was feeling like she was on top of the world.

"Did you see that light skinneded nigga with the braids? Tommy? He lookeded good as shit," Quanisha slurred as she took her pumps off to air out her feet.

"Yea, he was aiight," Trina answered with a jealous edge in her voice.

"Aiight? He looked betta than any of those other tired ass niggas in there," Quanisha said assuredly.

Trina felt a twinge of anger rise up in her as her envy overtook her for a second. She knew that Quanisha was right – for the first time, Quanisha had hooked the best looking brother in the bar.

"Man, fuck Pam, fuck Ma, fuck Tony," Quanisha rambled and ranted. "I'm my own woman. I'm gonna do my thing and fuck what anybody else got to say about it!"

When they got to Chrome they were caught up in the whirlwind of females that had entered the club thinking they were getting in for free. But it was well after 11pm and the admission had gone up to $10 for ladies. That was no problem for Quanisha and Trina who had only spent about $10 each at the bar and still had cash to burn.

Towards the end of the night, Quanisha was off to the side dancing by herself near the bar when someone grabbed her from behind and started dancing with her. She stopped instantly and whipped around to see who had the nerve to put his hands on her. Quanisha was in rare form – she became ridiculously cocky when she was drunk to the point where she didn't even want anybody, even guys, touching her.

To her surprise the face she met was familiar.

"What the fuck do you want?" she said as she laid snake eyes on Randy. Randy - the same guy who had done a 'tap and run' on her.

"Whoa, calm down baby girl. I'm just saying what's up!" he said as he held his palms up in surrender. He looked her up and down like he was a tiger and she was a tall piece of raw steak. He was obviously very drunk too.

Quanisha was turned off by his presence. "Man go ahead with all that corny shit," she said as she turned back around and started dancing with herself again.

"Come on ma, stop bein' like dat. What's your name?" he asked with his eyes dimmed from the effects of the Hennessey he had been drinking all night.

"What?" Quanisha said, turning her neck sharply to look him in the face again. "You don't even remember my name? Pffssh."

Quanisha gave Randy a flip of her hand as she made the sound meant to dismiss him, and walked right away from him. She left him standing there looking like a fool.

The whole night Randy watched Quanisha go throughout the

club and dance with all kinds of different men. But she didn't seem to care about any one of them – it seemed like she didn't have a care in the world. He liked that. He was still trying to figure out what her name was and where he knew her from though...

When he looked at his watch and saw that it was 2:45am, only a few minutes before the club would close, he made his way over to Quanisha boldly and snatched her away from the guy she was dancing with. He finally came to his senses and remembered that this was the girl he had kicked it with a couple of weeks before after *Fridays*.

"*What* are you *doing*," Quanisha pronounced her words clearly and loudly over the club music.

"I'm taking you home *Quanisha*. You popped ma. Don't worry, I'll take care of you."

Quanisha had no idea where she was as she leaned over the bed and let Randy pound her from behind. She was so drunk that she didn't even remember when he had pulled down her jeans and panties. She moaned and sighed, enjoying the feeling as the first orgasm started to build up inside of her.

When they were finished, Randy laid down on the bed next to Quanisha and smiled at her. How could he have forgotten Quanisha – she was the best sex he'd had in months. He then closed his eyes as if he wanted to go to sleep, but Quanisha stood up.

"Okay, I'm outta here," she said suddenly. Randy's eyes shot back open.

"What? Where you goin'?" he asked as he still lay there, not wanting to move.

"I'm goin' home. I got shit to do in the morning," she said

cheerily as she pulled back on her jeans and grabbed her cellphone.

"What you got to go for? You can stay the night," Randy said sincerely, as if he were doing her a favor.

"No thanks. I'll holla," Quanisha slurred as she stumbled to the door. Right before she left she turned back around and simply said, "Thanks for the bang out. I needed that."

She got all the way out to the street when Randy came bounding out the door after her. "Come on ma, you need to stay here for a while. You don't even know where you at and you fucked up."

"Gee, I wasn't too fucked up for you to fuck me though," Quanisha laughed and snorted through her nose as she called '215-333-3333,' the easiest taxicab phone number to remember in the city.

"Yea, whatever. I ain't beggin' you," Randy said before he slammed his front door shut.

When Quanisha finally got home, she gave the cab driver her last $15 and went upstairs so that she could crash out in her room. Only she didn't even make it to her bedroom – she ended up falling out on the living room couch.

* * *

Tony came in the door at 12 noon that day and saw Quanisha laid up, the top half of her body on the couch, the other half hanging out onto the floor. She was dressed in the clothes she had on the night before and her face was fully made up.

"Nish," Tony said as he stood over her, confused.

Quanisha was lost in deep sleep. If it was hard to get Quanisha up normally, it was impossible when she was hungover.

"Quanisha!" Tony said much louder this time as he shook her incessantly.

"What what what," Quanisha said sleepily with her eyes still closed.

"Why you sleepin' with your clothes on? Don't you have work today?" Tony asked her as he leaned down several inches from her face.

"Mmmmph," is all Quanisha said. It was completely quiet for a few more seconds, and then Tony heard her snoring again.

"Nish!!" Tony yelled as he grabbed her and sat her straight up on the couch. Her head slumped over to the side. "What's wrong wit you, you drunk?"

"No," Quanisha mumbled.

"You late for work ma, when you goin' in?" Tony asked her.

"I don't have no work leave me alone," Quanisha lied. She still thought she was inside of a dream. Tony wasn't really there.

"Why you drunk? You went out last night?" Tony asked again, but Quanisha wasn't responding. He didn't like the idea of his woman up in the club drunk. He scanned her body and his brows lowered at the sight of the tight jeans she had on, hugging every curve of her body. He wanted to snatch her up so badly, but he didn't want any Quanisha drama right now. He was exhausted and needed to lay down, so he decided to just get at her later on that day.

When Tony woke up he heard Quanisha on the phone.

"...I'm sorry, I told you I wasn't feeling too good. I'll just come in for second shift," she pleaded. "Amanda don't do this to me alright. You know I can't afford to lose this job!... I know, but this is the first time I ever missed my shift...I'm sorry, was I supposed to go in and throw up on the customers?...Yea I know I should've called...No I...(long pause)...Man this is some bullshit Amanda and you know it! I been there for almost five years and ya'll gonna fire me over one missed day? That's fucked up but whatever!...I don't got no attitude with the customers... and no I don't got no attitude with you either...Come on now, don't even go there with me, you and everybody in there know I'm a good worker, I do double shifts all the...Fuck that, I ain't even tryin' to hear that shit...Fine then ya'll keep your lil btich ass job. I got skills! I can get a better job than that anyway. Bye Bitch!"

Tony shook his head as he looked at the alarm clock that read 4:43pm. The time seemed to have flown by so fast.

Quanisha had slammed down the phone and was randomly screaming obscenities every few minutes or so in the other room. Tony did not want to get caught up in this whirlwind, and was plotting how he could leave without having to confront Quanisha. When he heard her coming to the bedroom he put his head to the side and played dead. Hopefully she would just go in the shower or leave. But no such luck.

"Tony!!!" she screamed at the top of her lungs in a way that made his body shiver.

Tony kept pretending to be asleep, so Quanisha came over and jerked up one of the sheets so hard that he went rolling off the side of the bed.

"Why the fuck didn't you wake me up when you came in!" she hollered. "I lost my fucking job!"

Tony just stood up and started putting his clothes back on.

"Do you hear me talkin' to your lazy, leeching ass? What the fuck is wrong with you! Now I don't have no job! What am I supposed to do??"

"I tried to get you up," Tony said in a low voice as he grabbed his hat and headed out of the room. He was getting the hell out of there.

"Where do you think you're going?" Quanisha asked incredulously as she followed him out of the room.

"I'll holla at you later Nish," Tony said as he opened her front door. Quanisha made a charge at him and punched him in the back with all of her power. Tony winced and threw his head back in pain.

"What, you think this is a hotel? You just gonna come here whenever you want and get some sleep and then leave?!" Quanisha said every note in a shrill high pitched scream. It was definitely heard throughout her hall. "I can't stand your bitch ass! What do you do for me!"

Tony wanted to turn around and punch Quanisha out so badly, but he restrained himself. Quanisha had a lot of uncles who were merciless killers – all she had to do was tell them that Tony had put his hands on her and they would be out for his blood. Instead, he just rushed out of the door as Quanisha followed him with blows to his head, neck and back. When she finally got tired she stopped in the middle of the hall and screamed behind him.

"Don't come back here you dumb motherfucker. You ain't no real man!" Quanisha yelled. "You ain't nothin' but a little pussy! Go ahead and run to your grandma so she can change your pamper you little bitch!"

chapter 17

Tony came around the bend of Spring Street sharply and pulled into Terrance's driveway. He hadn't seen his buddy for a long time, and needed a respite from the stresses he was experiencing with Quanisha, money, and Jenny calling his phone twenty times a day. He still couldn't believe that she hadn't just cut the phone off already.

Tony hadn't seen or talked to Terrance since he went to the hospital and was looking forward to talking to his friend, but Terrance wasn't home yet. It was close to 6 o'clock, and he should have been back by then since he did a 7-5pm shift.

"He'll probably be home soon," Tony thought as he settled back into his car to wait. This was a perfect time to give his jump-off, Tonya, a call. He had run into her on the block one day as she was heading to the grocery store and reconnected. She was looking good in a pair of white shorts and tennis shoes. The phone rang and rang until Tonya's voicemail picked up.

"Yo call me. 267-255-2152," Tony said and then hung up the phone. He turned up the radio and listened to an old Mary J. Blige song play.

Twenty minutes later Tony saw Terrance pulling up behind him in the driveway. Terrance parked and got out of the car.

"Yo man, why you park in my spot?" Terrance asked with an attitude. He had had a bad day. One of Terrance's so-called friends at work had stolen yet another one of his great ideas and passed it off as his own. The last co-worker that had done that had been promoted to a position that he wasn't even qualified for and Terrance was passed over. He was tired of his bosses not recognizing or rewarding his work. Now here was Tony, another so-called friend of his, taking his spot at home too.

"What's up dawg? I ain't seen you for a minute," Tony said, ignoring his question.

"Did you hear me? Don't park up in my driveway when I'm not here," Terrance said with his lip curled as Tony came over and gave him a pound.

"What the fuck is your problem?" Tony said, upset that after all this time the only thing Terrance had to say was about his parking spot.

"Nothin', just don't do it no more aiight?" Terrance repeated.

"Yea. Whatever." Tony followed Terrance up the stairs to his front door.

The last person Terrance wanted to see right now was Tony. His life had been so easy going for the past few weeks that he didn't have to see Tony's face. Now after a long horrible day of dealing with his overbearing boss and dishonest co-workers, here was another challenge.

"Yo Ran, you ain't even gonna ask me why you ain't heard from me for all that time?" Tony said when he had gone in the house and turned on Terrance's television.

Terrance didn't answer. He just threw his work bag down on the floor next to his couch and headed for the back.

"Man, that's fucked up," Tony said, turning his attention back to the television screen.

"Listen, Big Tone, I just had a fucked up day at work. I'm gonna jump in the shower. You can go ahead and get something out the fridge," Terrance said with his back to Tony as he walked down the hall to his bedroom.

Tony took him up on the offer and went into the kitchen to grab a soda. When he came back he leaned way back on the sofa and became interested in an episode of *Law & Order*.

He couldn't help but start to get angry at Terrance for not receiving him with open, friendly arms. He had been in the hospital for over a week recuperating and Terrance didn't even care.

"Some kind of friend this nigga is. He wasn't even worried 'bout my ass," Tony mumbled under his breath. He took a swig from his soda and thought about how nice it would be to smoke some trees.

"This nigga always talkin' that goody goody crap… and can't even be no friend when I need 'im," he complained. "Fuck that nigga."

Tony heard the shower running in the back and his eyes fell upon Terrance's work bag. He wondered if Terrance kept any cash in there. He could surely use just $20 right about now. He hadn't had a decent meal in days. *Naw*, he thought. He shrugged his shoulders and looked back at the television.

Terrance had some nerve to get an attitude over a parking spot. He was supposed to be Tony's friend, and hadn't even tried to get in touch with anybody to find out what had happened over the past couple of weeks. Tony could have been dead for all Terrance knew. Tony was really starting to feel some kind of way about that. And then Terrance didn't even bother to say what's up to his boy after all that time? That was really messed up.

All of these thoughts swirled around Tony's mind and before he even knew what he was doing, he was leaning over and grabbing Terrance's bag. Terrance had money, he reasoned, he wouldn't miss a $20 bill. He searched through the front pocket, then the middle pocket, relying on the sound of the shower running to tell him that Terrance was occupied.

But Terrance wasn't occupied. He was standing at the foot of the hallway watching Tony search through his bag.

Terrance stood there in a state of shock, as he watched Tony, his so-called friend, reach into one of his compartments and pull out his wallet. His eyelids dimmed with anger as he waited and then saw Tony pull two twenties out. He couldn't believe what his eyes were showing him as Tony put Terrance's wallet back in the bag, placed the bag back down in the same position as before and then stuffed the money in his pocket. Terrance opened up his mouth to yell, but no words came out. He decided against going on a rant right now; instead he backed up into the hallway. He was going to take this opportunity to see Tony's true colors so that he could get him out of his life for good.

Back on the couch, Tony leaned his body into the soft cushions and was satisfied with the fact that he had a little cash in his pocket again. He hadn't had money ever since Lil Joe took his last $10 for the stolen credit card. Now all he had to do was make a smooth exit from Terrance's house. What did he need to stay around there for? Terrance didn't even care if he was alive or dead. He heard the shower stop running and was bothered that he hadn't taken the chance to just call out the fact that he was leaving to Terrance while he was still in the bathroom. Terrance came out of the bathroom leaving a trail of the scent of Irish Spring soap behind him.

"So what's been up Tone?" Terrance said as he came right over and plopped himself down on the loveseat closest to his bag. He reached down and pretended as if he was going through it for some work papers. He was actually boiling with anger inside.

"Not much. Actually I'm 'bout to roll, I see you got a lot of things to do," Tony said, leaning forward as if he wanted to get up.

Terrance finally pulled out his wallet and started flipping through it. "Yo, you need any cash, or you straight?"

Tony immediately became uneasy at Terrance's question. He never asked Tony if he needed any money. "Naw dawg, I'm straight. Thanks for asking though."

"Hold up…" Terrance pretended to be shocked. "I had $100 in here? I'm missing 40 bucks."

Tony looked at Terrance curiously and then got up to leave. "Man, I don't know nothin' about that. Look, like I said, I gotta be out."

Tony offered his hand to Terrance, feeling guilty as sin, as Terrance eyed him closely and gave him a pound. Somehow Tony knew Terrance knew that he had taken the money. He turned around to leave before anything else could be said.

"You sure you don't know what happened to my money," Terrance asked, getting more bold with his questions. He stood up just as Tony turned back around to look at him, now with a look of indignation on his face. Terrance wanted so badly to rush at Tony and knock his ass out on the spot.

"What, you tryin' to say I took it?"

"I'm asking did you see it nigga, that's all," Terrance said, raising his voice. He cocked his head to the side and looked at Tony as if he dared him to say something smart.

"Well I didn't! You acting like a straight bitch right about now. Didn't even care if a nigga was dead, now you accusing motherfuckers of stealin'. Fuck you Ran," Tony raged on and then hustled out of Terrance's front door without another look or word.

Terrance stood in the same spot looking behind his asinine friend as he left. 15 years he had known Tony. He couldn't believe

Tony would ever steal money from him, not in a million years. Terrance had always been there for Tony in the hardest of times. He now knew that Tony was no friend. Terrance had wanted so badly to break Tony's jaw, but he was smarter than that. It was better that he just did exactly what Sonny from the movie *The Bronx Tale* said; he was going to look at it as if he had gotten rid of Tony for $40, a small price to pay. Terrance was done trying to talk sense into his so-called friend – as far as he was concerned, Tony was no longer able to be saved.

chapter 18

Scoop sat in his car staring out of the front window. He had been sitting still like that for close to an hour. He thought about where was the closest bridge he could drive off of. He thought about Shaquita's gun. He thought about all the pills in his mother's cabinet. But most of all, he thought about what the doctor had just told him. It hadn't fully sunken in yet.

His eyes were red and swollen into his head, and he hadn't even been crying. He couldn't even look at himself in the rearview mirror, because it would make the reality all too... real.

How could this happen to him? Things like this just didn't happen to guys like him. What was Shaquita going to say when he told her. Was he even going to *tell* her?

Tony would probably never so much as look in his direction when he found out. Tony was probably the last person on earth he would want to know about this. And his mother – his mother would be devastated.

The doctor had to be wrong. He had to retake that test. There was no way what he said could be true. He kept replaying the doctor's words in his head over and over.

"I'm sorry Mr. Boston, but the HIV test came back positive."

They were the last words Scoop heard said, even though the doctor kept talking for a good ten minutes afterwards. Everything else got lost in a blur.

He started to remember all of the warnings he had gotten from television commercials, public awareness campaigns, billboards and radio ads telling him to wear a condom *everytime*. They sounded so corny to him at the time. And despite his fears of catching the disease all he would say to himself was, *I can't feel anything with a condom on.* They warned that HIV was a real risk, especially to promiscous people like himself, but it never seemed real to him until now. He had figured up until now that he would just go unscathed by his frequent unprotected sex by screening his women – making sure they weren't on drugs, making sure they were clean and that they didn't act or look like skanks. Little did he know that he had been playing Russian Roulet with his life. And his head had just gotten blown off.

Keisha. Shaquira. Telia. Mabel from the Northeast. He wondered which of the women had given it to him. Which one of those trifling bitches had given him HIV!

Or could it have been that other thing… But he had worn a condom that time. It couldn't have been then. He shook the thought from his mind as quickly as it came.

Didn't they have a cure for this thing by now? he started to wonder as his mood shifted from shock to anger. Didn't they have a way to stop it? It just didn't make any sense. How could someone like him get it? How long had he had it? He had wondered why he had been getting those strange scabs all over his private area.

He was going to die? Well he might as well just get it over with then. He wanted to go drive off an embankment, or jump into the Schuylkill River, or slice his wrists. What did he have to live for anymore? He had tried to live a decent life, working for a living instead of being a bum like most of his homeboys, and here he was, ending up with a life threatening disease. It just wasn't fair.

The fury consumed Scoop as he started up his truck. He sat for a few more seconds letting his future crumple and die right before his eyes. He wanted to cry but he couldn't – he was too mad. It was him against the world now. He had gotten a raw deal. There was nothing that could be done for him at that point, he was going to die. And absolutely nothing even mattered anymore.

chapter 19

"Come on sis, you gotta have some money on you. Stop trynna play me," Tony pleaded.

"Tony, you know even if I did have some cash I wouldn't give it to your ass. You already owe me $200. I ain't giving you a dime," Tony's older sister Johnetta confirmed.

Johnetta was Tony's half sister on his father's side. He only called her when he was in dire straights. And there had never been a time in his life when the need for cash was so dire.

He had asked his grandmother for money. She told him that she didn't have any money and wouldn't have money to spare anytime soon due to the fact that she had to make up for the part of her emergency medical bills that wasn't covered by her insurance and medicare. Tony didn't know why she didn't just let that bill ride.

Quanisha wasn't talking to him. Even though she was furious with him for causing her to lose her job, he still had the nerve to call her up and see if she had any extra cash stashed away. She had just hung up the phone in his face.

Scoop told him he didn't have any money. Terrance was out of the question. He had spent up the money he stole from Terrance that same night on food, liquor, and weed, and Terrance probably wouldn't even want to talk. His other boys Rob and Belly didn't have two nickels to rub together at any given time unless they needed to eat, and then money magically appeared. So he had to go to his last resort – his half-sister Johnetta.

Before Tony even had a chance to say something about how he was getting a job that next day, which would have been a lie, he heard the phone click and then a dial tone on the other end of the phone. He hung up the phone and laid back on his bed. He was staying at his grandmother's house until further notice. It was like he just couldn't get any money to save his life. He was starting to regret taking that money from Terrance. Maybe he was being punished for stealing from one of the best friends he had ever had in his life. Terrance had had his back in 5th grade when the Too Fresh crew jumped him in the schoolyard. He had made sure Tony didn't choke on his own throw up numerous drunken nights in the past when everybody else had left him. Terrance was there for Tony when Tony's real mother died from a heroin overdose. He had bailed Tony out of some of the worst situations. When his mind's eye flashed back to the look of disappointment and anger on Terrance's face that night he had no doubt in his mind that he was wrong. These feelings of regret were new to him. He had no idea why all of a sudden he was starting to hold himself accountable for the things he had done wrong.

He shivered at the thought of calling Jenny the Psycho. He had almost been wooed to that point when he saw an ad for a succulent Arby's roast beef sandwich on his grandmother's living room television, but resisted. He didn't want Jenny having any reason for thinking that he was still interested. She had visited his grandmother's house on several occasions uninvited, and he was even afraid that she was stalking the house.

"Tony!" Tony's grandmother yelled from upstairs.

"What Ma?" he hollered back. She didn't answer, so Tony reluctantly got up from his bed and headed upstairs. When he got to his grandmother's room he first saw her TV on in the corner. Then he saw her standing at the window looking outside.

"That girl outside again," she said shakily.

"No she ain't," he answered as he went over to where she was standing to look over her shoulder. Lo and behold, right outside was Jenny getting out of her white Jetta, looking around apprehensively as she headed for his grandmother's front door. She looked like a crackhead as she glanced from side to side, slighlty cowered over.

"What is wrong with that child Tony?" his grandmother asked him seriously as she turned back to look in his eyes.

Tony didn't know what to say, because he honestly didn't know. Jenny had been rejected openly and rudely the last couple of times she showed up by his grandmother, and now here she was again. She didn't get the message. The last time Tony had seen or spoken to Jenny was when she was in her basement looking for something to tie Tony up with. She had gotten locked in her basement, and here she was, still pursuing him romantically. The girl seriously needed help at a mental institution.

"Do you need me to bust her ass?" Tony's grandmother asked out of the blue. "Because you know I will."

Tony started laughing at his grandmother, but she didn't laugh with him. She was serious. She was about tired of this foolish girl showing up to her house. She felt stupid for allowing Jenny to drop her off from the hospital that day. If Tony wasn't going to handle her now, it was time for Mrs. Jackson to break out the Vaseline.

Ding Dong.

Tony looked out of the window at nothing in particular as he explored new ways of telling Jenny that she was not wanted. Nothing worked. He had insulted her, told her the truth about why he had messed with her in the first place, and even threatened her with physical violence. Now he was thinking that maybe he should do more than just threaten her.

He and his grandmother stood by the window and tried to wait Jenny out. They hoped that maybe she would just leave. It was starting to get dark outside, and people in this neighborhood were so nosy. They waited for close to ten minutes and still Jenny continued pressing the doorbell every few seconds.

"I know someone's in there!" she suddenly called out as she looked up at his grandmother's window. They both ducked back to avoid her gaze. This was starting to become ridiculous.

When Jenny rang the doorbell again, this time obnoxiously long, Tony decided that for once in his life he had to be a man about the situation. He had to go down and confront this crazy bitch.

When he got to the door, he snatched it open and went outside almost in the same motion. He didn't want Jenny to get an opportunity to get inside the house. He stood with his back to the door.

"What the hell do you want??!!" he shouted with every fiber of his vocal muscles.

Jenny looked at him with eyes that said 'danger.' She was in a rare state that was accentuated by the fact that she had just snorted four lines of coke. It was a nasty habit that she had just recently taken back up after Tony left her.

"Did you hear me? What do you want?" Tony asked again.

"I want *you*," she said simply. She had wanted to say those words for the longest time. She hadn't laid an eye on Tony ever since she had hit him in the back of his head with her candy dish.

Tony opened his mouth to curse her out, but found himself at a loss of words. Everything that swirled in his mind to say had already come out of his mouth before. This girl was relentless. There wasn't a word or phrase that could turn her off of him.

"I want you to come with me, so that we can have some fun," she said with a smile that made Tony's stomach stir.

"Jenny, what is your problem? What the hell do you want from me? Why don't you go bother somebody else?" Tony said, almost in a pleading tone.

"I just told you."

"I don't want to go with you Jenny." Tony looked at Jenny intently and tried to get his point across to her. This was useless.

Then, just as if Jenny was reading into his innermost desires, she said the one thing that would sway him at that moment. "I'll take you down to the Outback Steakhouse, and I'll buy you a steak. You can drink all you want. I just want to talk for a little while."

Tony put both of his hands on his face and rubbed up and down in frustration. He was hungrier than a cockroach in a crackhouse. His grandmother barely had two end pieces of bread in the house and peanut butter. Was it possible to eat a meal with Jenny without digging himself deeper into the drama? Maybe not, but Tony was not much of a deep thinker on an empty stomach.

"Whatever, only if you promise not to come by here no more. I ain't hardly here no more anyway Jenny," Tony conceded.

When they got to the Outback, Tony instinctlively opened the door just as Jenny pulled into a parking spot. But Jenny grabbed his arm before he could get out.

"Hold on a second. Come back in," Jenny said with a smooth quality to her voice that Tony had never heard. Her mannerisms were almost attractive to him.

Tony sat back in the passenger's seat of her car and waited. Within a few seconds, Jenny produced a tablet from under her seat and placed it on her lap. She pulled out a small black plastic bag from her purse, and started emptying it out onto the tablet. Tony looked on in shock when he realized that she was sorting cocaine into neat lines.

"What the hell are you doing?" he couldn't help but ask as he watched her pull out a loosely rolled dollar bill and re-roll it tightly.

Jenny didn't answer, she just snorted up a couple of lines and then offered it to him. "Have some."

Tony laughed and shook his head 'no' in the same motion. "I've done some fucked up shit, but never in my life did I ever fuck with the snow."

"Come on," she urged. "It'll make the meal so much more enjoyable and fun. I really want to talk to you."

"I just said no. Get that shit out my face!" he yelled.

It was as if Jenny snapped. She shoved the remainder of the cocaine directly into Tony's face furiously and held it there as Tony struggled to recover from the attack.

"You dumb ass bitch!" he yelled when he finally smacked the tablet away. His face was covered with the white substance. White specks hung from his eye lashes. He rose the back of his hand up to smack Jenny.

But something in Tony made him hold his hand up in that position for a long time. For the first time in his life, he looked at someone in anger and was able to see their pain. He was surprised when he looked at Jenny's sullen eyes and saw the hurt she was experiencing for a split second. He couldn't believe that he was actually seeing that. He remembered how insensitive he had been to her in the past, and was almost regretful. The conviction made him lower his hand back to his lap.

"You make me miserable!" she suddenly screamed. "You don't even know what you've done to me! Go ahead and hit me, it won't hurt as much as you've already hurt me!"

Tony continued to look at her dumfoundedly.

"I gave you everything! I gave you all of me! You said you wanted to marry me!" Jenny bawled out. "Now you won't even see me? You should be dead!"

"I should be dead? See, what the fuck kind of crazy shit is that? That's what I'm talkin' about Jenny. You are psycho!"

"You should be dead because you don't care about anybody but yourself!" Jenny ranted on. She was obviously feeling the effects of the drug. "You've got a lot of fucking nerve! Who do you think you are?"

"I'm out of here," Tony said as he opened the door and got out of Jenny's car. He was tired of hearing and saying the same things from and to Jenny. Jenny got out of the car in record speed and ran after him. Tony was taking quick steps as he finished brushing the powder off of his face.

"I'm pregnant!" she screamed.

Tony stopped in his tracks, and so did Jenny. He half-turned his head, but stared at the large Outback sign instead.

"Stop fucking lying," he finally said. He waved his hand dismissively and then kept moving. This girl would say anything to have him, but he wasn't trying to hear it. How was she pregnant, yet she was doing coke like that? Besides, he had never even come inside of Jenny – she was tripping.

"Where are you going!" she screamed and he heard her boots clicking on the concrete behind him again. "Oooo, I'm gonna kill you!"

Only a few feet before Jenny could reach Tony, she tripped on a dip in the concrete and fell forward. Her hands and knees hit the concrete hard.

Tony turned around just in time to see Jenny looking at her

scraped up hands with tears in her eyes. He was shocked when he saw a 10 inch butcher knife gleaming in the sunlight right next to her. If she hadn't tripped, she would have been moments from possibly stabbing him in the back. He stood and looked at the knife and Jenny for what seemed like an eternity.

Tony finally went over and snatched the knife up off of the street. He looked down at this pitiful pile that was Jenny. She was really messed up, and he actually almost felt sorry for her even though she had just tried to stab him. He wished she would get some help. But that was it – the next time Jenny came anywhere *near* his grandmother's house he was going to call the cops. He disposed of the knife quickly – they wouldn't take kindly to a black man walking around with a big knife in the lily white suburbs of Springfield – and then hustled out of the Outback parking lot.

Tony rode the 119 bus all the way to 69th street using an old token he had, and then walked down Market Street back to his grandmother's house, still on an empty stomach. He couldn't believe that he wasted all that time with Jenny, only to go home hungry. He should have never given into the temptation. He could have gotten stabbed over a meal! All that drama with Jenny wasn't worth a steak.

He felt his cellphone vibrating in his pocket. When he saw that it was Scoop he was relieved. Surely Scoop either had some food, or some money to go get some food. Tony would have even settled for a double cheeseburger at McDonald's at that point.

"Yo, what's up man," Tony said with a newly positive attitude. He was walking down a small block parallel to the El towards his grandmother's house.

"What's up wit you? What you doin'?" Scoop asked. Despite his upbeat questions, his voice had a heaviness to it that Tony hadn't ever heard.

"Nothin', only almost just got stabbed," Tony said nonchalantly.

Scoop took a second to see if he misheard Tony. "What's that?"

"That crazy bitch Jenny was about to stab me in the back!" Tony said as he turned the corner onto Chestnut Street.

"Whoa, that's real," Scoop said, but wasn't really surprised. He figured at some point that someone would end up stabbing or shooting Tony.

"Yea, you sound real interested," Tony said sarcastically. It was times like this that he really missed Terrance. He was always genuinely interested in Tony's problems, even if it was just to laugh at him. He had wanted to at least tell somebody about Jenny's wild claim of being pregnant to make himself feel better about the situation. He still didn't believe Jenny. But Scoop obviously wasn't interested.

"I was gonna come scoop you, go get some drinks down the way," Scoop said without another word about Tony and Jenny.

"Yea, aiight. Well I'm walking down Chestnut right now. I'm comin' up on 63rd."

"I'm right around the corner from there. Hold up," Scoop said and then hung up his cellphone.

When Tony and Scoop walked into the Southwest Philly bar, their attention immediately went to three men who were arguing near the door.

"...Fuck you! I don't give a fuck about your kids, I want my money!" one of them yelled.

"Nigga and I don't give a fuck about you, so get your broke

ass out my face!" another shouted back.

"Get them niggas out my bar!" the harsh looking female bartender yelled from behind the bar with a pointed finger.

The third guy pulled his friend back out towards the door to leave before things escalated. They bumped into Scoop on their way out.

"Yo, watch yourself man!" Scoop said with a shove back at the irrational one.

"Nigga my money or your life!" the angry brother bellowed out once more to the guy he was beefing with before he and his friend exited the bar.

Once Tony was done viewing the spectacle he sauntered on into the bar with his hands in his army print jacket pockets. It was starting to get colder outside as they approached November. His black Timberland boots were loosely tied around his feet.

When they sat down at the bar Tony immediately ordered a forty of St. Ides poured into a cup. Scoop ordered a double shot of Hennessey and a beer.

"Ya'll kitchen still open?" Tony asked the bartender.

"Yea, what you want," she answered raucously.

Tony looked over at Scoop warily before he ordered. He wanted Scoop to know that this was on him without having to say it. Scoop wasn't even looking at him. He was looking down at the bar, something that Tony thought was weird.

"Let me get an order of wings and fries. Scoop you want something to eat?"

"Naw man, go ahead," Scoop said as he threw back the entire glass of Hennessy. "Let me get another one of these though."

They drank and sat in silence except for the music blasting and the people talking in the background. Tony could sense that something was up with Scoop – he was never this quiet. Even when the bartender came back with the food and told them the total, Scoop just pulled out a twenty and laid it down on the bar with no protest.

"Yo Scoop, what's up wit you man?" Tony finally asked between bites of chicken. He was starting to feel the effects of the malt liquor.

Scoop didn't say anything in response. Instead he looked over at the door and saw someone walk in that would change the course of his entire night.

"Ain't that that nigga Rock?" Tony said loudly as he turned in his stool.

"Yea," Scoop said weakly. He did and he didn't want to see Rock at that moment. On one hand, he was in a more laid back mode, but on the other hand, he wanted to finally confront this asshole who was dragging his name through the mud. The liquor in his system was making him lean towards the part of himself that wanted to confront Rock on the spot.

Scoop turned to look at Rock again, who was now leaning on the jukebox looking directly back at him.

"Look at that nigga, got the nerve to come in here grillin' you," Tony instigated as he glared at Rock with a screw face. "Faggot ass nigga."

Rock got up and walked over to them boldly. "Ya'll got somethin' you wanna get off your chest?"

"In fact, I do bitch ass muthafucka. Why you goin' around runnin' your mouth about me?"

"Pussy, ain't nobody talkin' bout you," Rock waved him off.

"Pussy?" Scoop answered as he stood up from the bar. "You the one always complainin' about a little money with your broke beans and rice eatin' ass."

"Yea, well it ain't my fault you don't know how to make no

dough. That's why don't nobody never see your black ass on the block. You scared of hustlin',"" Rock laughed, trying to hide his fury at Scoop's insult about him being Puerto Rican. "Just like I said, *puta!*"

"I ain't scared of hustlin' you dumb ass spic. Matter fact I could hustle you under a table."

"Man. You a pussy that likes dick!" Rock said suddenly. He pointed at Tony. "You probably like this nigga dick too don't you?!"

Rock was so intrigued by his own wit that he broke out laughing hysterically and fell into a brother that was standing behind him.

"Yo watch yourself," the guy said as he pushed Rock off of him.

Before Rock had a chance to respond, Scoop hit him over the head with his half full bottle of Coors Light. Rock stumbled and tried to reorient himself, but didn't get a chance. Tony came right behind Scoop and hit Rock with a hard right punch to the side of his head.

Rock fell to the ground and proceeded to get stomped by Tony and Scoop. The bartender was already on the phone to get the police at the bar. These types of things never ended harmoniously without the police. Inbetween stomps, Tony leaned down to run Rock's pockets. He found a stack of money and a couple of bags of weed and crack. The other pocket had a cellphone. If only he had checked Rock's sock though.

Rock's comment was inexcusable for Scoop. It was everything that he had been afraid of. Rock was probably telling everybody around the hood that he was gay due to one indiscretion Scoop had experienced.

One Sunday night a long while back, Scoop and Rock were

chilling at one of their customers' houses. It was at a time when Scoop was still dipping and dabbling with coke and wet. Their customer Rico was a functional crackhead who lived farther up North Philly in a Spanish area off of Norris Street. He had a job and his own apartment. He was also a fiend for dick, as a lot of the hood knew. He was a gay prostitute that worked the block down on 13th street. It was the only way he could afford his nasty habit.

Scoop and Rock had fallen asleep after a short session of smoking weed and snorting coke on Rico. When Scoop woke up, still high, he found Rico in his lap giving him head in a way that he had never felt before in his life. The sensation was so good that he just let his head fall back in the darkness and closed his eyes to focus on the feeling.

After Rico finished him off, he took Scoop's hand and grabbed him up off of the couch quietly so as to not wake Rock as they went into the bedroom. Rico put lube around his butt hole, gave Scoop a condom, and let Scoop take him from the back. Scoop wasn't in his right mind, but he was loving every moment of the experience. That was up until Rock came into the room and saw what was going on.

"What the fuck?" is all Rock said as Scoop whipped around. He was mortified to see his boy looking on in disgust at the sight of him with his penis inside of another man.

Back to the present.

The disgusted look on Rock's face that night flashed across Scoop's mind and it made Scoop so angry that he wanted to murder somebody. Scoop leaned down until he was only a few inches from Rock's nose and spit directly into his face.

What happened next went in slow motion for Tony, who was busy shoving Rock's money and possessions in his pocket.

In the commotion, Rock managed to lean down and grab his glock from his sock. He cocked it back and put the gun directly onto Scoop's forehead right as Scoop was about to strike again. Before Scoop could even move or react, Rock pulled the trigger and splattered Scoop's brains all over the place. Blood was everywhere.

Everybody ran and scattered out of the bar. Women were screaming and taking off their heels so that they could run faster.

And Tony was right behind them. His shirt was specked red with Scoop's blood. He had watched the scene in amazement and wonder. He thought he was watching a movie. When the scene changed from slow motion back to reality, his only thought was to get the hell out of there before Rock shot him too.

He ran down an alleyway to avoid the crowd and the police whose sirens could be heard close in the background. He stumbled and fell over a huge rock right into the middle of a puddle. He was almost certainly sure, since it hadn't rained in over a week, that he was now laying in a pool of piss.

"Ughhh!!" he screamed helplessly. He got up from the puddle and took off his piss soaked shirt. He felt as if he was in a really, really bad dream.

When he got to a safe corner, he looked around to make sure no one was watching him, and then started walking down the street as if nothing was wrong.

Tony clutched his army jacket together, not because it was cold, but because his chest was bare beneath it. The zipper on the jacket was broken, and there was no other way to keep it closed. It was only 8 o'clock in the evening and Tony didn't have any idea of what he should do.

He was trying hard not to think about the sight of Scoop with a hole in his head, the last image of his friend that he would probably ever have. He would never forget the look on Scoop's face when Rock put the barrel of that gun to his forehead. It was a mixture of fear, distress and relief. All at the same time.

He was starting to think about how maybe if he wouldn't have egged Scoop on, none of this would have ever happened. He didn't even know why he did things like that. He really didn't have to say *anything* when Rock came into the bar.

He started replaying everything that had just happened over and over in his mind. Then the reality started to hit him. This wasn't a dream – it was a nightmare. He had just watched one of his best boys get shot right before his eyes. Scoop was definitely dead.

"What the fuck is wrong with me?" he said to himself. He had to stop and sit down. This day had went from bad to worse to the absolute worst. He had to put himself on pause before things spun out of control. Before he did something else really stupid.

Tony put his head in his hands as he sat on the stoop in front of a corner grocery store. He let things sink in. His friend was laid up in a bar with a bullet in his head and here he was. He had left his friend without a second thought. How could he leave Scoop like that? But then again, what else could he have done? Maybe he could have grabbed the gun from Rock and shot him back, but where would that have gotten him? There were witnesses everywhere.

Scoop was his road dog. They had only known each other for about four years, but Tony felt like he had known Scoop for much longer than that. The time they spent together could better be described as 'dawg years' - they had been through some serious trials together.

However, through it all he had never really felt a connection to Scoop the way he felt with Terrance and his other best friend, Quanisha. Scoop leaving his life was more of an inevitability for him than a tragedy.

Then Tony remembered the money in his pocket. The way he had been losing and messing up money lately he doubted that it would last. When he flipped through the bills he saw that there was about $280 in there. Rock must not have been hurting too badly as he had been complaining to Scoop. Then a thought crossed his mind. Rock might still be alive and out there... and looking for Tony.

As soon as he thought about it he got up from the stoop and looked around cautiously. He grabbed Rock's phone out of his pocket and left it on the step. He kept moving down the street and thought about what to do. He thought about the only person in the world right now who cared about him at that moment besides his grandmother. It was Quanisha. She had been there for him in a lot of different ways, and had put up with a lot of his bullshit. And he was right around the corner from her apartment building.

Tony stood at Quanisha's door with a handful of flowers and his fist lifted up in the air, ready to knock. He was hesitating because he remembered the last time he saw Quanisha. She told him to never come to her house again. And she sounded serious. Something made him change his mind about going in there. She was probably still mad about losing her job. He knew how important it was to Quanisha to work and earn a living, rather than live off of welfare like all of her friends and family.

Instead he took the money out of his pocket and peeled off several bills.

"I can't believe I'm doing this," Tony said, shaking his head.

But he kept doing it before he changed his mind. He ended up stuffing $100 under the crack in Quanisha's door. It was the least he could do. He didn't even know if he would survive the night, so what was the point in having all that money on him when he could walk outside right then and get shot by Rock or one of his crew. He was certain that they were looking for him. And he knew Quanisha probably needed the money more than he did. And he knew Quanisha was tired of hearing him say the same things over and over again to get back in her house, even if this time it included, "Scoop's been shot."

Tony dropped the flowers in front of the door and left the building quickly. He caught a cab a few blocks down, a rare occurrence in that part of town, so that he could go back to his grandmother's house. He pushed the thoughts of Scoop to the back of his mind and tried to focus on his next move. He was just happy that he would live to see another day.

chapter 20

It had been a week since Scoop's death. Word had gotten all around the hood about what happened to him that night. Some said that the fight was over drug money. Some said Scoop had just said the wrong thing to Rock. Some people were even saying that Scoop was gay and on the down low, and that Rock was his lover.

But fortunately for Tony, not many people were putting his name in the story. He found out that Rock was still on the run from the police, who had him pinned as the main suspect in the murder. And now Tony was on the run from Rock.

Quanisha had left town to visit her Godsister in Virginia. She had heard all the stories about what had happened to Scoop that night at the bar, but hadn't heard anything from Tony since she kicked him out. She didn't even consider the possibilty that Tony was with Scoop that night. It was too hard a thought to bear. Fortunately she hadn't heard anything about him being there.

She needed the time away in VA to get her mind right, and to potentially find a new life out in the MD/VA/DC area. She didn't have any reason to still be in Philly. She didn't have a job or a life there. Her family wasn't supportive of her, and her worst fear had come true. Her mother had called her and ruined her day one day the week before.

"Quanisha, why the hell didn't you tell me you couldn't have no kids?" her mother asked immediately.

Quanisha was speechless. She never expected her mother to come right out with it like that. "What the hell are you talkin' about?"

"I'm talkin' about Pam's mother tellin' me you had all those abortions and now you can't have no kids! How could you be so stupid!"

"Ma, I don't—"

"Don't sit up here and try to lie to me girl. That's what you get when you ho yourself out there to death. I tried to warn you, don't be whoring around and think it'll just be a good time! Now look at you. You always think you know everything, but you really don't know shit you stupid little—"

Quanisha had hung up the phone right in the middle of her mother's sentence. She couldn't bear to listen to one more word. It was heart-breaking for her to hear her mother's seething hypocrisy. Her mother had whored around all of her life, to this day, and still had the nerve to lecture Quanisha on keeping her legs closed. She was the classic 'do as I say, not as I do' parent. She had left no legacy for her children and felt guilty about it, so instead of making things right she chose to make her children and everyone around her miserable right along with her.

To top all that off, someone had hit Quanisha's car while it was parked down the street from her apartment building. They hit it hard, causing the entire back side of her Mazda Miata to be crushed inward, and then apparently kept driving because she didn't have any type of note on her car. She was devastated, because she had worked so hard to buy that car and keep it in good shape. Even though the car was badly in need of a paint job and a tune-up, it didn't officially look like a hooptie until now. Now she would have to drive around in it with a huge dent in the right back side. Her insurance wouldn't cover it; her deductible was too high and she didn't have enough money saved to pay for the repair *and* pay her rent with no job.

When Quanisha crossed over the Delaware state line into Maryland, she thought about who could have left that $100 at her door. It had to have been a mistake. Somebody had to have left it under the wrong door. Nobody ever gave her money. When she saw the flowers a thought crossed her mind that it could have been Tony, but again, *nobody*, especially Tony, ever gave her money. Maybe it was that guy she met at the club, Randy, who had been calling her on and off ever since she left his house that night. Wherever it came from it came in handy. She was seriously in need of funds ever since she lost her job. The only way she was able to make the trip down to Virginia was with that money.

As she pulled out her directions her phone started ringing in her purse. It was that Randy again. She couldn't believe that after the way he had dissed her on their first date, he was sweating her so hard now. She almost wished he would have just left it at a one night stand.

"What you want?" she said into the phone nastily.

"That's how you answer a phone call?" he asked sarcastically.

"When it's you, yeah."

"Whoa. Now who ain't bein' nice?"

"I guess that would be me. But look I gotta go. I'm on the road."

"Where at?"

"Nonna your business. Why you always wanna know what I'm doin'?" Quanisha shot back.

"I don't care about what you doin'. Fuck you then," Randy said and then hung up the line.

"Stupid ass nigga," she said with a smirk. She couldn't stand the idea that Randy was probably just calling her for a booty call, but liked the fact that she had him in the palm of her hands. He was calling her at least three times a week and now she didn't even want to talk to him. *Payback's a bitch Randy*, Quanisha thought.

Quanisha arrived at her Godsister, Stephanie's, house an hour and a half later, after getting lost twice. She was so happy to see her cousin standing outside on the porch of her beautiful, large two story home awaiting her arrival. But she almost felt embarrassed to be stepping out of her banged up car in front of such a nice home.

"Sis!!" Stephanie yelled excitedly as she ran down the porch with her hands thrown up in the air.

"Heyyy Steph!" Quanisha ran towards her Godsister, leaving her bags in the car.

They embraced for what seemed like ages. Quanisha felt herself about to cry for a moment, but stopped herself. *This crying shit is getting old*, she thought.

"Sis, how you been?!" Stephanie asked as she pulled apart from Quanisha and took a good look into her eyes.

Stephanie was a caramel skinned sister with long straight brown hair down her back. She was thin but shapely, and had beautiful light brown eyes that shone in the sun. Something about her presence set Quanisha at ease.

Stephanie and Quanisha had been really close as kids. They were tight even though Stephanie was five years Quanisha's senior. Stephanie's family had uprooted and moved from Philly to Chicago when they hit the lottery for $270,000. From Chicago, Stephanie ended up moving to Virginia with her husband Karl, who she met at college. She now had a three year old son, Michael, who was the joy of her life. Stephanie had become a born-again Christian, and everyone raved about how much of a 180 degree change she had made from her old life.

At the age of 15, Stephanie's life had begun spiraling downward. She rebeled against her parents and ran away from home, becoming a statistic of the streets. She began prostituting soon afterwards, and one night was beaten so badly by one of her Johns that she had to go through a long rehabilitation at an alcohol and drug treatment center. Her family paid for her stay with most of the remainder of their savings from the lotto winnings. With her family's support, she decided from that moment on she was taking her life in a different direction. She went to a local community college in Chicago where she met Karl, a smart young brother who taught one of her business classes, tutored her and encouraged her to finish school. When Karl got the job of his dreams working for a law firm in Richmond, Virginia, they decided to start their own family there. Stephanie was now a stay-at-home mom with a small bookkeeping business on the side. She and Karl had paid her family back every dime of the money they spent on her rehabilitation and they were all doing very well.

Quanisha hadn't laid eyes on her Godsister in several years, but they had talked on and off on the telephone. She was looking good!

"I'm doing alright," Quanisha fibbed. She wasn't very convincing though because Stephanie turned her head and screwed her lips up at her young Godsister skeptically.

"Girl, no you ain't," Stephanie said and then went over to the back door of Quanisha's car and started to pull out one of her bags. "Come on, help me with your bags."

They went inside and immediately Stephanie made Quanisha feel at home.

"If you're ever hungry you just go right up in the fridge and get you something to eat. I also have a pantry full of goodies that I just picked up from BJ's. I got your room all set up, towels, washcloths, soap, toothbrush and everything. If you need anything, you just come ask and you got it," Stephanie said assuredly and then passed Quanisha a cup of tea.

"What's this?" Quanisha asked curiously as she sniffed the piping hot liquid.

"It's Chamomile. Tea. Taste it, it's good," Stephanie explained as she took a sip from her own cup. "It'll calm you."

Quanisha was about to protest about how it was 60 degrees outside, and what did she want with a cup of tea, but changed her mind. She sipped the tea slowly and let the warmth of the liquid permeate her body. She closed her eyes and enjoyed the feeling.

"I'm so glad you came out here girl. It's really good to see you," Stephanie said, and Quanisha really felt her sincerity. "So what's up with you sis?"

"Not much, tryin' to get my head together," Quanisha said nonchalantly as she leaned back on the couch and allowed herself to relax more.

"Oh yea, so what happened with that whole job thing you were telling me about?"

"Oh. It was fucked up. They didn't even care about what I was goin' through, they just fired my ass. I told that bitch she could shove that little grocery job right up her tight penny pinching ass if it would fit," Quanisha said, getting angry all over again.

"Dang, look who got the potty mouth," Stephanie said with a smirk on her face as she adjusted herself to lay back on the couch.

"Oh, my fault," Quanisha said apologetically. She had forgotten that her Godsister had become religious.

It was as if Stephanie read Quanisha's mind. She laughed. "Look, let me get something clear right now. Everybody in the family thinks ever since I got saved, I became this goody two shoes that nobody can relate to anymore. That's just not true. I gave my life to God, but that doesn't mean I don't still relate to what's going on out here. I still have my sins too, I'm not exempt from sin just cause I'm saved."

"I know but, you know, it's a little crazy when you get around some Christians. They think they know everything. And that shit – I mean, that stuff get's *sickening*," Quanisha said.

"I know. That type of thing turned *me* off of church a long time ago. But I realized that I shouldn't let that stop me from having a relationship with God. I still don't go to church all the time because sometimes it can be a negative experience with all the gossiping and self-righteousness, but I do talk to God all the time, and that's good with God so it's good with me," Stephanie said as she gazed over at Quanisha on the couch.

"Okay, I feel that," Quanisha said and then took another long sip of her tea. "So you don't curse or none of that?"

"Girl please. Once in a while I slip up, when I'm mad. But I just gotta catch myself. I'm human. But I ain't gonna be correcting you all the time you're here, all I ask is that you watch what you say around Michael. He is very impressionable."

"No problem."

"Another thing Nish, you are truly welcome to stay out here as long as you need to get yourself together. Trust me, I understand what that's like," Stephanie said as she closed her eyes and smiled.

Quanisha soaked in Stephanie's words and tried to analyze whether she was being sincere, or if she was just trying to be nice. She had only been in Stephanie's house for a few minutes, and already she felt so comfortable and peaceful. She felt as if she could just fall asleep right now on the couch. If Stephanie *was* just trying to be nice, she was doing a heck of a job at it.

chapter 21

Tony was a shell of himself. Nothing could make him happy. He was feeling like he had a ton of bricks hanging from his shoulders.

Every corner he turned, he was worried about Rock being right there waiting for him. He had been rolling with his other friend Rob a lot more lately. They weren't that close, but he needed somebody to have his back.

The only good thing was, he still had money left after robbing Rock. He had been sure that the money would be lost, the same way all the rest of his money had slipped out of his grip lately. But it was a week after the incident and he still had over $100 in his pocket. He wasn't even trying intentionally to hold onto it; it had just lasted.

"Don't you wanna eat somethin'? Damn, we been driving around for two hours!" Rob complained.

This was the reason why Tony hated hanging out with Rob. All he thought about was food. "Nigga tuck in your belly. I ain't hungry yet."

"Well I am! I ain't eat since noon," Rob nearly whined. "I'm sick of your stupid ass tellin' me when it's time to eat. I wanna eat *now*."

Tony rolled his eyes up into his head and sighed. "You sound like a bitch man. Where you wanna eat?"

They went to McDonald's on 52nd street and pulled into the drive thru. Rob leaned over Tony and ordered himself. "Lemme get a number five, super sized, an order of chicken nuggets, a double cheeseburger and a strawberry shake."

The girl on the McDonald's speaker paused. "Anything else?"

"Yea, anything else? Damn," Tony looked at his nearly obese friend in disgust. "You know they got chicken sandwiches too," he mentioned sarcastically.

"Yea, matter fact, let me get another small fry too," Rob answered, ignoring Tony's attempt at insulting him.

Tony and Rob sat in the parking lot and ate their food. Rob wolfed his food down, while Tony just picked at his fries. He wasn't that hungry. He hadn't been able to get the image of Scoop out of his mind. The sad look on Scoop's face at the bar while he was drinking, in contrast with the animated look on his face right before he died was etched in Tony's mind. He wished he could take back what he said to incite Scoop in the first place.

Look at that nigga, got the nerve to come in here grillin' you.

Maybe if he would have kept his big mouth shut Scoop would still be alive.

If he were honest with himself, he would have to admit that it was his own mortality that was really scaring him. Death by the hands of Rock was not so distant a possibility. Rock had never gotten picked up by the police, and as far as Tony knew after what happened at the bar, Rock was seven-thirty. He wouldn't hesitate to shoot Tony's ass too.

"Why ain't you eatin'?" Rob asked. Rob obviously knew what had happened to Scoop, but Tony didn't tell him anything about his involvement, or the fact that Rock was probably looking for him. If Rob knew everything that was going on, he probably wouldn't step within two feet of Tony.

"Just ain't hungry," Tony said dispassionately. The fries were crispy and hot fresh out of the oil, but they tasted as bland as cardboard to Tony. Rob on the other hand was eating as if this were *his* last meal.

"You ain't gonna eat that? Let me get that then," Rob said, grabbing some of Tony's fries.

Tony looked at Rob as if he had lost his mind, but didn't say anything.

"You can't be wastin' food like that, these fries is hot!" Rob said between chewing. Tony was starting to wonder if it was really worth hanging around Rob all this time just for the sake of having a partner. Rob had been grating on his last nerve.

"The food's wasted when it goes to your fat belly," Tony said as he shoved the rest of his food at Rob and started up his car.

Tony needed a drink badly. But he had been trying to avoid the bars like a plague in fear of running into Rock. He decided he would be safe at the little bar that he and Scoop had visited a while back in Germantown. As he pulled onto 76 West, he felt his phone vibrating in his pocket. When he looked he saw that it was an unknown 610 number.

"Yo," Tony said as he leaned back in his seat with his hat pulled down low over his troubled eyes. He was getting ready with his standard six word answer if this was someone for Jenny: "This ain't her number no more."

"Uh, hello? This is Dr. Stephens calling from Mercy Hospital. May I please speak to Jenny Storms?" a male voice asked.

"Doc? Yooo, how you? This Tony!" Tony said, and something inside of him sparked back to life for a moment.

"Tony Jackson? Oh hey, young brother! What's goin' on?" the doctor said cheerfully. He was surprised to hear Tony's voice.

"Ain't nuffin, just chillin'. How's everything over there at the prison – I mean the hospital," Tony joked. "I bet the Nazi Nurse is still terrorizing the other inmates – I mean patients."

"Very funny. It's going great. But I need to be asking you that

– how are you doing? You know you were supposed to come in and let me check the bandages after a week."

"Yea, I know. But it's cool," Tony said, slowly setting back into his reality.

"What about your hearing?"

"It's fine. Much better."

The doctor paused as he took in the tone of Tony's voice.

"What about otherwise? You don't sound too hot," he asked intuitively.

"I'm aiight."

Dr. Stephens paused again for a while. "So you and Jenny are still together I see? How is she doing?"

Tony couldn't help but laugh. He knew that as long as he kept this phone he was never going to be rid of Jenny's memory. "Uh, no offense Doc, but hell naw. I ain't never been with Jenny."

"What's that?" Doctor Stephens asked curiously. "She told me you all were engaged the last time I saw her. And isn't this her phone number I called?"

"Let me tell you something Doc. Ya'll should seriously think about getting Jenny 302ed, cuz she got a screw loose. We ain't never been engaged."

"Hmmm. That's interesting. Well, I was actually calling because her supervisor told me that Jenny hasn't been to work in weeks and she hasn't been able to get in touch with her. We're all a little worried about what happened to her. She hasn't even called to check in."

"Well I don't know nothing about that Doc, she must be doin' her own thing. Last I saw her she was tryin' to stab me in the back with a butcher knife," Tony mentioned nonchalantly.

There was an awkward silence as Dr. Stephens struggled to process what Tony had just said and find something to say in response.

"I told you she was crazy Doc," Tony said as he pulled off the Lincoln Drive exit. "But look I gotta get off this phone."

"Look Tony I gotta tell you something that's been on my spirit to say for a long time now. I think –"

"Oh no you about to get spiritual with me Doc?" Tony said lightheartedly, trying to make it into a joke.

"Just listen to what I have to say. I'll be quick. I've been wanting to say it since you left the hospital, but didn't think I'd ever get the chance. After all our talks, I believe that you are a very smart, insightful young man with a lot of potential. I just hope you think so too. I remember a lot of what you used to tell me when you were staying here, about the women, and your friends and the streets. I just hope that you're not falling victim to the negativity. You can do so much better with your life. I just wanted to let you know that I think you're a special young man, and no matter what happens in life, just know that God has a hope and a future for you. And that's it."

Now Tony was the one who was speechless. He stared emptily at the road passing in front of him as he drove the intricate twists of Lincoln Drive with his mouth half open in thought. Nobody had ever said those type of things to him, other than his grandmother. It was strange and different hearing it from a man that he respected like Dr. Stephens.

"Thank you Doc," is all that Tony could say in response.

"Alright, I'll talk to you soon son. And don't be a stranger, you can talk to me anytime you want. You have my number now," Dr. Stephens said, and then hung up the phone.

Tony closed the phone and went into a trance of thought as he drove the rest of the way to the bar. Now he *really* needed a drink.

chapter 22

"Aaaahhh!!" Quanisha screamed as she was dropped 100 feet from the sky. Her heart raced with a vengeance against her chest as she closed her eyes and waited for her inner organs to return to their normal places.

Stephanie's friend Michelle laughed hysterically at Quanisha when they settled down at the bottom of the Free Fall.

"Oh my God! I'm never doin' that again!" Quanisha said assuredly with a frown on her face as she pushed against the railing to free herself from the ride. She, Stephanie, Michelle, Karl and the baby had taken a trip down to King's Dominion, an amusement park in Virginia. Michelle had convinced Quanisha to ride the Free Fall with her. Quanisha had already changed her mind by the time the ride had risen halfway up into the air, but it had been too late.

"That was fun!" Michelle said excitedly as they exited the ride. Quanisha's legs felt like jelly underneath her, and they almost buckled when she started walking. "Whoa, you okay?"

"No!" Quanisha said seriously, but then laughed. She couldn't believe she had actually just done that.

Stephanie ran up to them and hugged Quanisha tightly as she laughed. "I saw you up there! You looked like you were gonna cry!"

Quanisha couldn't help but laugh too. "I shoulda kept my ass – I mean my butt down here with ya'll! That shit was crazy!"

They had been at the park for over five hours, and it was definitely time to go. Feet were hurting, stomachs were growling and the baby, Michael, was crying to be held. But it had been an absolutely beautiful day. Quanisha had had a good time.

Karl was a medium height light skinned brother with a goatee and reddish toned thinning hair. He was good looking in the way that Malcolm X was, and very distinguished and serious looking. Quanisha had been afraid that Stephanie and Karl would be one of those couples that were inseparable and disgustingly affectionate with one another all the time, even in front of other people. She hated being around a couple that flaunted their relationship among single people.

But it wasn't like that at all. Stephanie and Karl were obviously in love, but they didn't need to show it. It was apparent in the way they talked to each other, how they interacted in any situation, such as their mutual decision to pay for everyone's admission in the park, and the way they treated other people around them. They didn't need to be kissing each other every other moment in order for people to know that they were husband and wife.

As they walked back to the car, Stephanie fell back behind everyone to talk to Quanisha in private.

"So are you having a good time?" she asked.

"Girl, I ain't never had so much fun in my life. Thank you so much," Quanisha smiled. Her face was still flushed a deep red from the Free Fall ride.

"I'm glad. I was worried you would think we were too 'slow' down here," Stephanie admitted.

"What? Naw, I like it down here. I needed to get away from crazy ass Philly for a minute."

"So what all's been going on up there anyway?" Stephanie asked, and it was just the invitation Quanisha needed to get some things off of her chest. She sighed.

"Well, mom's trippin' again. I swear I can't deal with that woman. Sometimes I wish she woulda just had that abortion she always told me she was gonna get. I think she had me just to make somebody else miserable besides herself."

Stephanie was disturbed by what Quanisha had just told her, but not shocked. She had had points in her life when she had wanted to die, or wished she'd never been born. She could relate. But she felt sad that Quanisha was at that point in her life. She wasn't sure if she knew the right thing to do to help. All she could do was try to lift her spirits while she was there.

"Well, I'm glad you were born," Stephanie said simply.

Quanisha looked over at her Godsister for a moment, and then back down at the ground.

"Look sis, I've been there, but don't put yourself down like that. God put you here on this earth for a reason, and you'd better believe it," Stephanie continued.

When they reached home it was starting to get dark outside. Quanisha hoped that Stephanie had plans to cook or something because she was starving. She thought they were supposed to be going out to eat, but Stephanie had insisted that they go straight home. Before Karl turned down their block, he stopped the car.

"Okay Nish, we have a little surprise for you," Stephanie said as she turned to look at Quanisha with a smile. "So close your eyes. Michelle, make sure she keeps her eyes closed."

"What? Why I gotta close my eyes?" Quanisha asked as a smile grew upon her lips.

"Just do it silly," Stephanie commanded, and Quanisha finally just did it. Michelle reached around from the back and put her hands over Quanisha's eyes. Quanisha felt the car moving again and a twinge of nervous energy ran through her body. What was all this about?

Finally they stopped and Stephanie got out of the car. She grabbed Quanisha's hand to lead her out to the driveway. When they got there, Stephanie's husband and Michelle stood behind them as Michael tried to get his mother's attention by grabbing at her pants. Stephanie was busy holding her hands over Quanisha's eyes though.

"Okay… open them!" she said excitedly.

Quanisha's eyes slowly became transfixed on the sight of what looked like her Mazda Miata. But it was newly painted a solid black color, and the dent was completely gone.

"Oh my God!" she screeched.

"I hope you're not mad, we took the liberty. Karl has a friend over at the auto repair who gave us a great deal," Stephanie explained cautiously. She didn't know if the look on Quanisha's face was pleasant surprise or alarm at the fact that they had done something to her car without her approval.

"Oh my God Stephanie. This my car?" Quanisha finally asked in disbelief.

"Yea it's your car," Karl stepped in and explained. "My boy Bobby down at the shop hooked you up. Do you like it?"

"Like it? I love it!" Quanisha screamed and ran over to touch her car. She couldn't believe that they had even painted it! "But how much do I gotta pay him, I don't got any money for it right now?"

"Don't worry about it, that's my boy. He gave me a good deal. Just enjoy your car," Karl said sincerely.

Quanisha looked at Karl and Stephanie in disbelief as she came to realize what they had done for her.

"This is our gift to you Nish. I know you've been going through a lot, and I wanted to at least try to fix one of your problems. I wish I could solve them all sis. I hope you like the color, they couldn't find an exact match for the old one," Stephanie said.

Quanisha's eyes began to tear up as she ran her fingers across the area that had been dented before. Her car looked absolutely beautiful. It was good as new.

"Ya'll don't know how much this means to me. Thank you so much," Quanisha said between sniffles as she let the tears start to flow. Stephanie went over to her Godsister and gave her a big hug.

"Don't cry baby, you deserve this. You worked real hard for this car, and to have your own out there in Philly. I'm sure that everything else will fall right into place for you."

"Thank you Stephanie," Quanisha said in a muffled voice as she buried her face in Stephanie's shoulder. "Thank you so much."

Michelle and Karl stood off in the background and beamed as they watched the scene. Michael however wasn't concerned with that.

"Mommy, when are we going to Red Lobsters?" he asked as he tugged on his mother's pants leg again. At last, Stephanie let go of Quanisha, and it was apparent that she had been crying also.

"Okay, okay. *Now* we can go to Red Lobster!" Stephanie affirmed as she wiped her eye and grabbed her son's hand. She put her arm around Quanisha and led her back to their truck with her husband and Michelle close behind.

chapter 23

When Tony and Rob got to the small hole in the wall bar in Germantown, Tony immediately started ordering shots of Hennessey to help ease away his worries and fears. He couldn't be up in the bar acting all uneasy and on edge. There was only about five or six other people in the bar chilling – it was the perfect atmosphere for Tony to get drunk in. No drama, no noise and best of all, no Rock.

Rob had ordered a beer and then took it with him to the bathroom. Tony was left by himself at the bar downing his third shot of Henny.

About a half an hour later, Tony was dancing with one of the only women that was in the bar at that time of day. She was definitely not pretty by his own standards, but she had a fairly nice body, and he needed a temporary distraction.

"Ohhhh... hoooo... yoooo!" Tony yelled rambunctiously as he danced with his Coors Light and burning cigarette high above his head, looking down at the girl who was doing a two step in front of him to the uptempo beat of Beanie Sigel's *Rock the Mic*, which was playing over the jukebox.

He and Rob were making quite a scene in the otherwise quiet bar. They were acting like ballers in there, ordering drinks left and right. Tony was trying to spend up that $100 he had left as fast as he could. He didn't care anymore, all he wanted to do was have fun for as long as he had on this earth. Scoop's death had taught him that life was short. The liquor had taken all of his inhibitions away and he was having a good time.

That's when a stocky medium height brown skinned brother walked by Tony and intentionally bumped into him on his way to the bathroom.

"Yo, watch where you goin' man," Tony said with a screw face.

"Man, fuck you," the brother answered with an attitude. He grilled Tony down for a few moments, and then went on to the bathroom.

Tony was immediately turned off. "Who the hell do he think he is?" he said to Rob.

"I don't know man, just chill though," Rob warned.

"Fuck that little pussy," Tony said loudly.

When the guy came back out, Tony couldn't help but stare him down again. The guy looked at him and laughed as he sat back down at the bar with his boys.

"Man look at this clown," he said to them as he pointed a thumb back at Tony. "This nigga got a broke ass Easy Pickins army coat on."

Everybody within hearing distance of the guy started bawling. One guy was laughing so hard that he was doubled over.

"He got him a super extra large jawn. The inside of that coat probably says 'Baby Phat'," he cracked and had the whole bar dying with laughter.

Needless to say, Tony's ego was wounded. He struggled to recover with a comeback.

"Nigga I know you ain't talking with them fake ass busta Tims on," he said.

"Oh you got something to say now? These Tim's is fake like them sideburns is real," the brother kept going as he pointed at Tony's face. There wasn't a dry eye at the bar. Their slow day had just transformed into an entertaining evening.

"That's why you over there drinking Steel Reserve while I'm sipping on that Henny. Broke ass nigga," Tony bragged.

"I'm drinking on the Reserve cuz Boo pissed in the Henny," the brother returned quickly, referring to the huge bartender, Boo, who was shaking his head and chuckling as he poured someone a drink.

"Hook, you ain't right," Boo said with a chuckle.

"Suck my dick nigga," Tony said as he grabbed his balls to disrespect his newly created nemesis.

"Hey, watch your mouth. I think Doughboy gonna be jealous if anybody *else* suck yo dick. I ain't trynna step on nobody toes," Hook shot back as he pointed directly at Rob and laughed. He had a razor sharp tongue, and had within minutes offended both Tony and Rob now. "Right Doughboy?"

Tony and Rob felt as if they had just got caught up in a whirlwind. Things had been going so smoothly and now they were the jokes of the bar. If they stayed, their egos would continue to be hurt. If they left they would look like punks.

"Man why don't you just shut the fuck up," is all that Tony could say as he held onto his now empty glass.

"Why don't you just get the fuck up out my bar?" Hook asked. "This our spot, ya'll ain't welcome."

"Who's bar? Yours? I didn't see 'Pussy's Bar' on the sign outside," Tony responded. His comment drew a lot of "Ohhhhs" from the other patrons who were mostly still drinking, but listening intently to the exchange.

"Oh now suddenly you learned how to bust on somebody," Hook laughed and then hopped off his stool. He walked right up to Tony and got in his face. "You got a lot of nerve coming up in *my* bar talking shit bruh."

"Nigga, if you don't get the fuck out my face," Tony said as he put his finger up in Hook's face.

Hook grabbed Tony's finger and twisted it around so hard that Tony squealed out in pain. He heard something crack.

"Lemme go, lemme go!" Tony yelled as he struggled to break free of the hold.

"Yo Hook, chill with all that shit. You know the blue shirts been looking for a reason to fuck with my bar," Boo called out from behind the bar. He put down the bottle of Wild Turkey he was holding and started heading around the bar.

Hook let go of Tony's finger, which Tony was sure was broken by then. He pushed Tony back and threw a left hook that hit Tony so hard that he slid down the wood paneled wall. Now Tony knew how Hook had gotten his name.

"Hook!" Boo said as he pulled Hook away from Tony and back towards the bar. He was just in time because Rob was about to throw a punch at Hook. Tony was getting up from the floor. The blow had rocked him a little bit.

Tony couldn't go out like that. He charged for Hook and swung but missed. Hook hit him again. Rob came behind him and was confronted by some of Hook's boys. When they put his hands on him to push him back he swung at one of them and landed a punch to to his right eye. His other boy hit Rob out of nowhere and a fight broke out among them as well. Meanwhile Tony was ducking and protecting himself, trying to find an opening to get Hook just once.

Boo took over before an all out brawl could ensue. He grabbed Rob by the collar with his huge hand and pushed Tony forward towards the entrance with all of his power. Tony fell forward like a rag doll when Boo pushed him to the point where his hands had hit the ground.

"Get the fuck out of here!" Boo barked as he finished

dragging Tony and Rob out of the bar. He shut the door and looked out of the clear glass window, daring either one of them to try to come back in. Everybody in the bar was laughing hysterically. Tony and Rob had gotten embarrassed and played beyond belief.

Tony threw his hands down in disgust and anger. "Fuck them!"

Rob was straightenening himself out. "Man, come on Tony. You always gettin' us in some shit."

"And fuck you too nigga!" Tony spit. "What took you so long to get my back??"

"Nigga I know you ain't trynna blame that shit on me!"

Tony started walking towards his car in a huff. He was hopping mad.

"Ay yo!" Hook came out of the bar and yelled behind them, holding a pair of women's underwear up in his hand. "You forgot your panties!"

He let out an evil cackle and went back into the bar. There were only two women in the bar, and Tony had been with them. It had to have been one of their panties.

"I'm gonna kill that nigga!" Tony screamed at the top of his lungs and then headed back towards the bar. He was seeing red.

"Tony what the hell are you doing?" Rob asked incredulously.

"No matter fact," Tony said as he turned back around and took quick long strides back in the direction of his car.

"Thank you," Rob said, relieved, as he rubbed the back of his head and strolled behind Tony.

"I'm gonna shoot the shit out this muthafucka. Then we'll see who's laughing," Tony yelled angrily in a way that told Rob that he was serious.

"Oh no," Rob said in a low moan. Tony was tripping for real.

"Tony come on, you gotta just let it go man."

"Fuck that!" he screamed as he turned the corner.

Rob stopped in the middle of the sidewalk and looked up at the sky. He didn't know what Tony was about to do.

When Rob finally turned the corner and reached Tony's car, he reluctantly went to the passenger's side and got in. Tony was on the driver's side with the door open, rummaging through the car. He looked under the seats, and under the junk in the back seat of his car. Rob was hoping Tony was just going to eventually start up the car and leave all this mess behind. But he wasn't so lucky.

Tony finally pulled out what he had been looking for. It was the gun he had used to stick up the Arab man's grocery store. Quanisha's gun. He looked at it for a moment and then played with it between his legs, opening the revolver to check if it had bullets. It did.

"Tony, you ain't serious," Rob said as he looked at his friend in amazement. He surely had lost his mind.

"As a heart attack," Tony huffed. He closed his door for privacy as he maneuvered with the gun and got comfortable with it. His trigger finger was killing him after Hook bent it, but he didn't care – he was going to use it.

chapter 24

Quanisha had spent hours talking in private with Stephanie during her visit. She let it all out. She told Stephanie everything; from Tony giving her gonorrhea, his stay in the hospital and her problems with the nurse, to her innermost secret, which most of her family if not all knew about by now. That she was unable to have children because of the abortions she had when she was a teen.

She also told Stephanie about some secrets that she'd never told *anyone*, like when she went with Trina one night to a strip club to try out the job, and then felt so sick to the stomach that she left after one set.

Stephanie came clean too. She recalled a part of her life that she hated to bring up. Some of the stories she had to tell about her days in prostitution were so unbelievable that Quanisha was embarrassed to hear them. Like the time Stephanie had a train run on her by six men, and didn't even know about it until she got there because her pimp had conveniently left that part of the job out. She had been so physically worn after that episode that she had had to go to the hospital. The hospital personnel were treating her as a rape victim. Quanisha couldn't grasp that the woman before her was the same woman in those stories.

After their talk, Quanisha felt cleansed. Someone had finally let her talk without there being something in it for them. There was no accusing, judging or criticizing from Stephanie. She just listened. The only other person besides Stephanie that had truly just sat down and listened to her was Dr. Stephens, Tony's doctor.

And the car. It looked like it was brand new, and ran as smooth as butter. She still couldn't believe that Karl and Stephanie had taken it upon themselves to fix up her car and pay for it in full without asking her for a dime or favor in return. Again, nobody ever did anything for Quanisha without wanting something in return. A wonderful feeling came over Quanisha everytime she looked at her gleaming black car. It was something she hadn't felt in a long time - happiness.

Quanisha sat up on the bed in one of the guest rooms in Stephanie's house and looked through, not at, the television. She was thinking way too much to be interested in the episode of *Girlfriends* that was flashing across the screen. The room was dark except for the light from the television. Stephanie had to get up at 6am the next day with Michael, so Quanisha had to turn in early.

She wondered how Stephanie was able to make such a turn around in her life. Stephanie had been in an even worse situation than Quanisha, with a pimp and an incurable STD that she would never be rid of added to the mix. Now she had a great family and complete security in her life. Quanisha wondered if she could ever make the type of change in her life that was necessary to have a sprawling five bedroom home, a loving husband, a job she enjoyed and a beautiful life just like Stephanie.

Quanisha remembered when Stephanie said that she could stay there as long as she needed to get herself together. Maybe if she stuck around these people long enough, the positivity and happiness would rub off. It was worth a try. She could go to school down there in Virginia, like Stephanie had done in Chicago, and look into a new career.

Stephanie had even gone so far as to give Quanisha a key to her house. That was unheard of among Quanisha's family and friends. Quanisha barely had a key to her own *mother's* house! And after only a little over a week of staying with the family, Stephanie had entrusted her with the keys to her home. What Stephanie didn't yet realize was that in return, Quanisha had given her the key to her heart. Quanisha had been converted, in less than a week, into Stephanie's biggest fan. Stephanie was her new role model, and she would do just about anything that Stephanie told her to do.

Quanisha pulled the covers back and started to get into the bed. At 9 o'clock in the evening, this was officially the earliest she had ever gone to bed.

But before she laid down, something, better yet some*one* crossed her mind. She thought about the flowers and money at her door, and she saw Tony's face in her mind's eye. It was him. He was the only person she knew who folded his money in fours, lengthwise and then widthwise. The money had been indented in that way when she found it. She just didn't understand why he hadn't knocked on her door.

She grabbed her cellphone out of her purse on the nightstand and climbed into bed. She scratched an itch in her braids and looked for Tony's new number. She knew he probably wouldn't answer, as usual, but it was worth a try.

* * *

Tony sat in his car across the street from the bar and looked down at the gun in his lap. He still felt humiliated and unreasonably irate. When he thought about the way everybody laughed at him when Hook accused him and Rob of being gay lovers, he knew that he was going to do this thing. Now he knew exactly what had set Scoop off when Rock had basically called him a faggot in the bar that day. He was going to make Hook pay for the little bit of fun he had had with Tony. Hook would die in that bar.

But then he thought again about what happened to Scoop. He had gone into the bar, just like Tony, thinking he was just going to get a couple of drinks and chill. And he had ended up dead.

Did Tony want to risk that?

Hell yea. Especially after the way Hook had punched him into the wall. Tony didn't even get a chance to return the favor. He had just gotten chased out of a bar with all those people, including the women, laughing at him. The thought was unbearable.

When he grasped the gun again in his hand, Rob tried a last ditch plea to make Tony just let the whole thing go and drive home.

"Tony man, you don't wanna do this. That nigga ain't nobody. Don't none of those muthafuckas matter. Come on, let's just go home man."

Tony didn't answer him, he just kept looking down at the gun.

"Tone, this is crazy, you can't be goin' up in there like that," Rob reasoned.

"They came at me first! I gotta finish this. If you don't like it, get the fuck out my car!" Tony roared into Rob's ear.

"Fine, fuck this. You can go ahead and go to jail, get killed if you want," Rob said, opening the door and getting out. "Cuz you know all them niggas is probably holding heat."

Tony watched as Rob started walking down the block, trying to figure out how he was going to get home. But Tony couldn't be concerned with Rob right now, he had business to handle.

He pulled out a cigarette and pushed in his car lighter. He needed a cigarette badly to calm his nerves before he went up in there. There weren't any cops around that area usually, and it was fairly quiet during that time of the night. He would just run up in there with his gun low and his hat down over his eyes, find Hook and shoot once close range to be sure he got him. Then he would jump in his car and speed out. He never had to come up to Germantown again; at least not in a long while.

The lighter popped out and he snatched at it too quickly. He fumbled it in his hands and the red coils burned his finger. He winced in pain.

"Ouch!" he said, dropping the lighter and his cigarette on the floor of the car.

Something about that lighter burning his finger set off a chain of events in his mind. He remembered how he disrespected and bragged about that girl Tonya on 69th street and then got clipped by a speeding car as he crossed the street. He clearly recalled getting burnt with gonorrhea after having Keisha over at Quanisha's house while Quanisha was at work. The attack on his grandmother came the *same exact night* that he, Rob, and Scoop had attacked Gucci in the club! They had stolen all of Gucci's stuff, and in return, Tony had gotten all of his prized possessions stolen from his grandmother's house, as well as from his car. After robbing the convenience store, he was robbed and beaten almost beyond recognition by a brother who was nearly a foot shorter than him. He had messed over Jenny, and now she was stalking him and making his and his grandmother's life miserable. When did it end?

It was like there was some kind of force that was causing him to get Karma quickly and cruelly. It was like clockwork; he screwed someone and then he got screwed back almost instantly. Based on what had happened to him just over the last few months, what would happen if he went into this bar and started shooting people? He also thought about what the doctor had told him before he even came to this bar, about not falling victim to the negativity in life.

His cellphone started ringing and it caused him to jump. He picked out another cigarette nervously and put it on his lip before flipping open the phone.

"Yo."

"Hey," Quanisha's voice came clearly over the phone. "I didn't think you was gonna answer."

"Nish? Baby?" The sound of Quanisha's voice helped to put his soul at ease, even for just a few moments. He let go of the tension in his forehead.

"Yea, it's me," Quanisha chuckled at how surprised Tony sounded. "What you up to?"

"Nothin'. You?" he asked cautiously. He was surprised because Quanisha hardly ever called him those days.

"Well, I was just sitting down here… thinkin' about you," Quanisha admitted.

"You was thinkin' about me? You lyin'," Tony said as a smile cracked at the corner of his mouth.

"No I was! I was thinkin' about how nice it was for you to leave that money and those flowers at my door. Thanks."

"You're welcome Nish. How you know it was me?"

"I just did. But anyways. I'm down here in VA with my Godsister you know," Quanisha said, changing the subject. She didn't want to get too mushy about the gift.

"No, I ain't know. You don't tell me nothin' no more," Tony said. "I thought you was done with me for good after I made you lose your job."

"Tony, it wasn't your fault I lost my job. It was my own lazy ass – I mean my lazy butt not getting up on time. I ain't mad no more," Quanisha explained.

"You ain't? Then how come you ain't call me?" Tony asked.

"How come you ain't call *me*?" Quanisha came back.

"Cuz I thought you was mad!" Tony answered enthusiastically. He looked around and almost forgot where he was at, and what he was about to do. He had even let go of his anger. He lit his cigarette and took a long drag from it.

"Well I ain't mad no more, so you better call me!" Quanisha said in the same tone and then laughed. Tony chuckled. It felt good to laugh with Tony again, like they used to when they were teenagers just starting out together.

"I think we got a lot we need to talk about Tony. I'm gonna be back in Philly in a few days or so, so just come by then," Quanisha said. "You're welcome to stay at the house too, if you need to."

"Thanks Nish."

"You aiight? You don't sound too good," Quanisha said, picking up something in his voice.

"Naw, naw, I'm aiight. Just a little tired, and drunk," Tony said as he flicked his butt out onto the street and looked back over to the bar entrance. He saw one of the patrons leave and head down the block.

"I told you about drinkin' them St. Ides forties. Call me later then, aiight?"

"Aiight, talk to you later."

"I love you Tony," Quanisha said with an anxious smile, and then held her breath.

Tony was quiet for a little while, and then it finally came out. "I love you too Nish."

Quanisha closed her eyes and took in the moment for all it was worth. She heard the phone line disconnect in her ear, and knew that Tony had hung up. She opened her eyes and put the cellphone down on the nightstand. She was utterly blissful as she settled herself underneath the covers.

Tony sat in the car for what seemed like an eternity, thinking. For some reason now he couldn't shake the memory of how he had opened his big mouth when he and Scoop were robbed off of Kingsessing.

You wouldn't be doing shit without that gun in ya hand.

That comment had gotten him the ass whooping of his lifetime. When he looked down at the gun, he thought about how that same comment actually might apply to him right at that moment.

He finally just shook those thoughts out of his mind. Regardless of the past, he knew what he had to do now. He took the gun and put it in the inside front of his pants. He got out of the car and walked slowly across the street until he reached the entrance of the bar.

He took two long deep breaths before opening the door and stepping inside. There was no turning back now. He struggled with himself even as he walked in about whether this was the right decision to make or not. The choice he made in this bar right now could potentially have an effect on his entire life. It could mean the choice between whether he even had a life to live.

Everyone in the bar was carrying on as they were before, talking and drinking, until Boo noticed Tony standing on the inside of the door with a very strange look on his face. It was not quite anger, but it was not exactly happy either. Something was about to go down.

"Yo, didn't I tell you to stay out of here?" Boo said, frozen in place as he was about to pour a shot of straight vodka. A fear now came over him that something really bad was about to happen, and he wouldn't be able to do anything in time. He looked over at Hook, who was also looking over at Tony with a very serious look on his face. There weren't anymore smiles in the place like before.

"Yea, but I got something I need to tell ya'll," Tony said loudly so that everybody in the bar could hear him. He pulled the gun out from the front of his pants and pointed it right at Hook. Everybody in the bar started bracing themselves for what was about to happen. Hook immediately put his hands up in the air and started begging for his life. He was trying to figure out how he was going to make a dash for the back entrance without getting shot. Maybe he could throw one of the females out in front of him and get out of there unharmed. Rob was wrong – Hook wasn't holding anything.

"Come on man, I was just kidding before. Come on, don't shoot me man. I got kids!" Hook pleaded.

But all Tony did as he held the gun was reach into his pants pocket. He pulled out one of the last two $20 bills he had and tossed it onto the floor.

"Look at ya'll bitchin'! Ha ha. Ain't shit funny no more though huh? Ya'll ain't even worth me ruining my life. Just go 'head and get a round of Steel Reserves on me," he said with a sly smirk, and then backed his way out of the bar with the gun still pointed in the air.

8 Months Later

Tony was hustling to catch the bus that had just pulled up. The driver looked like she didn't even want to stop. If Tony missed this bus he would probably have to wait another hour for the next one in the darkness; not something he wanted to do. Fortunately, he got there just in time.

"This bus go down Philly right?" Tony asked the driver once he had climbed aboard.

"Yup," the driver said and closed the door.

Tony sat in the window seat at the center of the bus and looked out of the window. He was dead tired, having just finished his second week of work at the restaurant in King of Prussia where he now worked. They had him doing basic kitchen duties, but it was pretty good pay at $10 an hour.

These days, Tony was not only working, but also studying to get his GED. He had never passed the 10th grade in High School, and needed some serious brushing up on his skills. He wanted to go to college, or a technical school one day.

Tony had finally decided that there were two options for his life. To go in the wrong direction and fall victim to the streets, or to go in the right direction and try to become a responsible young brother. He spoke to Dr. Stephens just about every other week and updated him on what was going on in his life. Sometimes the doctor even helped him with homework problems over the phone. Dr. Stephens had become a big influence on Tony's life. It was no instant transformation however – Tony still had some of his bad habits to shake, like yearning for other women and opening his big mouth when he shouldn't, but he managed to keep both vices under control, at least temporarily.

Quanisha was back and forth from Philly to VA every few weeks. She would stay with Stephanie for the weekend and then head back. It was like her respite away from home when she started to feel the pressure of family and life in Philadelphia. In the meantime, she had found a new, better paying job at a supermarket in the suburbs, where the conditions were a lot more pleasant. She was saving up every penny she could spare for her plans to move to the Virginia area within the next couple of years. She and Stephanie were talking just about every other day, and Stephanie was trying to help Quanisha enroll in a community college near Philadelphia now, so that when and if she did move to Virginia she could then go to a four year college. Quanisha was also considering going to a reputable beauty school instead of college, so that she could be on the right path towards opening the beauty shop she had always dreamed of owning. She decided to take a few more months before making that final decision about school and save up as much money as she could in the meanwhile. To help Quanisha save, Stephanie and her husband would give her the money to cover her frequent trips to see them in Virginia. She was like part of their family now.

Tony and Quanisha were doing okay. They still fought, just about every day, but Tony was now contributing to the bills and spending more time with his woman, which caused a very big weight to be lifted off of Quanisha's shoulders. She definitely couldn't complain about the fact that Tony was no longer giving her reasons to suspect that he was cheating.

Even Jenny had stopped coming by Tony's grandmother's house when Mrs. Jackson invited her in and sat her down for a long talk. She made it clear to Jenny that Tony didn't live there anymore, and even if he did he was simply not interested. There was something about a third party, an older female, telling her those things to her face in a loving way that made her finally grasp that she was wasting her time and should move on to the next stalkee. Jenny surprised Mrs. Jackson when she revealed that she had lost the baby; Mrs. Jackson hadn't even known that Jenny was pregnant. *Maybe that was why she was tripping so much*, Mrs. Jackson thought. In any case, she breathed a silent sigh of relief when Jenny left; no strings attached. She didn't know if she got through to Jenny completely, as far as getting off whatever substance she was on and getting psychological help, but what she said was enough to make Jenny stay away from the house. The very next day, Jenny had turned off the phone Tony was holding. It was the final indication that Jenny was moving on.

Tony's fears about being tracked down by Rock were squashed when he found out by word of mouth that Rock had been picked up for drugs, and as a suspect in Scoop's murder. Word was, just based on the amount of drugs Rock had on him when he was caught, he was probably going to be going away for a very long time.

Scoop's girlfriend Shaquita went through a mental breakdown after she found out that Scoop had been killed. She tried to kill herself by taking a bottle full of Percocets, but was found alive ironically by her jump-off Tim, a brother who she had been dealing with off and on during her entire relationship with Scoop. Tim had been the distraction she needed when she knew Scoop was out there doing his own thing, and one of the reasons why she didn't always make a big deal about Scoop's affairs. Tim came in the house that day and found Shaquita laid out on the couch passed out. He was just in time, because as the doctors said, just a few more hours and she would have been dead. Unfortunately, after taking some blood tests, they discovered that Shaquita was HIV positive also.

Tony had been nervous about approaching Terrance for weeks, but finally got up the courage to do what he needed to do to get his best friend back.

He showed up at Terrance's house one Saturday with a basketball that had two $20 bills taped to it. It was his way of apologizing to Terrance, and admitting what he did wrong. Terrance understood immediately. He didn't say anything about the money; he just went inside and got his keys so that they could go down the block to the park to shoot some hoops.

A small miracle happened a few weeks after Tony walked out of that bar and went on with his life. Someone had dropped Tony's silver box off on Grandma Jackson's porch. It was missing a lot of things of value, but it still had the picture of Tony's mother and the baseball cards inside. On top of that, every page of Tony's rhymes that he had written was stacked neatly underneath the other items. There was no good explanation for it, other than a thief who also had a heart. Either that, or someone close to the thief had returned it — it was a good thing that Tony had written his grandmother's address on the bottom of the box. Seeing his mother's picture gave Tony an added dose of encouragement and strength to go on.

As Tony looked in the distance and saw the brightly lit Philadelphia skyline against the darkness approaching, he thought about how far he had come in such a short time. He had made some hard decisions in his life, but none as hard as the one he had made to change his life around for the better. He still wasn't perfect by any means, but he was trying. He was really genuinely trying.

He sat on that bus and smirked to himself as he thought of

how good it felt to finally be on the right track. Who would have ever thought that Tony, the asshole of West Philly, would start doing the right thing? To have everybody love him, have faith in him and see the change in Tony for themselves was way more valuable than any stolen watch or ego boost to Tony now.

"Stop the fucking bus! Stop!" a brother in his thirties who had been standing at the back exit yelled in distress, causing Tony to lose his train of thought. The brother hustled up to the front with his half open raggedy looking bookbag slung over his right arm and started cursing out the husky female driver.

"Didn't you hear the fucking bell? I rang that shit three times! That means to STOP you dumb ass bitch! Now I gotta walk all the way back there. Man, I'm tired of these stupid ass bus drivers!" he raged on as he stomped down off the bus. When he stepped down off the last step he just missed the curb, tripped and fell flat on his face. The contents of his bookbag fell out all over the sidewalk.

Everybody in the front of the bus saw, including the driver, and started screaming with laughter. The bus driver leaned over and pointed to a small sign near the entrance.

"Didn't you see the sign? That means to 'Watch Yo Step'!" she cackled and then shut the door behind him, feeling glad that at least one thing had gone right for her that day. She put the bus back in gear and pulled off.

Tony stood up and stretched his neck to see what everybody was laughing at. When he couldn't see, he got up from his seat and looked out the window, just in time to see the man getting up from the pavement. He smirked.

"Damn nigga, Karma's a bitch!" he said and then laughed hysterically. After recovering, he looked at the brother until he passed out of view, and then went back to sit down with an amused smile still plastered to his face. Tony was so glad that that wasn't him anymore. He glanced up at the sky again and by chance saw one unusually bright star shining in the midnight black sky. He nodded his head as he thought to himself that that star was made just for him. God had been trying to reach Tony for a long time to get his life right, and he was finally listening.

It had been long overdue for Tony to man up and take responsibility for his life. He pounded his fist on his chest once as he looked at that star and made a personal vow to God, Quanisha and his grandmother at that very moment. He had a lot to live for, and nothing to gain by living his life like an ignorant fool.

Tony Jackson vowed then and there that he would never be Karma's bitch again.

Karma's a Bitch

by J.Gail

To the killers, rapists and thieves who think nothing of their victims: Karma will think nothing of you... Karma's a Bitch.

To the child molesters: you think you've gotten away with something, but you're *dead* wrong... Karma's a Bitch.

To men who beat women: no blow can match the one you'll feel when Karma comes for YOU... Karma's a Bitch.

To rappers who speak poison into the minds of young kids everyday and allow women to be disrespected in formulaic songs and videos... Karma's a Bitch.

To you so-called friends, talking behind people's backs and plottin'... Karma's a Bitch.

To the jealous, envious, and bitter who have nothing better to do than plan someone else's downfall: you'll *never* succeed, and... Karma's a Bitch.

To all men who are out there cheating on good women, including down low brothers who only think about themselves when they do what they do... Karma's a Bitch.

To anyone that's done somebody dirty, you should really work on making it right, because there's no doubt that **what goes around comes around**.

about the author

J.Gail has been writing creatively on and off for the past decade. She currently has three novels, *Thugs are for Fun*, *Thugs Ain't No Fun At All*, and *Karma's a Bitch*. *Karma's a Bitch*, J.Gail's third novel, is the story of an ignorant young Philly brother who experiences Karma almost instantly. She is currently releasing her fourth book, entitled *Stop Looking at Me!*, about a young woman who is besides herself with paranoid delusions and working on her next novel *Cap'n Save a Bro*, the story of a woman who spends her whole life, from school girl to career woman, trying to save the bad men in her life, but instead they end up corrupting her soul. The author currently resides near Philadelphia.

acknowledgements

Thank you to God and my family — for believing in and being there for me. A special thank you to L.W. for being the face of this book and helping me make it the best seller it has become. This book is dedicated to you. - J.Gail

Give the gift of this exciting book
to your Family and Friends...

Give it to somebody you don't even LIKE.
Maybe they didn't know that

KARMA'S A BITCH !

Check your Local Bookstore or Order Online

Get it at **karmabook.com**!

Get them at **thugbooks.com**!

Want to order through the mail?

Karma's a Bitch by J.Gail
Price: $14.00
Shipping & Handling: $1.75 each book
($1 S&H for each add'l book ordered)

All books will be shipped via USPS Media Mail, which takes anywhere from 3-10 business days. If you want your book quicker, send $4.25 S&H so that your book will ship via USPS Priority Mail.

Call 888-715-9599
Fax 888-645-1615
if you have any questions that can't be answered on our website: http://www.JazoliPublishing.com.

Truth Hurts Publications is an imprint of Jazoli Publishing.

Make your check or money order payable to *Jazoli Publishing* and return with this form to:

Jazoli Publishing
P.O. Box 1316
Code B-OF144-1
Brookhaven, PA 19015

www.JazoliPublishing.com
This is real life.
It ain't no fairytale.